A SHADOW AND STONE NOVEL

THE CURSE OF SIGHT AND SONG

RUE VOLLEY

DRAGON'S KEEP

KINGDOM OF SILVER FLAME

KINGDOM OF STONE

KINGDOM OF NIGHT

THE ISLES OF
ELLIAN

KINGDOM OF SHADOW

KINGDOM OF THE CRYSTAL GARDEN

THE
SORROW

THE OBSIDEON VEIL

Book Design: Rue Volley
Additional Graphics: Rue Volley
Interior Design: Rue Volley
Edited By:
Tasha Berkenstock and Jodi Laux
Wordsmith Editing

Published by Rue Volley Books LLC

THE CURSE OF SIGHT AND SONG

A SHADOW AND STONE NOVEL

THE ISLES OF ELLIAN
BOOK THREE

RUE VOLLEY

Thank you for buying this eBook.
To receive bonus content, special offers,
and info on new releases and other great reads
please visit us at https://linktr.ee/RueVolley

For all other business inquiries, please contact us at
ruevolley@gmail.com

Enjoy the song list here

"We need women who are so strong they can be gentle, so educated they can be humble, so fierce they can be compassionate, so passionate they can be rational, and so disciplined they can be free."

Kavita Ramdas

For my Babes in Bookland

THE CURSE OF SIGHT AND SONG

CONTENTS

Trigger Warnings:

SA (off-screen)
Violent Death
Cannibalism
Religious Trauma
Graphic Sexual Scenes
Gore
Physical and Mental Abuse
Torture
Forced Captivity
Thoughts of Suicide
Incest

CHAPTER 1

THE SORROW

O dette Ender leans over the cauldron, gracefully swirling her fingers, using her borrowed magick to mix the contents. Talen Freeborn's stomach knots up as the scent wafts through the air.

The young Witch turns her head, eyes lit with fury.

"Did you kill him, Odette?"

Odette's eyes narrow, choosing to show concern. "Talen, you must eat—it is unwise to refuse." She pulls her hand back, but the contents inside keep swirling.

The young Witch recognizes Odette's new ability. The power of magick can only be obtained through either natural inheritance or deliberate pursuit. Although she is curious about the shifter's ability to cast spells, she decides to temporarily set it aside. Keeping Odette engaged in conversation is crucial, as it might be helpful.

With her shoulder aching and her back curved, she makes a hissing noise. With every passing hour, her discomfort has become increasingly intolerable.

"You eat it," she says while examining her bound hands.

The Witch cannot cast any spells because of the smooth metal binding her wrists and thumbs. It's something she's never seen before. It's likely a war artifact. Yet, who gave them to Odette? She ponders. If she had to make an assumption, it would have to be a mortal.

A man, no less.

She knew neither vampires nor the Fate harbored any hatred towards her kind. Wolves and Witches, united by a common cause, fought side by side in the past to secure their freedom. No, it has to be men from the Kingdom of Stone. Whether it was her role in the events that unfolded within their walls or simply her connection to Naya Freeborn. This implies that Odette Ender had been actively working against them since the start.

Rising, the shifter blocks out what little sunlight is left in the day.

Speaking with a rolling hand gesture, her voice lacks any hint of emotion. "He was still breathing when I took flight."

Bravely, with tears threatening to spill from her eyes, Talen musters the strength to ask, "How certain are you?"

The shifter chooses not to answer her question, remaining silent and avoiding eye contact.

Talen's pulse quickens. "Odette, I can't rest until I know he is safe. Please, I beg of you. Tell me the truth. I would think lies would prove useless now."

Odette's eye twitches, showing her frustration. The once endearing quality of Talen's personable nature is becoming a source of irritation for her.

As the shifter scans the room, she is immediately drawn back to the cauldron, noticing its steam rising and filling the air with a delicious scent.

"I'm not worried about the wolf, rather my concern lies with your well-being."

"My well-being?" Talen derides. "You abandoned that when you shackled me."

She lifts her wrists as high as they will go, feeling the strain in her muscles, but swiftly drops them. Her current state makes it impossible for her to bear the weight of the metal.

"Have I not provided?" Odette inquires, gesturing towards the cauldron.

The Witch averts her gaze, refusing to acknowledge the effort Odette had put into their meal.

In order to warm their bones and fill their stomachs, the shifter has prepared a delicious and hearty broth. She spent hours boiling the bones of the small creatures she had captured and skinned. Talen holds such value to her that she made an exception and put in the effort, which she rarely does for anyone else. The young Witch must eat and remain strong because she is no good dead. Odette carefully dips a bowl into the simmering contents and advances toward the young Witch.

Speaking with concern in her voice, Odette urges her to sip from the edge of the cup.

"Now eat."

Talen firmly shakes her head, showing her refusal.

"How is it possible for you to offer your help and then betray us? Have you no loyalty, Odette?"

With a swift motion, Odette hurls the bowl with all her might, causing it to crash against the cave wall. Rather than looking away, Talen keeps her gaze fixed on the shifter, demanding that she provide an answer.

"How could I? How could I!" The sound of Odette's voice

is reminiscent of a crack of thunder, rumbling with power and intensity. With each passing moment, her aggravation mounts, causing her muscles to stiffen. To find relief from the pain in her neck, she twists her head, hoping to relax the muscle causing her discomfort.

She takes a slow breath, centering herself. It's pointless to let her anger get the best of her. Instead, Odette expresses her disapproval by clicking her tongue. It is important for her to remember that Talen Freeborn is significantly younger than she is. Compared to Odette's actual age, she is practically an infant.

Dismissing her question, she lets out a tired sigh. "I do not wish to hear any discussions about loyalty from you, Witch."

Talen flinches as the waves crash against the jagged rocks along the shoreline, creating a mesmerizing display of black water that takes the shape of wings behind Odette's striking silhouette. The young Witch recognizes the deep symbolism that is present in this situation. Some might perceive the shifter as an angel of death. Although it may appear ominous, there is something mesmerizing about it. Talen has an inherent attraction to the enigmatic nature of darkness. Cullen Moore serves as a perpetual symbol of that fragility.

A tiny quiver runs through her lip, betraying her inner turmoil. Her bones are feeling the chill, which has been gradually settling in. If she had the choice, she would prefer to be anywhere other than here, even if it means relying on a vampire who both fascinates and frustrates her.

As she closes her eyes, a symphony of silence greets her.

Murder is not out of the question.

The Witch knows this. Odette has brought this out of

her. She yearns to quell this churning hatred which burdens her heart. If she permits the shifter to damage her inherent nature, then the battle is already lost.

If she were freed, she knows the shifter would have to engage in a fierce battle to survive. Even in a weakened state, a Witch poses a significant threat, her powers still potent and dangerous.

Talen Freeborn grapples with the challenge of reclaiming her lost compassion. Even now, in this desperate hour, she remains steadfast in her aversion to causing harm to anyone. Odette Ender's actions pale compared to her unwavering determination to preserve her own identity. Without that, Talen has lost everything. She tamps down her irritation.

"I apologize. I'm not feeling like myself," she half-whispers.

Talen hopes to remind the shifter that she is growing weaker. Unable to tap her chest, she coughs, her throat feeling tight and constricted. As the Witch observes the shifter, she detects a faint hint of anxiety flickering in her eyes. It's possible that her efforts are paying off.

The Witch knows she must go to great lengths in order to persuade Odette that she poses no threat. The shifter never was who she claimed to be. In order to navigate this treacherous situation, Talen must accept this if she wishes to find a way out. Once again, she readjusts her position and lets out a hiss of pain as the cold, unforgiving metal digs even deeper into her delicate wrists. Sores are forming. If the wound has not already festered, it is just a matter of time before it becomes infected. With a subtle movement, she glances at her wrist, hoping that Odette will notice.

The shifter instantly senses Talen's deteriorating health.

Odette paces back and forth with growing frustration. With each pass, she effectively blocks out the sunlight. The brightness of the sun forces Talen to squint each time it hits her face. They've been in this cave for what feels like days. The current situation renders that unimportant. Failing to make her escape, the Witch risks losing everything. With each passing day, her resistance weakens and the inevitability of surrender grows stronger. In this moment, she can't help but feel a twinge of envy towards Cullen Moore. If only the embrace of death could empower her.

The shifter is right. Talen must eat.

"You do this to yourself," Odette claims.

Talen clenches her jaw, feeling the pressure in her teeth. The mere thought of Cullen Moore has left her feeling unprotected in a way that she deeply resents.

"You did this to me. This is your fault, not mine."

The shifter rushes in and grabs the back of Talen's head, twisting her fingers through her hair. The Witch gasps as Odette forces her head back. Swiftly, she reaches for another bowl, plunging it into the swirling contents of the cauldron. She lifts it like she is about to pour the broth down her throat. But the shifter takes pause as their eyes meet. A crooked line of dirt marks Talen's pale skin where a single tear has left its trail. The weight of her sadness bothers the shifter, even though it shouldn't affect her. She releases her and takes a step back. As Odette drinks the broth, Talen's stomach churns with knots, causing an uneasy sensation. Despite the powerful temptation, she resisted, knowing that this was not the right moment to give in.

Not now. Not yet.

It is imperative for her to select the appropriate moment. When it will be of the utmost benefit to her.

He will come for me—he will.

Talen silently reminds herself while thinking about the vampire prince. He gave his word to safeguard her. He took action when his mother hurried toward her, and once more when he feared that Koa would cause her harm. In order to ensure that she would remain undetected, he resorted to biting her. Even though he claimed he couldn't, he had proven his care for her in countless ways. Ways she cannot forget.

Cullen Moore will not let her die this way. Talen Freeborn will hold onto this hope, like a lifeline in a stormy sea.

Odette lowers the bowl, her hands trembling, before it slips from her grasp and crashes to the ground.

"What does it feel like to be cast aside?" Her tone is emotionless as she poses the question.

Talen narrows her eyes. Odette's assumption of being able to discern her thoughts greatly upsets her.

She defiantly juts out her chin. "What's it like to be a traitor?"

Odette smirks. "You know nothing, Witch."

"I know you injured Koa and shackled my wrists as if I'm your prisoner."

Talen raises her arms, but the heaviness promptly causes her hands to return to her lap. Although she may feel defiant, she acknowledges Odette has the upper hand.

Memories overwhelm the shifter's thoughts, taking her back in time.

"Those like me were coveted above all other things in this wretched world, Talen Freeborn. Our power surpassed even that of the mighty dragons who held dominion over the sky above us. The true power in this world lay in the hands of the shifters. Shifters! Not mortals, not vampires, not Fate or Witches. My kind."

Her emotions are apparent in the way her breath has quickened, a visible struggle to regain composure. Taking a moment to regain composure, she meticulously arranges her hair, carefully tucking away any loose strands. Then, she smooths down her ruffled feathers, ensuring they lay neatly against her chest and sides. She crooks her neck before continuing.

"In Ellian, where truth was scarce, we stood by each sovereign as equals, offering them the advice they so desperately needed."

"What advice would my mother need?" Talen asks.

The shifter straightens her shoulders.

"Little did you know, Witch, that your own kingdom had become a breeding ground for wickedness, a place where evil flourished." Odette says, her eyes locked with hers. "Each kingdom sought our help, and we offered it despite the dangers. When our usefulness ended, they discarded us as if we had no value. Including you mother."

With an intense glare, she focuses her attention on her trembling hands. The memory of her fallen brethren consumes her thoughts. Gradually, the sorrowful wails of her kind become less prominent, fading into the background of her thoughts.

"Like an anchor, I have held onto this truth, unable to move forward. I long to be rid of it, to never have to deal with it again. To be rid of all of you."

The silence settles between them.

Talen's voice carries a soothing quality as she speaks. "In this desperate hour, my view of you, Odette, remains unchanged. I find you deserving of life and all its blessings.

The anger you feel is completely justified given the harm that has been done to you and others like you. But listen to me. You can turn back. Your decision holds the power to prevent a disastrous outcome for this world. I can help you. I know I can—but only if you help me."

Odette looks at the young Witch leaning on a rock. Her face is pale, her skin stretched taut and glistening with sweat from the lingering fever. She will soon sleep due to exhaustion. The only thing that is keeping her alive now is her magick. It will sustain her for a bit longer, but she knows it will not last forever. This truth irritates the shifter. It is detrimental to her cause.

Talen parts her lips, ready to plead her case further, but the shifter reacts before she can convince her any further.

"Help you? Liar!" the shifter cries out before rushing in, curling her spidery fingers in the Witch's face, but Talen does not look away, instead choosing to gaze deeply into the shifter's eyes. She will drag empathy from her bones if need be. She must. There is no choice left but this. It is possible that her life hangs in the balance.

"I do not lie," she insists, refusing to look away.

Talen can feel her stomach cramping. It emits a fierce growl reminiscent of a wild beast. She longs to satisfy her hunger, quench her thirst, and finally put an end to her suffering, but it remains out of reach. Instead, she must carefully unravel Odette's true character.

In a moment of clarity, Odette lets go of her rage, feeling a weight lifted off her shoulders. Her head tilts, mirroring the movements of a bird, as she closely observes the Witch. She respects her bravery.

"It's a shame that things could not be different. In other times, perhaps we could've been friends," she admits.

Talen capitalizes on Odette's vulnerability.

"Odette, you spoke to me like a friend in The Kingdom of Shadow. You promised to speak with my mother. You warned me to be prepared for war if she marched upon that kingdom. Can't you remember? We parted as friends—you and I, our bond strengthened by the shared victory of saving Everleigh and reclaiming the book of dark magick. I'm confused about what has changed. Why have you turned against me and everyone else?"

Talen waits for an answer, but receives none. The shifter seems indifferent to her pleas, but the young Witch is determined to establish a connection with Odette, hoping to alter her intentions.

"Odette—"

The shifter abruptly cuts her off, causing her to fall silent.

"The sky seemed to beckon me when I was a child. Its endless possibilities stretching out before my eyes. Among my kind, they saw me as someone extraordinary—a true blessing. Ruling the sky is a rare gift that only a handful of shifters share with the dragons. Very few would be brave enough to fly alongside them." She points to her chest. "But I did without fear—without question, because I believed I was doing something worthy. Something that would bring everlasting glory to our people and secure our place in this world."

Odette pauses, lifting her head high before continuing.

"I am chosen, Talen Freeborn. I am of royal blood. My dream was for the inhabitants of Ellian to show respect and gratitude towards my kind, acknowledging our role in bringing peace to their once troubled land. We have completed that task. Those just like me. But what did we receive in return for our unwavering loyalty and guidance? I'll tell you. We received nothing of worth. In contrast, this world has turned its back on us. In our time of need, not a single person stood by our side, not even your mother."

Talen leans forward, using her strength to hold herself upright.

"Your life matters to me. I don't know what else I can say to convince you."

Odette clucks her tongue.

"I have a clear memory of the way you looked at me as we stood on the stairs that day. Like everyone else in this world, you also passed judgment on me. You thought I was inferior to you, belittling my worth. Beneath you. You believed I wasn't to be trusted." She chuckles. "I guess you were right, Talen Freeborn—second daughter, inheritor of lies and deceit. The curse seethes in your veins, a dark force that refuses to be quelled. You cannot escape it. It is who you are. Does it not call out to you when the vampire prince is near?"

Talen conceals her anger, opting for diplomacy.

"I admit I wasn't kind. But my mother is ill. She has been unwell for a while, and I didn't know you like I do now, Odette. I'm sorry for the way I made you feel. I didn't trust you, and my lack of trust extended to anyone in her company. In her twisted mind, the lines between reality and imagination blur. I'm sure you are aware of this. It's that book. In her misguided efforts, she has tried to draw darkness from it, failing to comprehend its intended purpose of providing light. Moonrise harmed her while shielding itself."

Odette crouches before Talen. With a delicate touch, she reaches in and twists a piece of her long light-green hair.

Curiously, she lifts it to her nose and inhales the scent. Not only did the Witch's appearance change, but her very essence seemed to alter in ways unseen. Could it be her attraction to the vampire?

"I liked your hair before. This doesn't suit you," she jabs while observing her.

Talen Freeborn differs from her mother. It's possible that she is not like any other Witches. She possesses both bravery and a compassionate nature. Odette can sense the sincerity in the young Witch's words, although they leave her feeling bewildered. Talen's expression remains tender. It's challenging to comprehend. Odette bares her teeth, a low snarl rumbling in her throat, but the Witch remains unfazed. She must fight for freedom without backing down. Talen has no choice.

"I admit you have shown me kindness, Witch."

Reluctantly, Odette admits her uncertainty while she rummages through different scenarios in her mind. She finds herself trapped, compelled to do what she must. Without the Witch, she has no leverage against The Holy Scribe.

Talen adjusts her shoulder against the rock. "Then let me go. Odette, please. You can't trust what they've told you, regardless of any promises that have been made. The person who wants me is neither your friend nor ally. There's a chance you'll be killed while delivering me."

Now willing to engage in a civil conversation, she asks, "How would you know?" aware of the limited time they have left.

Talen's gaze shifts beyond her, fixating on the book that is concealed beneath a layer of cloth. "Because taking me and Starfall means only one thing. There is a misconception that I have the power to control it, but I want to make it clear, Odette, that I cannot. The pursuit of controlling that book will lead us all down a path that ends in death. The consequences of this action will lead to the destruction of the entire world and everything that exists within it. I am not its steward. I never will be."

Odette rises, her towering figure casting a shadow over the Witch once more. "You have your aunt's magick in your blood, do you not?"

Talen's brow furrows, her face contorting with concern.

"There is no such thing as two identical Witches. My mother and her sister were complete opposites, despite being twins. It's the same for you, right? According to you, flying is a skill that only a handful of your kind possess. Moonrise and Starfall are no different. I have no control over that book. It won't listen to me. Moonrise is my inheritance. Eventually, my magick will make that claim. But not Starfall. It doesn't and won't ever answer to me. You have to believe me."

Odette leans in, her eyes filled with curiosity.

"Convince me with truth—your truth."

"About what? I have nothing to hide."

With a sigh, Odette shakes her head, her disappointment clear.

"Do you think I don't know how you truly feel about the vampire?"

Gritting her teeth, Talen tries to suppress her frustration.

"Cullen?" she asks.

Odette almost laughs, finding amusement in the Witch's refusal to acknowledge her own feelings. "Is there another vampire?"

Swallowing hard, the young Witch tries to steady her nerves.

"No. There is no other vampire that I know."

Odette crouches in front of her, locking her gaze.

"So, tell me. How does he make you feel?"

Talen experiences a rush of adrenaline. "He is a formidable ally, nothing more."

Odette's disappointment is palpable. "Even now, you choose to lie." Without diverting her gaze from the Witch, she adds another piece of splintered wood to the flames.

"I—I'm not." Talen's stuttering voice undermines any chance she had of persuading the shifter.

The edge of Odette's lip curls. "And I thought we were becoming friends."

Talen's tongue glides over her cracked lips, trying to alleviate the dryness. The temptation to quench her thirst was strong, but she resisted, aware of the advantage it would give Odette. If the Witch keeps weakening herself, she will become less important to the person who convinced Odette to betray her. Odette is also aware of this, so she needs to act quickly.

Talen winces while shifting her weight. "We can be."

"Friends do not lie, so perhaps it's time to go—"

Talen's nostrils flare. "Fine. Should I discuss the vampire prince in the north?" she looks around, "I mean, what I assume is north."

As Odette tosses another piece of wood on the fire, the crackling sound fills the air and the flames dance with renewed intensity. In an instant, a comforting warmth floods the cave. Talen sighs with relief.

"I thought all Witches could tell where they are in this world?"

Laughter escapes from Talen's lips. "If not starved and held captive."

A mischievous smile plays on Odette's lips as her eyebrow quirks upward. "The first of which is your choice."

With a grunt, Talen raises her wrists. Despite the obvious reminder, Odette ignores it. "Give me your truth in what you claim is a desperate hour, as if you've ever really known desperation, living as lavishly as you have— protected with privileges."

Odette's teasing irritates her. Without the restraints on her wrists, she would go to extreme lengths to liberate herself. She understands this now.

"I find him disagreeable and irritating," Talen turns her wrist to ease the pressure.

Odette smirks. "I'm sure he found you to be as well."

With a slight tilt of her head, Talen's eyes narrow in concentration. Odette's curiosity might benefit her.

She elevates her chin. "In addition, he's condescending. He looks down on everyone around him."

With a focused gaze, Odette studies the mesmerizing patterns created by the dancing firelight.

"Yes, vampires are notorious for their egotism and tendency to seize opportunities. They fixate their thoughts entirely on themselves. I fought far more than I care to admit. Some I killed; others injured."

The shifter pushes up her black sleeve, revealing a winding scar that snakes around her forearm. The unusual markings are indeed claw marks, rough and uneven in texture. Seeing that Talen is staring, she pushes it back down and releases a sigh.

"As I tried to take flight, a female vampire viciously attacked me, nearly ripping my arm off. Just in the nick of time, a blue dragon appeared and unleashed a torrent of flames, obliterating the vampire. Otherwise, my life would have ended. But sometimes I wonder if that would have been a more desirable outcome."

"I'm sorry," Talen offers.

"Don't offer me sympathy, Witch; it's demeaning, given our current circumstances."

Talen accepts her claim and shifts his focus onto Cullen Moore.

"Well, Cullen angers me. He's a selfish child."

With a chuckle, Odette shakes her head in disbelief, her amusement clear. "Child?"

"I know he's older than I am, but I believe he's been sheltered—spoiled—he's a brat."

Odette observes Talen Freeborn with a sense of disbelief spreading across her brow.

"Allow me to introduce you to Cullen Moore, the enigmatic Vampire Prince of Darkness—Heir of Shadow. While he may come across as civilized, it's crucial to remember who turned him. It was Lord Raiden, son of Dracula, ruler of death and destruction. Cullen possesses a darkness within him. He is a force to be reckoned with—a terrifying, ruthless predator. Despite his eloquent speech and expensive attire, don't be swayed by his outward appearance. He craves what you have. He is consumed by that desire. That longing. His kind do not sleep—nor rest. Like predators, vampires are in constant motion, circling us with an eerie grace. Young Witch, do not allow yourself to be seduced by this, or you will regret it."

Talen's face turns a shade of red, betraying her embarrassment.

Odette experiences a sudden rush of protective instincts.

"He has an insatiable desire for the blood coursing through your veins. The flesh on your bones. His kind considers you to be their source of nourishment. People like you—innocent and untouched—are the target of their cannibalistic appetite. They have an insatiable desire to consume girls with your unique essence. Your exquisite flavor makes you a sought-after delicacy."

Talen can feel the warmth rising on her skin. Odette's curiosity about her purity is unwarranted, but she is power-less to protest.

"Well, he can't have me," Talen states.

"Your emotions give away your true intentions, Witch, despite what you say. If I can feel the intensity of your desire for him, he can sense it as well. It appears that your fate has been determined, and there is no altering it. All he must do is reach out and pluck that juicy, ripe fruit from the vine."

Avoiding eye contact, Talen shifts her focus elsewhere. The rush of excitement made her cheeks flush and her heart pound in her chest.

"I grow tired of this game, Odette."

"Perhaps if you allowed him to do as he wished, you would not be so disagreeable."

Talen lets out a half-hearted chuckle. This was the first time since Odette attacked them and brought her to this cave overlooking The Sorrow that she had felt entertained.

Her back straightens. "The vampire will never touch me that way—I won't allow it."

As the shifter crosses her arms over her chest, a low growl rumbles in the back of her throat. "Does his charm not entice you?"

Talen's gaze intensely refocuses on the shifter. "I don't

need a man, living or dead, to want me so that I may think I have worth. That is not who I am or ever will be."

Odette is savoring the newfound depth of Talen's personality. She must admit, this is proving to be an enjoyable way to pass the time.

"I would not deny him if I were lonely and bored," she jests.

Talen reacts with an eye roll. "I'll tell him you said that when I see him again. Maybe you can date him."

Odette laughs. "Such fight in you."

"Well, I am my mother's daughter."

"True." The shifter nods. "I must remember that."

"Perhaps it would benefit you to experience love, Odette Ender."

Odette parts her lips, revealing a glimpse of her pearly white teeth. The weight of her mother and sister's story presses on her, urging her to confide in Talen, yet she chooses to keep it hidden. The opportunity will arise when she can leverage it to her advantage. Possibly as a means of diversion. The shifter understands that her most powerful tool is the knowledge she holds and the timing of its disclosure.

The intense coldness in her gaze could put out the flames.

"Love. There is no real love in this world, Talen Freeborn"

"I guess it would be easy to lose sight of the beauty in this world when you close yourself off from it."

With a sigh, Odette unfolds her arms and tenderly places a hand on her chest, as if seeking comfort.

"Oh, sweet child. You speak of a beauty that only exists in your mind. Do you think anyone held to their word in this world? That kingdoms did not rebel against the treaty meant to end the suffering?"

Talen narrows her eyes, studying the scene before her with an intense focus. "I know that my mother did. She only wanted her sister to come home. She is suffering from grief, Odette. You, of all people, must know this. She must have confided in you. Please remember this before you speak ill of her or make uneducated assumptions about me."

Odette claps her hands, the sound growing louder with each rhythmic beat. Finally, she stops. Her face shimmering from the heat of the flames. The light glides across her skin like a hand against silk.

"I would love to think that this is a bit of theater you've afforded me, but I fear you are growing weak from hunger and lack of sleep."

Odette reaches out, her fingers tenderly cupping her cheek. Desperate for sleep, the Witch leans into her hand, resisting the urge to surrender to exhaustion. This might be her last opportunity to persuade her.

"Everything changed when my sister—"

Talen pauses, her breath catching in her throat. She hadn't thought of Averill in this way for a long time—as her sister, someone she had grown up with and cherished.

"Yes, tragic as it was, but necessary," Odette is quick to offer.

The furrowed line on Talen's brow becomes more pronounced.

"Necessary?" she asks.

Odette tilts her head again, unable to hide the truth any longer.

"Your mother held the belief that a curse plagued your bloodline. She believed that Moonrise yearned for Starfall's company just as strongly as she yearned to be reunited with her sister, Naya. However, it was your mother's wickedness that truly cursed your family. It wasn't a matter of heritage, but something deeply ingrained within her. Darkness clung to her like an intoxicating perfume, a reflection of her deep longing for it."

Talen shakes her head, her long hair swaying with the motion. "I don't believe you."

Odette leans in, her voice barely audible as she whispers in Talen's ear. "Jealousy was a constant presence in her relationship with her sister, who, despite being born just a few minutes earlier, always came first in everything. First born, first to master a spell—first to love."

Talen is fixated on Odette. The young Witch had believed she was manipulating the shifter, but Odette's clever tactics had been in control all along. She sees this now. A soft whisper escapes her lips as she realizes Odette had been a part of their lives far longer than she could have ever fathomed.

"You were there when my mother and aunt were born."

"I held them in my arms and swore to protect them. To love them, and I did with all my heart," Odette admits.

Talen shakes her head. "Why didn't you tell me this?"

Odette lifts her hands toward the fire and warms them.

"It matters not. The only thing that will set things right in Ellian now is war."

"War!?" Talen exclaims.

"Yes, it is the only concept that any of you comprehend. The relentless quest for power and domination. Owning land or having security is never sufficient. None of you desire peace; instead, you all crave chaos. I've seen this happen over and over again, and it's become so tiring. All of you exhaust me."

"I had hoped to have a heartfelt conversation with you, seeking your understanding and empathy. But now, all you talk about is war? War leads to nothing but the proliferation of animosity and division. I would expect someone claiming wisdom to be aware of this."

Odette's eyes, once bright and vibrant, now narrow with a hint of darkness. Her patience has worn thin, leaving her on edge.

"You were not there when the water turned black and began to rise, eating up precious crops and the ground beneath our feet. Unlike others, you did not have to witness the heart-wrenching scenes of thousands of innocent people perishing in camps because of hunger and disease or smell the stench of rotting flesh that saturated everything around you. You didn't have to witness the merciless slaughter of those deemed unfit for survival, all in the name of conserving resources, nor were you forced to take part in the lottery that sentenced many to death in the rising tide simply because of the color of their skin, their gender, who they chose to love, or what God they worshipped. There is a reason it is called The Sorrow, Witch. It is a graveyard littered with the bones of millions scattered in the deep. Sent to their deaths for what?" Odette takes a slow breath, wishing the visions of such things could be erased from her mind, "No—instead, you speak to me of animosity and division, your words laced with a false sense of understanding, child. By choosing to judge such things from a place of privilege, one cannot understand the experiences of others. Ellian has hidden its cursed past by rewriting narratives that simply did not exist. But I have witnessed all of this first-hand. I remember every torturous detail. Every scream, every mother's cry. I am a living testimony to this darkness that festers in the hearts of men. I have been forced to navigate this wretched place among disgusting creatures. I have served those who think me less than simply for existing. I speak of war because it is all any of you understand. You are violent by nature. You will betray each other in moments of weakness and desperation without mercy. So don't assume you know me—understand me or can comprehend what I have endured because I know you all too well."

Talen's eyes brim with tears, blurring her vision. Struggling to find her voice, the young Witch feels a tightness in her chest, as if her words are constricting her.

"Odette. Know that I would never do such things. Never."

Odette shakes her fist, "And you know this how?! Have you been judged for simply existing? No—you have not."

"My people have. I know this," she states.

"You—not those before you, Talen," Odette clarifies. She shakes her head. "You will never understand."

Talen's eyes grow larger. "Then help me. I want to learn. I'm willing to listen and understand."

Odette's lips part, but any rational words she might have said to Talen are silenced by the presence of a growing shadow looming on the horizon. The large ship emerges from the mist, its majestic bow adorned with shimmering silver inlays that added to its awe-inspiring sight. Talen Freeborn's time to convince the shifter to set her free has simply run out.

With her remaining strength, she laboriously drags her feet toward the cave's entrance. Frozen in horror, she stood there, her eyes fixated on the flag bearing the shield from

The Kingdom of Stone, a symbol that represented her worst fears. Talen takes a step forward, her shoulder now in perfect alignment with Odette's. The shifter is clutching a bag to her chest. As the breeze catches the cloth, Talen catches a glimpse of two books, their spines boldly displayed. Gasping in disbelief, she realizes that Odette has not only stolen Starfall, but also Moonrise. How did she take the book from her mother's tower without being caught?

She is suddenly overwhelmed by a terrible realization, which almost causes her to lose her balance.

"What have you done, Odette?" she begs.

Odette clutches the books securely against her chest and, without even a glance, utters her words with little compassion.

"What I should have done decades ago and saved myself."

CHAPTER 2

CROSSING THE RIVER WILDE

A young girl, no older than seven rotations of the Springmoon, stands in silence while admiring the River Wilde. Her eyes widen in awe as she takes in the breathtaking view. The crisp northern air fills her lungs as she gazes upon the majestic river, a sight she had only dreamed of until now. Her mother had carefully weighed the risks before deciding to embark on this treacherous journey. Many had not returned in the past while collecting much-needed water for their village. The cause of death varied, with some being attacked by Wolves, others by Vampires, and a considerable number meeting their demise at the hands of those living in the Kingdom of Silver Flame.

The girl, with her pastel pink hair and burnt orange eyes, hails from the Wayward Divide. At the southern edge, there lies a narrow strip of land that serves as a barrier between the Wolves and the territory under the Fate King's dominion. Even though she was born long after The War of Brumah had ended, its lasting impact had profoundly influenced her upbringing and that of her parents. In the face of war, her people remained steadfast in their commitment to peace. In the end, they found themselves banished as a consequence of their rebellion. The King of Silver Flame, consumed by rage, ordered his dragon riders to descend upon the land, their destructive presence leaving a trail of desolation. Amidst the ruins, only a small group managed to survive, working tirelessly to cultivate the barren soil, construct settlements, and protect themselves from the menacing Wolves in the south and intermittent raids from the north. No one expected the ways in which they would prosper and flourish. With unwavering dedication, they labored to restore the land, ensuring its fertility for crops and sustenance for all. This includes a well filled during each full moon, collecting water from the northern River Wilde.

The King of the Fate was furious, leading him to dispatch a spy to infiltrate their ranks. Nonetheless, the power of love disrupted their mission, causing this spy to become a traitor. Thwarting King Elio Efhren's desire for retribution. The longer these rogue Fate remain in the south, the stronger the temptation becomes for others to join them.

And now a mysterious sickness is spreading.

Elders carry a cough they cannot shake. It weakens them, causing some to slip into a deep slumber, never to wake again. The males struggle to catch their breath while tilling the earth or tracking down the few remaining animals, while the females suffer the anguish of losing their unborn while still in the womb.

There are those who believe that by refusing to join their people to the north, they have brought a curse upon themselves. As the disease claimed more lives, a message arrived, beckoning them to return to the realm of the King of Silver Flame. He is extending to them forgiveness, a source of nourishment, and a fortress of protection.

It is a true blessing, but unfortunately, they have been deceived.

For it was none other than the King's servants who poisoned their water source.

The young Fate loses her footing, her body lurching forward with an unsteady stumble. With care, the mother holds her daughter's hand and steadies her, then raises an eyebrow.

"Be mindful of your steps, Maliah. You must appear well when we arrive. The King will not accept us if he suspects we are sick. You must be strong."

With a tender gesture, her mother wipes away the dirt from her cheek, revealing a rosy glow underneath. The young Fate had always been headstrong, preferring to secretly trail her father on the hunt rather than learn domestic skills. However, she had now embraced her mother's guidance, leaving behind her untamed spirit.

"And don't mention your father. I will speak in his place. I will tell them he died in battle protecting us from the wolves if asked. Do you understand? This will protect us."

Giving her small hand a little shake, she receives a confirming nod from Maliah. She's always been strong— stronger than most. She's inherited that trait from her mother, just like the way she smiles when amused.

The girl bites her pouty bottom lip, feeling a surge of determination. However, the terrain between the Wayward Divide and The Kingdom of Silver Flame is notorious for its treacherous nature. Little do they know that the poisoned well is nothing compared to what awaits them.

Her gaze falls upon the other side of the river, revealing a picturesque scene of lush green grass and a thriving forest. Maliah's eyes sparkle with awe and curiosity. It is the farthest north she has ever traveled, and the beauty of it is captivating—even the aroma. The Silver Flame contained the key to reestablishing their connection with The Isles of Ellian. Unfortunately, the king had built his entire kingdom around this invaluable spring and spared no effort in safeguarding it. Sharing something like that with others, especially those from the southern region, made him feel uneasy.

Maliah's small bag hangs from her back, its strap digging slightly into her shoulder as she walks. The young Fate had carefully chosen two books and three outfits—a couple of shirts, a stylish vest, and a dress that was destined to remain untouched. Despite her reluctance, her mother insisted she bring it along to appear more feminine. While Maliah's mother holds out hope that the king will view them as an asset and allow them to join the other royals, she understands that if they are accepted, it will be in a position of servitude rather than as members of the ruling class.

Just as the woman turns, the piercing howls echo through the air behind them. It seems that the Wolves have somehow found out about their migration, exposing them to grave peril. With a sense of urgency, she reaches in and swiftly lifts the girl, carefully positioning her on her side, as she quickens her pace. The rushing waters stand between them and the freedom they seek.

"Mama?"

When Maliah turns her head, she catches sight of the swift movement of fangs and a thick coat of fur. A group of three wolves is chasing them at a rapid speed. With each powerful stride, their claws penetrate the unyielding terrain, occasionally propelling stones and clouds of dirt behind them.

One of the male Fates from the caravan manages to safely reach the other side and proceeds to securely wrap a thick rope around his arm. Several more follow suit, repeating the process in various spots along The River Wilde. These males form bridges as their teeth grind and muscles tense.

Crossing the rushing water is crucial for their survival.

The wolves will soon arrive, and the thought of facing them with so many trapped in their path fills Maliah's mother with dread. Glancing behind them, she feels a rush of fear as her wide eyes dull with terror. Without hesitation, she would sacrifice herself in order to ensure her daughter's safety.

She lets her maternal instincts take over, guiding her every move.

"Maliah, do not wait. I'm right behind you."

Frantically, she removes the necklace from her own neck, a present from Maliah's father, and quickly puts it on her daughter. In a state of panic, Maliah shakes her head and silently mouths words that are impossible to hear.

"I will always be with you," she whispers before releasing her daughter with a whimpering gasp.

Maliah tightens her grasp on the rope, feeling its rough texture against her skin. Her hand barely wraps around it. She growls, pushing through the water, ignoring the icy sting on her skin. Just as she looks back, a piercing cry echoes through the air. An enormous wolf has knocked one man to the ground, growling fiercely before tearing into his flesh and ripping it away from the bone. The air is filled with cries of terror as the river sweeps away those desperately clinging to the rope he had wrapped around his arm. With desperation in her voice, she cries out for her mother, who wields a sharp blade to defend the man clutching the sturdy rope that Maliah depends on to navigate the rough currents.

As her eyes narrow and jaw ticks, her mother warns the approaching wolf with an intense gaze.

"Not this day."

She effortlessly demonstrates her skill as she twirls the blade in her hand. The edge of her lip curls into a smirk. If she is to fall, let it be in this way as she defends her kind. It will be an honorable death for someone with more Fae blood than Elven coursing through their veins. Calling upon her ancestors, she lunges forward with a newfound strength and determination. Her war cry fills the air, momentarily freezing the wolf in its tracks. Without hesitation, she thrusts her blade into its side. Despite her efforts, another wolf swiftly latched onto her forearm, the bones shattering like fragile glass. Her mother tilts her head, listening intently, before the wounded wolf emits a low, menacing snarl and charges forward.

As she loses sight of her mother, Maliah desperately clinks to the rope, feeling its rough texture against her palms. Another woman gracefully dives into the water and swiftly swims towards her, gently encircling her waist with her hand. The shoreline is alive with a cacophony of howls and war cries blending together. The woman urges her forward, shielding her from the unfolding tragedy on the shores. Yet another man's life takes a grim turn as he becomes the prey of a wolf pack. The helpless cries of those clinging to the rope he had wrapped around his arm fill the air as they plead for assistance, their voices trembling with fear. Now there are only two ropes left. The woman swings Maliah onto her back. The other side is rapidly coming into view, but out of nowhere, the rope goes slack, and the woman lets out a muffled cry of pain, her teeth clenched tightly together as she fights to hold on. Maliah's heart races as she looks behind them, the sound of raging waters filling her ears, while the male holding the rope fights against the violent shaking inflicted by the enormous wolf's sharpened teeth gripping his waist. As his body is tossed into the water, it disappears beneath the surface, carried away by the current. The wolf approaches the shoreline, its eyes fixed on Maliah. In response, she quickly looks away, her grip tightening on the woman's neck, but a powerful wave strikes her, causing her to be thrown around until she collides with a rock and loses consciousness.

The woman's desperate cries for help echo through the air as people on the other side rush to save Maliah from being swept away and disappearing forever. As she is lifted from the water, her body hangs limp in the rescuer's arms, water dripping from her hair. The woman hurries to her side, falling on her knees and placing her head against Maliah's chest. Despite detecting a faint heartbeat, the girl remains unresponsive. As she extends her hand and touches the back of her head, she recoils upon seeing blood. A look of fear washes over her, causing her eyes to widen.

"She is injured!" she exclaims.

"Leave her—the king will think she carries the sickness," someone warns..

The woman scowls. "Did you not see that her mother saved many of you!? She fought valiantly as we reached this shore, shedding her blood for us." She cradles Maliah in her arms. "Has it come to this, where we abandon her and let a child die with no one by her side? It pains me to think that we would be so unkind. No—her fate will be the same as ours. She comes with us! I will be responsible for her now. I will be her mother. If the king chooses to kill her, then he will have to kill me, too. We stand together, as we always have."

One by one the remaining Fate step forward, showing their solidarity, until none are left who would refuse.

The woman rises with Maliah in her arms. Her eyes scan the Forest of Blood Roses and she sighs.

"Our future lies beyond those trees and I don't plan to be caught out here after the light leaves the sky. Unless any of you want to face the vampires from the north?"

As she progresses, the others follow. Suddenly, a man approaches her and kindly offers to take Maliah, to which the woman agrees. Folding her arms, she shivers as a cold sensation rushes over her. She can't tell if it is the lingering chill from the raging waters or the haunting sound of the wind whistling through the trees. Lifting her chin, she ventures into a forest that has been untouched by her kind for generations. She knows they must move without delay.

LETTI KNEELS DOWN and gently wipes a smudge of dirt from Rowe's cheek. The twinkle in her bright eyes echo the same light that dances in his. It is a stunning shade of lilac. Rowe's features resemble his mother, while his brother, Noble, takes after their father, Elio Efhren, also known as the King of The Silver Flame.

As the doors swing wide, the sound of their creaking fills

the room, and in rushes the king. His queen immediately captures his attention, whose beauty and grace mesmerize him. Then, his eyes shift to his youngest son.

"Rowe, leave us—entertain yourself with a book. I would like to speak with your mother."

Letti stands up, bringing Rowe closer to her legs.

"Let the boy go," Elio demands.

With a nod, she lets him go, and Rowe, like a spirited young Fate, bounds out of the room in a flurry of movement.

The king glances behind him. "He is getting too old to cling to you in such a way."

"Elio, my King, he is only six rotations of the Springmoon."

"I was a skilled archer at his age and quite skilled with a blade."

Letti sighs. "You are king. Elio is a second-son. I ask that you allow him to enjoy what you were not afforded."

Letti notices that the young woman who walked behind the king avoided eye contact with her. It seems like her clothing is in disarray, and her hair is messy. It is common knowledge that Elio has a tendency to engage in romantic relationships with those who serve them, but the Queen of Silver Flame has chosen to ignore this and focus on the two sons she has given to her king.

Her eyes narrow with a harsh glare as Elio turns his attention away.

"Prepare a luxurious bath for my queen, using the warm waters from the natural spring."

The girl nods, her dress shimmering in golden hues that highlight her slender frame. She is a beautiful creature; her eyes are bright, and her hair shimmers like silk. The queen's age is nearly triple hers. Letti's heart aches at the thought of her husband shamelessly parading his lover, especially after just being intimate with the girl.

"Obey your King," she hisses.

The Fate Queen's shoulders slump as the girl closes the chamber door, and she lets out an audible sigh of resignation.

"They seem to get younger and younger, do they not?" she asks.

As Elio nears her, his fingers trace a soft path along her cheek, leaving a tingling sensation in their wake. Her skin is heavenly soft, reminiscent of the luxurious texture of silk. Letti is a stunning Fate, adorned in regal attire, with the bloodline and stature of nobility. From the moment Elio laid eyes on her, he knew she would be his queen. Their love affair became the stuff of legends, and their sons were born in quick succession, a testament to Elio's unwavering desire for his queen.

Letti's gaze locks with the piercing eyes of her king. She cannot fault him for his burning desire. But maybe she should grant herself the same little delights? Yes, without a doubt, she will. In her secret plotting, she desires the same level of attention that Elio seems to relish from the never-ending stream of servant girls.

"I am grateful to you for providing me with new guards to protect and watch over me. I find them—absolutely delightful," with a mischievous smile, she jests, her voice laced with a hint of flirtation.

His brows knit together, forming a line. "Do you? These measures are designed for your safety, not for your amusement."

She takes a step back, her fingers delicately tracing the curve of her neck. Her beauty entrances Elio.

"I desire to have more quality time with them. Perhaps one could stand guard as I bathe."

Elio exhales slowly. He is well aware of her annoyance towards his promiscuous behavior. Quietly approaching her from behind, he encircles her waist with his hands. He firmly presses her against his chest, holding her tightly. She lets out a quiet gasp as she feels his strength behind her. It has been quite some time since he last entered her bedroom. Left alone, she had no choice but to satisfy herself.

With a gentle lean, he brings his lips close to her ear, lightly grazing the edge of the finest point with his teeth.

As she closes her eyes, she can't help but picture his playful grin in her mind.

"I have a gift for you, my love," he whispers.

Curiosity dances in her eyes as she turns to face him.

"I have jewels that sparkle like stars, clothing that flows like silk—an entire kingdom at my fingertips. Elio, what is it that you could possibly offer me? And please refrain from suggesting a dragon. You know how I feel about those creatures. My distaste for them is undeniable." As she pauses, she can hear the distant chirping of birds and the rustling of leaves in the breeze. Her gaze briefly shifts towards the open window. "Such filthy things. I still don't understand why you keep them on that wretched island. You could kill them once and for all—instead, you allow them to linger like ghosts."

"My dearest. You forget. The dragons helped us win the war."

"Win?"

Her mocking tone latches onto Elio's pride, digging deep like a relentless parasite. Admittedly, she takes pleasure in tormenting him as a form of revenge for his unfaithfulness.

A frown forms on Elio's face as his brow furrows. He turns his head and peers out of the window that faces south. Letti had insisted on a room that offered a view away from The Sorrow to avoid any reminders of their past.

"They brought peace when there was none, my lovely queen."

"If I am to be exposed for my fearful nature. I will admit that I'm afraid they will retaliate and pose a threat to us."

Elio closes his eyes, shutting out the world around him. "My beautiful bride, their fortunes will never improve. As the treaty demanded, I carried out the act of taking their wings."

"You certainly did, with your powerful longsword and forceful strikes," she purrs.

He lingers near the window, captivated by the expansive view of the lands they can proudly claim. With a sigh, she acknowledges the immense effort he put into creating this kingdom for their people—for her. With guilt as her driving force, she cautiously approaches him from behind. She pauses briefly before choosing to embrace him by wrapping her arms around his waist. His gaze drops, and a sense of relief eases the wrinkles that have developed on his forehead.

Elio is of Elven descent. It's commonly referred to as pureblood. His wife is not. Because she has Fae blood, she has given birth to two sons who are a blend of both races, known as Fate. He did this to unite their people, but not everyone chose to reside in the kingdom he worked tirelessly to establish. No—some chose to live in the Wayward Divide, free from the rule of a single king and forging their own path. Elio's father, an Elf king, harbored a deep hatred for the Fae, yet he knew that without their presence, both races would have faced certain destruction. Once his father fell, Elio resolved to bring them together despite his hidden disdain for the Fae and their brutal customs in times of war.

Their salvation was owed entirely to the strength of the Fae and dragons. Nevertheless, Elio would never acknowledge it. In a display of unwavering confidence, he insisted that the credit for their survival belonged to him alone, demonstrating that traces of his father would forever exist within him.

But Letti had changed all of this.

The beauty she possesses. The level of her intelligence.

Her blood may be muddied with the Fae, but she holds her chin up high, refusing to let it break her spirit. She represented the future, and he selected her to bring their people together and shape the Fae into a civilized society, as he referred to it.

With his hands now gently resting on top of hers, Elio and she share a serene moment before he decides to break the silence.

"I have sent word to the south and invited the Wildlings home."

Letti tries to free herself, but his grip on her wrists tightens, causing her discomfort.

"It is time to end this last separation," Elio demands.

She pulls with all her strength, and finally, he is compelled to release her, not wanting to leave a mark on her flawless skin.

With eyes growing wider, she makes no effort to hide her distaste for them.

"Elio, they are diseased, like the dragons."

Elio takes a deep breath before turning to face her. He

knows it will take some convincing, but he is the one with authority, not her.

"I am taking precautions."

Her eyes search his for reassurance.

"What kind?"

His head tilts.

"Do you not trust your husband?"

Her posture stiffens. "Trust is a word I would not use in our case."

"Please don't," he begs.

"You will put us all in danger!" she presses.

Elio ticks his jaw. He loves his wife beyond measure despite finding her occasionally tiresome.

"I would not allow anyone within these walls that would bring harm to our people."

Letti lifts her hands in protest.

"And who has convinced you of this? Our children live here, Elio. Your sons are the future of our realm."

Elio blinks, his jaw clenching in frustration.

"Do not speak to me of our children, Letti. You know I would burn this world to the ground for them."

"Would you?" She glances toward the chamber door. "Your young companions seem to receive more of your attention than either of your heirs. If you do not take care, your name will fade from their memory, along with the echo of your voice. The children will be convinced that the chambermaid and guardsman are their real parents, never suspecting their true origins."

Moving closer to her, he forms a tight fist at his side, a visible sign of his growing aggression. She has once again provoked him, as she tends to do when they spend extended periods of time in each other's company.

He reaches in and grabs her arm, pulling her close against his chest, feeling her heartbeat through her racing pulse. Elio's eyes narrow, filled with an intense desire to lash out at her for her disrespectful behavior, though he restrains himself. He has never physically harmed her, even though she could have benefited from it, just like his mother did from his late father's heavy hand.

Letti stands her ground, deviant as always. It is in these moments that Elio is reminded of her heritage. Fae have always been stubborn by nature, with underlying currents of anger. It was their secret to winning wars.

"Tell me they are mine," he demands.

He increases his hold on her upper arm despite her laughter, causing her to gasp.

"Elio—of course they are yours! They come from *your* seed. I gave birth to them. They are of *your* blood. How could you question my loyalty?"

The way Elio openly shares his jealousy with her ignites a primal desire within her, causing a surge of moisture to gather between her legs. Despite her temptation, she resists the urge to invite him to her bed as pride consumes her.

They are locked in this aggressive embrace, their bodies pressed tightly together, until Elio reluctantly releases his grip. She takes a step back, her neck bent at an awkward angle as she struggles to rein in her emotions.

"Letti, the world is changing. We need to be united."

"Changing? In what way?"

Elio manages to compose himself after suppressing his anger towards his queen. He is incapable of causing her any harm. The existence of his heirs strip him of power, leaving him impotent. They need to view him as both their father and their king.

A ruler who can command with authority, yet also show compassion, even if that compassion is often used to his advantage.

"Whispers on the wind suggest that other kingdoms are failing to honor their part of the treaty. Without confirmation, the decision to let people like us stay in the Wayward Divide would be seen as a sign of vulnerability. This demonstrates my inability to govern my own people. I must show force. I cannot allow myself to appear weak in the eyes of anyone—especially our enemies."

"That's absurd. Your power as a ruler is widely recognized by everyone. If you had fallen out of favor, the Silver Flame would not offer guidance. That is the only way you would lose authority over this kingdom."

Elio tilts his head up. Her compliment brings him a much-needed warmth that she seldom shows.

"Your belief in me is deeply appreciated, but it's important to remember that you are my Queen. Vampires, witches, wolves, and mortal men perceive me differently than you do."

"They are fools. You should be the rightful ruler of all these magnificent lands. Ellian should be yours, my love," she coos.

He watches as Letti moves past him, her presence leaving a trail of warmth in the air. The scent of her sweetness ignites his senses. He would not hesitate to take her right now, provided he believed she wouldn't put up a fight. As she moves closer to the fireplace, he turns to face her. She stares up at the portrait of their family painted by a skilled hand in happier times. Her hair is swept up by a cool breeze, creating a graceful and flowing movement. He steps up behind her, his fingertips lightly grazing the thick braid that cascades over her shoulder. His lips yearned to brush against her skin, craving the sensation of its velvety smoothness.

Letti closes her eyes but is quickly reminded of his infidelity when a knock comes on the door, and behind them a young girl stands, one-half Letti's age and often heard moaning from pleasure behind her king's chamber door.

As Elio catches sight of her, he notices the dullness in Letti's eyes, filling him with remorse. His lack of self-control had been detrimental to their relationship, but the allure was too strong. His father had also been this way. It seemed to linger in his blood.

"Why do you interrupt us?" Letti demands.

The girl lowers her head, "I was told to bring word to our King."

Elio positions himself between the two women. He knows that his queen's temper can sometimes erupt without warning.

"What news do you bring?"

The girl lifts her chin with a mixture of anticipation and curiosity as Elio draws nearer. Her lips, swollen and tender, curve into a mischievous grin.

"They have entered The Forest of Blood Roses, my King."

Her gaze travels down his body, fixating below his waist. He clears his throat, his voice coming out in a raspy, strained whisper.

"Anything else?"

Shaking her head, she glances past her king to find Letti comfortably seated on her plush velvet couch. She lifts her teacup and takes a sip.

The queen grimaces, peering into her cup.

"I need hot tea." she says.

The girl bows to her, "Of course, my Queen. I will let your chambermaid know."

Letti cocks a brow, "I want *you* to fetch me some hot water."

The girl gazes intently at Elio, studying his every feature. With a simple nod, he silently agrees.

"Do as your Queen commands of you."

"The wolves have taken half," the girl blurts out without being asked.

Elio's irritation is clear as the girl shares the news, aware that he never wanted his queen to discover his deliberate endangerment of the Wildlings.

"Your queen has given you an order. Obey her."

"The wolves?" Letti asks, leaning forward on the couch.

With a respectful bow, the girl catches Elio's furrowed brow before gracefully leaving the chamber. Despite being aware of his potential harshness, she still prefers the strength of his firm hand over a weak touch as he forcefully takes her within his private chamber. What brutality Elio wishes to bestow upon his queen is spent on her.

He turns to face Letti, her eyes fixed on the ground, refusing to meet his gaze. He joins her on the couch, sinking into the soft cushions. As he reaches in to touch her face, she subtly shifts away, denying him any contact. His hand descends.

"What have you done, Elio? You just spoke to me of unity."

Elio crooks his neck, feeling the tension release as he stretches his muscles. He fantasized about bending her over the end of the couch, lifting her dress, and savoring her treasures, but her disdain for him was evident. Elio is aware that he will unleash his frustrations on the girl who delivered the information.

"I want you to know that I am selectively permitting only a few of them to enter the kingdom. I want to ensure that there are no males present, and that all women and children are thoroughly inspected before they engage with anyone, especially you and our sons."

Letti raises her hand and touches the delicate area at the bottom of her neck. Elio is captivated by it.

"I appreciate your concern for our safety. It seems I spoke in haste, and for that, I apologize to you, my king."

Elio nods to her, a small smile playing at the corners of his lips. This was the most they've communicated in quite some time, their voices carrying a tinge of both familiarity and distance.

"As I said. I would never place you in harm's way. I meant it, Letti. I will protect you, now and always."

"It's unfortunate that my heart isn't shown the same courtesy."

Elio stiffens.

Just as she was about to speak her truth, the girl arrives with a kettle of hot water, interrupting the moment.

With his queen's eyes fixed on him, Elio suppresses the nervous knot in his throat, hoping for a flicker of the love she once had for him. He yearns for that connection, even though he knows he is responsible for her intense animosity towards him.

The girl carefully kneels in front of the small table, her eyes fixated on its intricate carvings. Her gaze shifts towards her queen, seeking guidance amid uncertainty.

"Would you like something sweet or savory, my queen?"

Letti grins, stealing a quick glance at her husband, a twinkle of affection in her eyes.

"Virginal tea leaves. They are the sweetest—once they are plucked, they tend to become bitter. Would you not agree, my king?"

Elio's eyes twinkle with mirth, but he quickly composes himself, hiding his amusement. Clearly, her anger towards this girl is palpable, and she's plotting to make her suffer.

"Speaking of bitter. Perhaps you should bathe," Letti says while sniffing the air. "It seems work has not agreed with you today."

The girl is clearly upset but chooses not to speak her mind. Anything she says to her queen will surely result in punishment. As she opens one small box, a delightful aroma wafts up to her nose, causing her to break into a smile.

"Would you prefer I go now before serving you, my Queen? I wouldn't want to ruin your tea with my stench."

Letti bites her lip. The girl possesses a sharp wit. Elio's attraction to her is clear; her wit and charm captivate anyone who meets her. However, she should be careful, or Letti will ensure she regrets it.

"Mmm, you can join me. A bath is being drawn."

Elio's eyes brighten.

"Alone," Letti adds.

She knows her husband's taste more than most. He would prefer more than one female in his bed—and has, on many occasions, enjoyed it. But Letti could not bring herself to share him. Not yet. Perhaps one day.

Elio's shoulders droop.

"I would like for you to start bringing me tea every day at this time."

Letti looks to her husband. "If you will allow it, of course."

Elio nods. Despite his skepticism about Letti's plans, there is a growing sense of anticipation stirring within him. He must rise, feeling the growing tightness beneath the fabric of his pants. Letti, fully understanding the circumstances, lifts her hand to suppress a delighted grin.

Without warning, a guardsman interrupts the silence by knocking on the half-open door. All attention is on him as he respectfully bows to his queen and king.

"They have arrived," he claims.

Elio's perplexed expression is obvious for all to see.

"Who?"

"The Wildlings, they await at the gates for entry, my King."

"Why was I not informed of this?"

The guardsman's gaze lingers on the girl kneeling on the floor, but he remains silent. In this moment, Letti realizes the girl has deliberately withheld the information, leaving her to wonder about her ulterior motives.

Letti rises, her hand waving enthusiastically at the girl.

"What is your name?" she demands.

"Shalee," she offers.

"Shalee, you shall tend to them in the bathhouse."

With fear, the girl's eyes grow wider.

"They are diseased, are they not?" she asks.

Letti squares her shoulders, demonstrating her sovereignty.

"Do not question me—now go, prepare the baths for them. They will need to be inspected and cleaned before they are to be presented to the royal house."

"One appears to be injured, my queen," the guardsman states.

"Injured?"

The guardsman lowers his eyes, hoping he hasn't spoken out of turn.

"Yes, my queen—it is a child. The only one among them."

The girl stands up as Letti pushes past him. With a scowl, Elio snaps his fingers in her direction.

"Do as she commands. I will speak to you later."

The girl lowers her head as he hastily exits the room, chasing after his beloved.

"Letti! Where are you going?" he calls out.

With a firm grip on the hem of her elegant gown, Letti makes her way to the wide staircase that descends to the lower level. Carefully gripping the railing, she descends the steps, her heart pounding with each hurried step, until she finally emerges into the checkered foyer. Glancing behind her, she sees Elio hurrying to catch up, but she continues sprinting towards the entrance. As she darts down, two guardsmen graciously open the heavy doors adorned with intricate vines and other captivating natural elements. Her flawless skin is gently kissed by the cool air as she rushes across the courtyard, creating a sense of exhilaration in her movements. Pausing at the gates, she finds herself captivated by the barrier that separates her from the outside world. The mere thought of leaving the kingdom after all this time fills her with excitement.

"Open the gates!"

She demands. Elio, panting heavily, reaches her.

"Letti—please."

Without a glance in his direction, she brushes off his attempts to get her attention.

"I said open the gates! Do as your queen commands!"

The guardsmen glance at their king, but he nonchalantly waves his hand, fully aware that she will not be turned away.

The doors creak and moan on their hinges, creating an eerie symphony that echoes as the last bits of sunlight cascade through the opening, illuminating Letti like a divine presence.

Straining her eyes, she can make out just twelve figures standing before her. With Maliah cradled in his arms, a man takes a step forward. As a result of being violently thrown against the jagged rocks in The River Wilde, she remains in an unconscious state.

Unafraid, Letti closes the gap between them, her eyes locked onto the girl, her heartbeat quickening. With a hesitant gesture, her fingers brush against her ashen cheek. The scent of drying blood fills her nostrils.

Elio joins his wife but is momentarily frozen as he eyes the necklace around the girl's neck. As soon as he saw the necklace, he knew it instantly - it was the same one worn by the spy he had entrusted to gather information from their villages in the Wayward Divide.

The sound of his racing heart fills his ears, drowning out all other noises. His skin feels the rising heat. Despite his burning desire for revenge, he reluctantly decides that keeping his enemies close would offer him more advantages than rejecting this innocent child.

"We shall heal her and then give this child to Noble as a companion," he states.

Shaking her head, Letti reflects on her youngest son.

"No—I ask that she be given to Rowe. He longs for a friend. She could be that to him and more if he so chooses."

Elio hesitates and then stares at the necklace once again that sits against the young girl's chest.

"As you desire, my queen. The girl shall be his to do with as he wishes."

"Who claims this girl?" Letti asks, looking at those who made it to their gates. "She shall serve my son and her mother along with him."

The woman who plunged into the frigid waters steps forward to claim the girl.

The man holding Maliah glances in the woman's direction. She is brave to take on the role of mother to a child she doesn't know, but she is unable to ignore the situation.

The Fate Queen directs her attention towards her king.

"I want both brought to the bathhouses. Your companion, Shalee, can tend to them."

Elio's jaw twitches.

"So be it."

Inquisitively, Letti leans in to get a closer look at the girl, studying her intently.

"Yes. You shall bring my son joy."

CHAPTER 3
INTO THE VOID

Maliah's fingers gracefully brush against the necklace before she lets it settle against her throat. It was the one thing from her childhood that she had kept with her, a small trinket that held immense sentimental value. All other things were thrown away as she was prepared to be Rowe's companion. The thought alone is enough to tie her stomach in knots. She has come to realize that she was held captive in that realm, yet she developed an affection for the young successor much faster than anticipated. Along with her mother, he was the determining factor for her decision to stay.

"Dreaming while awake?"

Maliah pivots, bracing herself against the ship's edge as it sways with the motion of the waves. With her vibrant purple hair flowing in the wind, the dragon rider playfully tosses a fish into the air. With ease, one of her two dragons snatches it mid-flight, while its twin lets out a hiss of disappointment at missing out on a tasty morsel.

Maliah is caught gazing at the two dragons, both of

which played a crucial role in her survival and the survival of everyone else. Nevertheless, their presence leaves her spellbound. Dragons had always been forbidden to her, but in such a short time, she had already encountered four of these awe-inspiring creatures.

"Thinking of the past."

She makes the decision to lean against the rough, sturdy wood, only a couple of feet from the approaching dragon rider. She can't help but smile as she gazes at her dragons, their playful antics bringing her joy, one snapping playfully at the other.

"My father always emphasizes the importance of living in the present, as memories can vanish without warning."

With a slight turn of her head, Maliah folds her arms over her chest.

"I have few childhood memories. I suddenly felt like the light was turned on one day."

"Did a Witch cast a spell on you?" The girl's brow contorts with curiosity as she asks her question.

Maliah shakes her head. "No—I was injured and lost my memory. But I was born in the Kingdom of Silver Flame. This I know."

"Perhaps that is merciful." The dragon rider gives her a once-over. "From what I understand, those your age lived through hard times."

Maliah bursts into laughter, but it quickly subsides.

"Hard times? No—I was sheltered within the walls of the kingdom. I grew up with privileges, or so I thought until I was told—"

She hesitates, unsure if she should reveal her truth so readily to the Witch.

"How can you grow up with privileges and not?"

With a swift motion, the girl rolls her hand and reveals yet another fresh fish. When she throws it up, the other dragon emerges victorious and claims the prize. Heavy vibrations reverberate through the wooden floor as both dragons stomp their feet. She puts her fingertips on her lips and emits a high-pitched whistle. The two dragons settled down, their scales shimmering in the sunlight.

"Hunt."

With each word she utters, they slowly begin to take off, their beautiful crimson wings causing Maliah's bangs to flutter away from her forehead. Lifting her chin, she watches as they soar above the boat and vanish into the sky, their shadows merging with the billowing clouds above.

With a sigh, Maliah gazes across The Sorrow, letting her barriers crumble.

"I was given as a gift to the King's son."

"Oh, shit. As a slave?"

After nodding, Maliah twists her neck slightly. She winces as her shoulders throb with pain.

"It's very much an 'oh, shit' type of situation."

The dragon rider looks beyond her.

"Was it the one who tried to kill our dragon queen?"

With a surge of anger, the Witch squints her eyes as memories come rushing back.

Taking a deep breath, Maliah slowly exhales.

"Um, no. I was gifted to the one who is healing below. The other one was his brother, Noble Efhren, first son of the King of Silver Flame."

A look of surprise crosses the dragon rider's face as her eyes widen at the unexpected turn of events.

"Well, that's unfortunate."

Maliah shakes her head. "Noble was a terrible Fate. If he had gotten his way, I would be his and he would have—"

To offer empathy, the dragon rider gently touches Maliah's arm, conveying understanding without words. Her compassion touches Maliah.

"You don't have to explain. I am well aware of how awful some men can be. Most, actually, in my experience."

"Not all of them," Maliah half-whispers while looking down.

"Oh—oh!" The purple-haired Witch is grasping the depth of Maliah's struggle.

After pushing off the hardwood, Maliah shakes her head in frustration.

"It's complicated."

"Love often is."

"I don't love him," Maliah protests.

The dragon rider smirks. "No—of course not, I shouldn't assume."

Maliah extends her hand. "I should introduce myself. I'm Maliah Bazzel."

"Bazzel?" the dragon-riding Witch asks.

Maliah nods, "Yes. What is it?"

"Oh, nothing. It just sounds familiar."

Maliah grins. "Well, I have no siblings that I know of."

With a hearty laugh, the dragon rider firmly shakes her hand, her strong grip leaving an impression. Her oval eyes match her purple hair that is braided over her shoulder to keep it out of the way when she is clinging to her dragon's back.

"I am Faeryn Zabina, and my twin dragons are Ori and Sable." Her grin dimples the middle of her bottom lip. "I am a free Witch, under no ruler, as were my parents before me, and those before them."

As Maliah withdraws her hand, her eyes sweep over Faeyrn's red outfit, finally settling on the distinctive patch attached to her outer arm. With a quick glance at her patch, the dragon rider's attention returns to Maliah.

"You must be curious."

Maliah nods.

Faeryn places a hand on her shoulder to reassure her.

"I promise you will receive all the answers you seek once we reach my home."

Maliah, feeling relieved now that Noble is no longer a threat, is eager to press further. However, time will eventually turn against them when Elio Efhren, the King of Fate, discovers that his eldest son has died.

"Where is home?"

Faeryn's eyes light up, as if a memory has just sparked within her.

"Beyond the Veil—."

Maliah's eyes narrow in concentration, assuming the dragon rider is speaking of Obsideon.

The soft breeze tousles her bangs, creating a gentle movement against her forehead. Maliah's gaze lingers on her perfectly sculpted jawline and the dainty contours of her petite nose. Her beauty is captivating and impossible to ignore. Maliah won't deny it. The pull towards both males and females had always been there for her, but the weight of her obligations to Rowe Efhren kept her from pursuing any romantic interests. But now... well, she can't think about such things as Rowe lies below deck, his wounds slowly mending.

"I want to thank you for what you did."

Faeryn's eyes briefly meet hers, a silent acknowledgement passing between them. Her skin is bathed in the soft,
gentle light of the sky, giving her a luminous complexion
and a sparkle in her eye. Maliah senses a deep connection
with this girl, as if they share many similarities. She may be
taking unnecessary risks and putting herself in danger
without reason. There is a noticeable mark on the neck of
the dragon rider that catches her eye. The curious shape
almost seems to be a symbol, hinting at a hidden meaning.
Embarrassed, she quickly looks away when Faeryn catches
her staring. She reaches up, her fingers brushing against it.

"It is a tattoo, not so unlike yours." She looks at Maliah's
arm and then her chest.

Maliah rubs the side of her neck. "All Fate have them
once you drink of The Silver Flame. It draws them to the
surface."

"Well, I think they're lovely. They suit you."

Despite Maliah's efforts to hide her grin, her eyes betray
her true emotions.

As the dragon rider's hand moves, it accidentally grazes
against the side of Maliah's hand, which rests gently on the
smooth hardwood. As Faeryn parts her lips, the tranquil
silence is shattered by the emergence of Arren and Grim
from below deck. Waves of hearty laughter reverberate,
filling the atmosphere like the sound of a ship's bow cutting
through water. Grim slaps his hand on Arren's shoulder and
shakes his head.

"So, I chucked the empty bottle into the swirling waters
and dropped my pants right there to relieve myself in front
of everyone, seeing as I was too far gone to know I had an
audience."

Maliah's face contorts in a grimace, while Faeryn adjusts

her posture, no longer appearing as relaxed as she was during her conversation with the captivating pink-haired beauty.

"Charming," Faeryn states while rubbing the side of her arm.

Grim tightens his lips before shaking his head.

"I wasn't aware that all of the beauty was collected in one place. Surely you might spread out a bit so I will not have to fight such temptation."

"And a talented liar," Faeryn smirks, her full lips tugging at the edges.

Maliah smiles before noticing Arren is staring at her. He remains alluring. Nevertheless, there are other matters that occupy her thoughts besides the fascination with a wolf who can change forms.

Arren glances below. "Rowe is doing much better, it seems."

"And Wennie?" Maliah asks.

"Curled up next to him. She refuses to leave his side."

Arren turns his attention to the dragon rider, puzzled by Maliah's decision to stay here instead of joining Rowe below deck, and a silence settles between them. Perhaps she desired the company of someone new and some fresh air after their ordeal.

As Grim takes a step toward the dragon rider, the heat from the fire-breathing creatures intensifies. Suddenly, a blur of red scales appears before them, as one of her loyal dragons lands forcefully in between, its presence commanding attention. Grim is compelled to retreat a few paces. Faeryn reaches out and strokes Sable's side.

"She does not know you."

Sable bares her teeth and gives Grim a menacing glare.

He lifts his hands, palms open and facing outwards, to signal that he poses no threat.

Nervously, Grim observes the dragon and says, "She looks like she wants to eat me."

Her long and thin head gives her a sleek and elegant appearance. Her snout, boasting a set of perfectly aligned, menacing teeth, completes her formidable look. She stands firm, her chest vibrating with a low rumble that refuses to go unnoticed.

"Well, you do carry her favorite scent of rotting fish."

Grim sniffs at his underarms, wrinkling his nose in distaste, and waves a hand to dissipate the smell.

"I can't dispute that claim." With a mischievous expression, Faeryn casts her gaze upon him, her eyebrow lifting. "But she won't eat you unless I say. Give me no reason and you'll remain safe."

With a laugh, Grim leans sideways and nods to let Faeryn know he wholeheartedly agrees.

Arren speaks up.

"Allow me to introduce myself. I am Arren Verrick, assigned as a guard to Arcadia Miakoda, the daughter of Althea, Queen of the Kingdom of Night. And this is Grim Dashiell. We appreciate everything you have done."

The increasing winds tousle his black hair as he reaches up, flexing the muscles in his arm to tuck a loose strand behind his ear. The light dances on the earring hanging from his right ear. He treasures the gift from Arcadia, a symbol of their eternal bond.

Grim nods, his shaggy brown hair tickling the sides of his face and intertwining with his scruffy beard. "I am—or was, an Umbra. I left my Gen to sail alone on The Sorrow. This is my ship—an inheritance from a lifetime of work reduced to wood and sails, but she gets me where I want to go. I offered safe passage to Maliah, the small dragon, this canine beast, and the Fate who rests below."

The touch of gray at his temples only served to amplify his appeal. Without speaking, he might seem more proper than he actually is, despite the growing stench.

With their matching athletic builds and bronzed complexions, the two men appear remarkably similar. They even share the same humor. It's no surprise that the two had formed such a strong bond.

Leaning into Sable's ear, the dragon rider whispers something, causing her to huff before she takes a few steps back, creating space for her to speak. With a low growl, Sable raises her paw and proceeds to give it a thorough lick. Grim angles his head. If she wasn't a flesh-eating dragon with fire for breath, he would imagine she would be a delightful pet.

"I am Faeryn Zabina, a proud Witch, dragon rider, and —" she looks to her arm, "Cleric."

Arren's arms are folded tightly across his broad chest, and Grim absentmindedly rubs his jaw, running his fingernails through his stubble.

"Religious?" Grim asks.

Faeryn grins. "In some ways, yes. But no, not how most would assume."

She pauses, her gaze fixated on something beyond them.

"I will explain in due time, but first we have to navigate that."

She points beyond the bow, where the sound of rushing water grows louder with each passing moment.

"No—no—no!"

Grim exclaims in a frantic voice as he rushes toward the

wheel. He pops his knuckles before seizing it. He puts all his strength into turning it, but it refuses to yield, firmly stuck in place.

"There is no need to panic," Faeryn states while inspecting her nails.

"No need to panic?! We are approaching the Void! It is the edge of the world, we will all die!"

Maliah's brows knit. "What is the Void?"

The sound of Grim's frustrated grunting fills the air as he battles to maneuver the wheel. With a forceful slam of his black boot against the pole, he strains his muscles, desperately pulling with all his might, yet it proves futile. Faeryn has taken control of the ship. With little effort, she effortlessly guided the ship by casting a spell.

"The Void means death. It devours entire ships, swallowing them whole and taking their crews down with them. No one who falls over that edge is ever seen or heard from again. The depth is unfathomable, invisible to any eye."

Maliah glances at Arren with a rush of panic in her eyes.

He hurries to assist Grim in redirecting the ship, but both men end up gasping for breath as they tire themselves out, attempting to rotate the wheel.

"Do you think I would save all of you only to let you die now?" Faeryn asks, lowering her hand and placing it on her leather-clad hip.

With a quick sprint, Grim rushes past her, seizing a spear with a hooked end, then promptly heads back to the wheel, firmly jamming it into the spokes. Trying once more, he gives it his all to pull, only to have the handle break and send him tumbling onto the deck with a loud thud.

As the vessel lists, he quickly stands up, feeling the tilt of the floor beneath his feet. Despite not being religious, Grim instinctively makes the sign of the cross and holds on tightly. Rushing to the edge, Maliah's eyes widen with fear as the Void steadily approaches. Arren growls fiercely, then moves to join Maliah. He wraps his arm tightly around her waist, steadying her with a firm grip as he pulls her back against his chest. Even in this most dire moment, she couldn't deny the excitement coursing through her veins.

In the center, Faeryn stands tall, radiating an unwavering sense of confidence.

Grim's heart pounds in his chest as he watches the front of his ship teeter on the edge of the crevasse.

"You have doomed us all, Witch!" he cries out.

The collective screams of horror merged into a chilling chorus as the ship disappears from view.

During the ship's freefall, a majestic blue dragon emerges from beneath it, its wings gracefully slowing down the descent. With a graceful yet menacing movement, the blue beast wraps its body around the vessel, its scales scraping against the wood as it effortlessly snaps the mast in two. With immense power and meticulous navigation, the ship is carefully lowered through the dense mist caused by the cascading water from above, until it finally settles onto the pristine, sapphire sea that has remained unseen by outsiders for centuries.

As the blue dragon retracts its sharpened claws, the sound of scraping metal fills the air, and the vessel rocks on the surface, showing signs of damage but remaining whole. As Grim finally gathers the courage to stand, he is taken aback by the incredible scene that unfolds before his eyes, leaving him in awe. Joining Maliah and Arren, he stumbles forward towards the bow. Faeryn makes her way towards them from behind.

In their view lies a picturesque land, abundant with lush greenery and a magnificent snow-capped mountain in the background. At the island's edge, there lies a port, and just beyond it stands an architectural marvel reminiscent of an esteemed academy. Adorned with lofty towers and meticulously placed shimmering stones, this structure basks in the radiant glow of sunlight that seems to embrace every nook of this mystical place. With her fingers resting on the necklace draped around her neck, Maliah turns her gaze towards the sky. As the two red dragons soar through the air, their synchronized spins create a mesmerizing display of joy and grace. As Grim surveys the scene before him, a mix of disbelief and confusion washes over his features, rendering him speechless.

"Have we died?" he asks. "Is this paradise?"

Faeryn smiles. "No—you are very much alive."

"But how—we just—"

Looking behind the ship, he is greeted by the sight of a towering wall of water, descending with a thunderous roar. However, it is no longer as dark as the night sky. Now, it is as clear as a polished diamond. Ignoring the damage the ship has taken, he leans over the side and peers into the water, curious about what lies beneath. The underwater world comes alive as he gazes down into the depths, where a thriving coral reef teems with an array of colorful fish he has never seen before. His laughter starts to bubble up, growing louder and more uncontrollable as he starts to strip naked. Making his way up to the edge, he effortlessly dives into the water, promptly coming back up to vigorously shake his head, resulting in an explosion of water spraying in all directions. He tousles his hair and creates a splash with his hands. His face lights up with unmistakable joy.

With a sense of urgency, Maliah, Arren, and Faeryn all rush to the edge. In a state of disbelief, her eyes become brighter.

"It's so clear—so beautiful."

Arren glances at her from the corner of his eye and quickly looks away when Faeryn catches him staring.

"Come in! It's perfect! Cool, clear—tastes sweet!"

Grim drinks some water, then gestures with his hands while waving his arms and kicking his legs.

Choosing to keep his clothing on, Arren backs away from the edge and then takes a running leap into the water. Maliah shakes her head. Faeryn watches as the two men splash and play in the refreshing water.

Maliah directs her gaze towards the shoreline and observes some movement. More dragons seem to have gathered, their wings casting long shadows as they descend into the water. She looks to Faeryn, her eyes filled with curiosity and anticipation.

"They will not harm them," Faeryn insists.

With her eyes fixed intently on the horizon, Maliah strains to see as the dragons emerge, their sleek bodies moving through the water with a synchronized grace that mimics the flight of birds. As they pass under the ship, Arren and Grim remain unaware of their presence until a golden dragon emerges from beneath them. Suddenly, they find themselves marooned on the dragon's back, floating on the water. As Grim stands up, he hastily cups his groin, casting wary glances at both Maliah and Faeryn.

Arren stays seated, eyes wide open, while the other dragons emerge from the water. The range of sizes and colors among them is quite diverse. Among them, some are gold, others are green, a few are bronze, and finally, the red twins return and land on the ship's deck.

"They came to welcome all of you," Faeryn calls out loud enough so Grim and Arren can hear.

Maliah catches movement from the corner of her eye and notices Wennie approaching. She comes closer, bending down to softly caress her head. The dragon emits a purring sound. All eyes are drawn skyward.

After gliding over the ship, the blue dragon gracefully reaches the shoreline. Flapping his wings with determination, he gradually gains altitude, until he finds the perfect spot on top of the academy that extends across the horizon. With a graceful motion, he arches his back, causing his wings to fan out.

"Where are we?" Maliah asks.

The majestic blue dragon raises its head, releasing a deafening roar that reverberates through the air and causes ripples to dance across the water.

As Faeryn stands tall, strength surrounds her. She confidently speaks with a noticeable sense of pride.

"What remains of this ship rests in the clear waters of the Iron Reef, beneath the towering Mountain of Ember of Flame, where mighty dragons rule and freedom is born."

She pauses, taking in the sight before her, then turns to face Maliah.

"Welcome to Ashland."

CHAPTER 4
THE KINGDOM OF SHADOW

L eaning in closer, Cullen Moore carefully examines Koa, making sure to catch any subtle changes. His breathing, once labored, had eased, and it appeared that the fever was finally subsiding. The wolf would either perish or battle through its injuries to survive. Cullen retreats, gently pressing his fist against his mouth. His worry is evident, etching lines into his otherwise smooth complexion. He is not able to bite Koa or give him his blood. Due to the bite he received from his mother, his blood is now tainted. Lowering his arm, he carefully studies the rapidly spreading disease. The looming uncertainty of how much time he has before his mind deteriorates, similar to his father's, weighs heavily on him. If he could only find a method to treat all of them, including himself, his mother, and even his father, who had mysteriously vanished from the kingdom. With unwavering focus, he stares out the window. His eyes fixate upon the churning waves of The Sorrow. It reflects the chaos that rages within him. With desperation, he tries to feel his father's presence, but all he finds is emptiness. It's an odd sensation, difficult to describe. Lord Raiden had always been a constant presence in his life, but now there was an emptiness in his absence. The future for the King of Shadows hangs in a shroud of uncertainty. Has his life come to an end?

Detecting movement, his eyes shift. Everleigh is awake. He knows this, but she hasn't uttered a word since she found herself trapped once again in her gilded prison. But Cullen cannot trust himself with the gnawing sickness that continues to spread throughout his body.

"Are you hungry?" he asks.

Everleigh swallows, feeling the dryness in her throat. She draped the furs over her shoulders to protect herself from the increasing cold in the room. Although she would have preferred a cozy fire, she understood that Cullen's intention was to assist his friend.

Cullen redirects his attention towards her when he's met with silence.

"I realize this is not ideal," he admits.

"Is he doing any better?" Everleigh asks, her eyes filled with concern.

Cullen is enchanted by the way her voice carries through the air, resembling a beautiful melody. The strength of her scent has increased, enveloping him with an ever-growing craving. Unable to control the impulse, he bites his lip, wincing at the sharp sting and discreetly wiping away the blood. Soon, this will not suffice. His desire for her will persist until his resolve shatters. In that moment, he would transform into his greatest fear, something he had always dreaded.

A monster just like his father.

"Please, let me out of this cage so I can try to help him," she begs.

Cullen pauses, motionless like a statue, before contemplating the offer. He is quickly running out of options.

"In what way do you think you could help him?"

The Stone Maiden adjusts her mask. She's chosen to use it to shield herself for now, although the vampire has seen her face.

"Talen showed me how to give life in your beautiful garden. Surely you watched me?"

Cullen narrows his eyes, his gaze focused and intense. The mere mention of her name is excruciating. Over time, the bond they shared from the bite had diminished. Unsure of her survival, he remains confined in his kingdom, tending to a newborn Witch, burdened with extraordinary powers, a loyal companion wounded in their service, and a decaying royal bloodline entombed beneath them.

"I witnessed sparks and flame."

Everleigh's moistened lips shimmer in the candlelight. "I'm still learning."

Cullen lifts his hand, motioning toward the bed. "I want him saved, not incinerated."

The young Stone Maiden is feeling discouraged. With a sense of defeat, her shoulders sag. Cullen experiences a twinge of guilt. He recognizes that she is making an effort to help in any way possible.

He rubs the side of his neck.

"You said I have a beautiful garden. You are aware that it is filled with poisonous things that I planted. There is nothing there that cannot kill you if used correctly."

Everleigh shifts on her knees, feeling the soft furs slide

off her delicate shoulders. Braving the cold is a small price to pay if it means convincing the vampire prince to release her.

"Those plants are simply misunderstood." she states with confidence.

Cullen's curiosity tugs at him, urging him to take a step closer to the gilded cage. With an innocent demeanor, she sits upright on her knees, catching his gaze.

"They're dangerous—deadly. Some of those plants can kill you simply by touching them."

She experiences a fluttering sensation in her chest. The vampire may be providing a description of himself. She finds herself oddly drawn to this beautiful boy—or maybe she should refer to him as a man? One should not be quick to judge based on appearances alone, as they can be quite deceptive. It is quite clear that he is significantly older than he appears.

She regains her composure. "And yet, I'm fine."

The edge of his lip curls. "So, it seems."

Leaning on her hands, she shifts her weight forward while asking. "Are you?"

The soft fur caresses her palms. She flexes her fingers. Cullen is curious about the sensation of her touch. His mind wanders aimlessly, drifting from one thought to another. He can't shake the memory of her weight pressing firmly against his lap. Despite his best efforts, he is unable to let go of this desire.

"Am I what?"

"Fine?"

Her head tilts in curiosity. Cullen Moore remains an enigma in her eyes, shrouded in mystery. It's puzzling how he can switch between being warm and caring one moment and then distant and evasive the next.

Cullen parts his lips. Her gaze falls upon his fangs, which are wickedly sharp and impossible to ignore. He lifts his hand to keep them hidden.

"I am a vampire."

Everleigh cocks her brow. "Does that mean nothing affects you?"

He chuckles. "No—it means everything does. That is my curse."

A mischievous grin spreads across Everleigh's face, revealing her excitement. She is pleased that he has decided to talk to her. Several days had passed, and each morning she woke up to find meals and beverages prepared for her, yet he remained silent, solely focused on taking care of Koa. His compassion had a way of melting away her previous judgments of him. Despite his inherent danger, she couldn't help but feel a hidden attraction that she wished she could suppress.

"You sound as if you are describing a mortal."

Cullen effortlessly glides his chair across the floor as if it is weightless. Taking a seat directly in front of her, he leans forward and intertwines his fingers, resting his elbows on his knees. A sudden flutter in Everleigh's heart catches her off guard, causing the vampire's eyebrow to raise in intrigue. Naturally, he has the ability to detect it. Despite its annoyance, there is an undeniable allure to his knowing.

"You act as if you don't remember placing a knife to my throat."

"I admit that was a bit dramatic," Everleigh admits.

The vampire prince purrs under his breath.

"So," Cullen sits back and places his hands on his knees. "Tell me, why should I trust you now?"

"Because he needs more than you can give him."

Everleigh's gaze shifts past him, fixating on the bed where Koa begins to stir. Despite not looking, Cullen has the ability to sense his discomfort, but her claim affects him even more deeply.

"He is healing."

As Everleigh looks at him, her captivating bright green eyes delve deep into his core. He is forced to adjust on the chair. He finds her ability to do this deeply unsettling. However, he must accept that it's the illness spreading through his body, not a concealed attraction.

Or so he hopes.

"I could make him heal faster."

Cullen shakes his head. "You only wish to be free so you can torment me."

"Torment you?" Everleigh's tone digs into his pride.

"Yes. You seem to enjoy it."

With a snort, she glances sideways and rolls her eyes.

Cullen leans forward once again. "I don't trust you."

Frustration etches across Everleigh's face as she locks her gaze.

"Trust me? I'm the one in a gold cage."

She carefully observes the vertical bars that ascend, joining together at the top, creating an impenetrable barrier.

"This is the safest way."

Moving closer, she reaches out and clasps her hands around the golden bars, her flesh now dangerously within his reach. As his fangs grow, a primal instinct takes over, causing the hairs on the back of his neck to stand up. As he stares intently, his eyes dilate, revealing his heightened state of alertness. This girl arouses all of his senses. Despite growing tired of it, he finds himself unable to break free from the gravitational pull of her essence.

"Safest?"

With careful precision, she reaches her hand behind her head, slowly untangling the ribbon while keeping a firm grip on the mask against her skin. Motionless, he sits there, his mind reeling from her unexpected decision. In an act of grace, she takes it off, giving him the chance to fix his eyes on her captivating face. The delicate movement of the dim light in the room brushes against her skin, reminiscent of a hand gliding over silk.

She possesses an unmatched level of beauty.

Her skin, as pale as fresh snow, appears flawless. A hint of a smile plays on her swollen, rosy lips. Her bright green eyes, framed by thick black lashes, sparkle with intensity. This action has a seductive quality that surpasses the act of undressing. Everleigh is fully conscious of her actions. Allowing the vampire to experience a moment of intimacy with her. She couldn't deny that he had a knack for coaxing such inappropriate actions out of her, much like venom being extracted from a snake.

"Do you fear me, Cullen Moore?"

With a shimmer, his eyes betray a flicker of emotion, revealing his inner thoughts.

"Fear you?" he asks through breathy laughter.

She lifts herself to the bars. Now, she has made herself vulnerable. Her plan is to tempt him, deliberately provoking his anger in order to manipulate him into releasing her. She is willing to go to great lengths in order to obtain her freedom. Even if it means embracing the inevitable end.

She moistens her bottom lip with her tongue before taking it inside her mouth. Cullen is captivated, feeling the warmth of her breath and the pulsating rhythm of her heartbeat. She is a thought that lingers, teasing and enticing. It's been decades since he last felt such a strong longing. He had secretly asked the *Old Gods* for someone to challenge him—someone who could reignite the fire within him. And it seems his wish had been granted. He felt a mixture of gratitude and an increasing sense of remorse. He could see himself with this girl—this Witch, this raven-haired siren—feeling the warmth of her touch and the electric chemistry between them. He possesses the ability to bring her unimaginable pleasures, evoking euphoria that originates from the depths of her being and leaves her breathless. It is a skill only a creature like a vampire could offer.

Talen's warning echoes in his mind.

"She is poison to you—I want you to know this. Her blood. She's been weaponized against your kind."

Yes, he must deny himself. Talen Freeborn spoke truthfully. Everleigh Aeress had been fed a blend of teas that turned her blood against him. He knows this, but her sweet scent is driving him mad.

Everleigh willingly engages in this never-ending game of cat and mouse. She is proving to be a formidable opponent who may possess a similar level of skill despite being mortal. Perhaps this is part of her irresistible charm.

Her fragility is like a delicate glass sculpture, easily shattered by the slightest touch.

He desires her weakness, which he sees as her most enticing quality. In contrast to Cullen Moore, she is capable of embracing death, and he cannot help but feel jealous. The thought of your own mortality can be both terrifying and strangely thrilling, and he yearns for such emotions.

"Perhaps I misspoke," Everleigh claims, despite her disbelief.

The vampire had given her more than one reason to

believe she may be able to sway his decision, such as his lingering gaze and the subtle smile that plays on his lips.

"I will permit you to walk for one hour to ensure your muscles do not suffer from atrophy."

She perks up, her eyes now brighter and skin flush at the thought of besting him.

He steps closer. His crimson eyes caressing her delicate fingers.

His eyes darken. "Please let go of the bars."

She retreats, carefully observing his every gesture. With a hesitant pause, he unlocks the cage, his hand lingering on the door as if unsure of what lay inside. Everleigh feels a momentary pang of fear, worried that he might reconsider, but it appears he is committed to keeping his promise. Despite his best efforts to hide it, his inner turmoil is evident as he struggles with his decision.

She slowly advances as he retreats, extending her hand to grip the bars and rising to her feet. Her legs tremble with an unaccustomed weakness due to spending too much time lounging on the sumptuous furs he had provided. As she sways, he can't help but feel a magnetic pull towards her, but he forces himself to stay away. A small muscle twitches in his jaw, betraying his inner tension.

Everleigh Aeress cranes her neck, feeling a slight strain as she looks up. She takes a deep breath, her chest expanding and contracting in rhythm with her movements. She won't let her body show any signs of weakness. Cullen's eyes trace her figure from head to toe, taking in every inch of her. Her beauty is impossible for him to ignore. His desire grows, and he nervously clears his throat, his hands clasped tightly behind his back. It's possible that by restraining himself, he can avoid looking so anguished. However, the girl recognizes and understands his struggle. Since birth, she had been trained to please others, which made her ability to attract any man, whether mortal or supernatural, quite evident.

His eyes shift to his shadow, a dark silhouette creeping ominously towards the gilded cage. Its arm was now extended, fingers splayed like twisted branches. He forcefully stomps his foot, causing it to recoil in fear.

The lingering shadow captivates Everleigh, leaving her in awe of its mysterious presence. In a curious manner, she crooks her head and raises an eyebrow.

"Is your shadow—alive?"

Cullen grazes the edge of his lip with his sharpened fang, feeling a slight sting.

"Annoyingly," he acknowledges, casting a swift glance downwards.

Stepping out of the gilded cage, she gingerly lets her toes touch the cold stone floor, taking in the sensation. As she flinches, Cullen's shadow mirrors her sudden movement.

With each step she takes, her eyes gleam with curiosity. The shadow shifts towards the left. She raises her foot, and it eagerly anticipates her next action. As she hops, it darts away in a blur to the right, leaving her momentarily stunned. With a lifted chin, she locks eyes with Cullen, who can only watch helplessly as she continues her game.

"I think your shadow likes me."

"It wants to devour you."

His words penetrate the depths of her being. Like a gentle tide, desire lapped at the edges of her innocence. Everleigh's fingers softly glide over the side of her neck. Cullen's eyes, a vivid shade of crimson, track the motion of her hand, observing every subtle movement of her fingers.

He has never come across anything so difficult to resist. As the disease continues to spread, his resolve falters, leaving him feeling increasingly helpless.

Resolute in her decision, Everleigh moves forward, leaving behind any doubts. Each step she takes seems to effortlessly merge with the next, creating a seamless rhythm. As the shadow moves behind her, it engulfs her from all directions. To her surprise, the presence of it oddly provided her with comfort. She stops abruptly, just a few feet away from Cullen Moore. His back, once arched, is now straight. Her gaze is drawn to him, as she observes his form steadily growing in stature. If she were to hold him close in this manner, his chin would naturally come to rest on top of her head. She is aroused by his size. His shoulders are wide, dwarfing hers, and his hands are noticeably larger. Everleigh's mind wanders without focus. Looking behind her, she notices the shadow inching closer to her ankle. Out of nowhere, Cullen's fingers tightly grasp her upper arm, forcefully turning her around so that his back is now positioned towards her gilded enclosure. The shadow sways from left to right, but Cullen hisses in response, refusing to allow it to pass. It pauses, sensing the vampire's displeasure with its playful behavior.

Their eyes stay fixed on each other as her hair, as black as ink, settles around her shoulders. The vampire prince lingers, his intoxicating scent filling the air and drawing her in. Her eyes, the color of emeralds, widen with excitement. She longs to press her lips against his, but the knowledge of him being her captor holds her back. However, it doesn't extinguish the fire of her desire. In fact, it only amplifies her attraction towards him.

She glances at her arm, feeling a shiver run down her

spine as she watches his pale fingers tightly gripping her flesh. Their connection crackles with electricity, sparking excitement between them.

"Cullen," she whispers.

Two sharp fangs gleam from behind his swollen lips, adding an air of danger to his presence. His eyes darken, revealing a storm brewing within. Cullen is battling against his inner demons, resisting every temptation to claim her as his own. He can sense her purity.

"What do you want from me?" Everleigh demands.

With each passing thought, he becomes more entangled in a web of inexcusable actions.

"Mmm," he growls.

In the depths of his mind, their lips crash with an electric spark, his hands wandering freely as their bodies entangle in a fiery embrace. Despite this brief period of vulnerability, the vampire swiftly recovers and regains his composure. He is actively trying to distance himself from this impurity. In an act of self-preservation, he decides to bury his longing to consume her in a graveyard of his own creation. This weakness must be contained, or he will destroy her with the growing strength pressing against the fabric of his pants. In the past, he had seen how others struggled to handle his imposing size and intense demeanor. He adamantly refuses to expose Everleigh to such peril. If she ever permitted him to seek refuge in the intimate space between her thighs, she would assume the risk, not him.

As he releases her, she notices the fear etched on his face, making her heart race. He takes a few steps back, wincing as he flexes his hand to alleviate the cramping in his muscles. In many ways, the vampire prince fully understands that this girl is far from weak despite her delicate appearance. She is his most treacherous foe, crafted to entice, captivate his attention, and deceive him into falling in love with her, and ultimately, sealing his doom. With a heavy sigh, he averts his eyes to the floor, determined to drown out the steady pounding of her heartbeat in his ears. Despite the moan lingering in the back of his throat, he regains his composure, fighting against the rising tide of emotions.

As Cullen lifts his chin, his eyes shift beyond her, capturing the movement of Koa beneath the black satin sheets.

"In what ways can you help him?"

Everleigh's hand instinctively goes to her stomach as it growls. The hunger within her is as undeniable as her longing for this breathtaking boy with white-blonde hair and a mouth that begs to be kissed.

"I can give him my life."

With a slight quirk of his eyebrow, Cullen's intrigue becomes evident.

"Your life?"

Everleigh nods. "Yes, it is how I can heal. Talen showed me—it is what created sparks of light in your garden."

"If I recall, that winged creature turned to dust."

Her brow furrows. "Well, I didn't say it was perfect."

Cullen chuckles. "I would say not."

"But," she glances behind her. "He needs help, and I know you are helpless in this way."

Cullen places his hands behind his back and clasps them.

"Helplessness is not something I've ever been accused of."

"Perhaps I should choose another word then— should I say impotent?"

Cullen smirks. "Definitely not."

Everleigh's cheeks take on a rosy hue. Despite her attempts to tease him, she ended up embarrassing herself instead.

She turns to face the wolf, but Cullen's swift movement brings him to her side in an instant. He extends his arm, his hand open and hovering just above her abdomen. Her eyes cast downward, filled with a desire for his touch that manifests in various ways. It's not just the vampire prince who is struggling with his growing needs.

"Wait." His voice comes out soft and pure.

Everleigh is moved to hear him practically beg her.

His eyes graze her. "You should eat first."

"In the dining room?"

The muscles in his jaw tighten, and he instinctively curls his hand into a fist, bringing it back to his side.

"Although entertaining the last time, I would suggest the kitchen."

Everleigh lifts her hand, her eyes sparkling with mischief as she tries to conceal her wide grin.

"How about the garden? I can eat and then practice, so you can feel more at ease before I offer assistance to your friend."

"You keep insisting he is my friend."

Everleigh looks up at him, but Cullen avoids making eye contact with her.

"I've watched you secretly tend to him." She gently clears her throat. "You care for him—deeply. I can tell."

Cullen releases an unneeded sigh. "He has served me for

as long as I can remember. Never leaving my side in times of need. I reward his loyalty, nothing more."

"Mmm." Everleigh folds her arms over her chest.

"What?"

"Oh, nothing."

Cullen faces her. "I would like to know what you're thinking."

Everleigh smirks. "It must annoy you not to be able to read my thoughts."

Cullen narrows his eyes. "I don't need to read your thoughts. I can feel—" he stops short of admitting how his body reacts to her every whim.

She swallows hard. "Feel what?"

"Come. You need to eat."

With a gentle gesture, he lifts his hand and motions for her to head towards the door. Just as she is about to reach it, his speed causes her loose curls to sway against her chest and back. The door opens, propelled by a flurry of movements so quick that even the keenest mortal eyes cannot perceive them.

Everleigh exits. The cold wind greets her, causing an immediate reaction of chattering teeth. As she reaches up and rubs the sides of her arms, she can feel the slight chill in the air before the furs wrap around her, providing warmth and comfort. Cullen's response to her needs has been immediate.

As she looks at him, her eyes soften with a deep sense of appreciation. Nevertheless, her focus is captured by the stone bridge, which to her dismay, lacks a railing, making it the only link between this part of the structure and the rest. She had rushed across it before without much thought. Her mind splintered from her near-death experience. The memory of which seemed like a dream, but now she is fully aware of the danger.

Mesmerized by the breathtaking scene, Everleigh leans forward to catch a glimpse of the tumultuous waves of The Sorrow as they mercilessly crash against the jagged rocks below. The violent motion, although befitting of The Kingdom of Shadow, was not in line with the vampire prince's character, who displayed tenderness towards the wolf that shared his bed. Deep within Everleigh, there exists the knowledge that his mortality must remain intact, even if it is concealed. Her desire for that is strong, but it is surpassed by her intense fascination with his beastly nature. His teeth, sharp and gleaming, could tear through flesh with ease. Dangerous energy ignites a fierce longing within her, resonating in the depths of her soul.

However, what does this imply about her? Is evilness an intrinsic part of her nature? Does she yearn for the very thing that would undoubtedly bring her downfall? Despite her captivity in a gilded cage, her heart still yearns for him above all else in this miserable world. Her destiny to serve is draped around her like a wedding veil, a constant reminder of her purpose.

A hand gently rests on the small of her back, sending a shiver down her spine.

"I will not let you fall," Cullen promises.

Everleigh's gaze shifts towards the vampire, her eyes revealing a depth of emotions that he has yet to comprehend, for she has fallen in ways that remain hidden from him.

In a mesmerizing spectacle, the sky crackles and illuminates with a sudden flash of light. Delicate tendrils emerge and gracefully sway, teasingly reaching out to touch the edges of the billowing clouds. The wind takes hold of her. She lets out a gasp, falling to her knees.

"Let me carry you!" Cullen shouts.

"I can walk!" Everleigh replies.

Cullen shakes his head, but she is unwavering in her determination to cross the stone bridge without assistance.

Rising against the backdrop of roaring waves, pounding rain, and gusting wind, she gathers her courage.

With arms lifted for balance, Everleigh carefully begins to proceed across the stone bridge, taking a deep breath to steady herself. She must conquer this challenge for Cullen Moore to trust her, but more significantly, Everleigh must have faith in her own abilities.

With her eyes fixed on the turbulent water below, she cautiously takes a step forward. If she were to plummet from such a great height, it would undoubtedly result in her death. A spark of excitement quickly spreads throughout her body. The experience fills her spirit with an electrifying energy, activating the magick in her blood. Her hands pulsate with light to the beat of her heart. The soft glow emanating from her palms guides her through the darkness.

Cullen is utterly mesmerized by the effortless display of her magickal abilities, a reminder of her immense power. Without warning, the vampire's shadow lunges forward, and Cullen quickly reacts by slamming his open palm against the wet stone, effectively trapping it. The shadow falls just short of reaching her.

A gust of wind comes close to knocking her off her feet. With unmatched speed, Cullen swiftly pauses behind Everleigh. His presence is a protective barrier, shielding her from the gusts of wind that sweep up from the madness far beneath them. Everleigh raises her arms, finds her balance again, and continues moving forward. Left standing in the middle of the bridge, Cullen watches her with wide eyes, amazed by her bravery. Rushing forward with excitement, she finally reaches the other side and turns around. Her back is now pressed firmly against the imposing black door.

Cullen advances towards her. The wind and rain pelts him, but he remains unfazed. No storm could tear his attention away from her now. Her breathing is labored. Everleigh can feel the excitement coursing through her veins, making her heart race and her hands tremble. As his awareness intensifies, he can't help but feel his fist tightening at his side.

Cullen's shadow trails behind him as he walks, slowly inching up the wall beside her. It won't dare touch her, but the creature yearns to bask in her aura like its master.

The wet fabric of her dress perfectly outlines Everleigh's body. Her breasts, stomach, and thighs fill Cullen's view, captivating his attention. She is a desirable beauty—delicately wild, a flower yearning to be picked.

In a rush, he moves towards her, his lips hovering just inches away, but he resists the urge. Reaching down, his arm brushes against her, causing her breath to catch in the back of her throat. He proceeds to open the door while she stumbles backward. Cullen swiftly drops to one knee, his arm instinctively wrapping around her waist, preventing her from hitting the hard stone. Desperate, she reaches out and grabs his side, tightly gripping the fabric of his shirt in her hand. With a storm looming behind them and uncertainty ahead, they remain frozen in this moment. Their minds hold onto the memory, their eyes stubbornly fixated on each other in a dangerous connection.

The maiden in need.

The vampire who is ready to save her.

The curse of their love ever growing like a song.

Rising to his feet, Cullen effortlessly lifts her up, their bodies pressed close together. She clings to him, her grip tight and desperate, but eventually, she releases her hold on him. Everleigh instinctively takes a step back, her body tensing as he remains steadfast in his position. As lightning flashes across the sky, the loud roar of thunder fills the air, and at that moment, the vampire is compelled to confront his innermost truth.

There is no escaping the fact that she will be his, just as he will be hers.

Yet, this will result in his ultimate demise.

CHAPTER 5
THE KINGDOM OF STONE

Visha conceals herself in darkness, adorned in a black cloak. Despite the limited lighting in the long corridor, her eyes still manage to shimmer, adding an ethereal quality to her presence. The door is being guarded by two Stone Guardsmen who are standing watch. With intense focus, she gazes downward at the scroll clenched tightly in her hand. Finally, after careful consideration, she makes the decision to come out, fully aware that the guards will remain steadfast in their positions unless given explicit orders from the King. Luckily, she is well-prepared to lure them away.

Advancing one step, she halts upon catching a male voice from behind. She clings to the corner's edge with intense focus, listening closely. Another voice emerges, filled with laughter. It seems to be a girl. Glancing behind her, Visha realizes she has missed her opportunity. However, she chooses to investigate who interrupted her upon realizing that the couple has entered the atrium, which connects to the royal garden.

Staying hidden in the shadows, she skillfully follows their voices, her presence unnoticed. Finally, she finds respite behind a towering statue of their beloved Queen. The sculpture, made of bright white stone, has accumulated moss over time, giving it an organic touch as the green foliage clings to its shoulders and hands. The face on this statue seems to have a touch of melancholy, with a subtle downward curve to its smile. It was after the birth of their son, Arrowe Brumah, that Cassius had the statue placed in the atrium. A sense of mystery surrounded the memorial, dedicated to a Queen who had chosen to stay out of sight for many years.

Leaning forward, Visha steadies herself against the statue's base as she gazes at the couple sitting near the fountain. She is mesmerized by the ornate vines and roses intricately carved into its bowl-like shape. The water, sourced from a hidden spring, flows without interruption, serving as a vital resource for the plants and the bustling bathhouses.

The blonde-haired man's fingers gently caress the girl's cheek, leaving a trail of warmth. His affection leaves the girl's bronze skin with a rosy glow. Judging from her dress, she seems to be a servant in the royal house and older than Visha.

He leans in while moving her hair over her shoulder and kisses her neck. His hands wander, one cupping her full breast and the other wrapping her waist. Again, she giggles, enjoying his attention.

"Trystan," she gasps but doesn't fight off his advances.

His fingers coil around her erect nipple. It's impossible for Visha to avert her gaze. The intensity of his passion causes the girl's lips to part and her breath to quicken.

Impure thoughts start to creep into Visha's mind. The cathedral beckons to her, a sanctuary where she can silently plead for absolution. Acheron must excuse her behavior. Her wants and needs had been tightly contained for so long, a result of her grooming to serve a king, and it had taken a toll on her. Her understanding of pleasure is restricted, but she possesses the skill of speaking softly, always yielding, allowing a man to assert his dominance over her. Acheron's instructions for all women in the Kingdom of Stone are clear. Men know better—they're physically stronger and smarter—and take on the role of providing. Women are expected to provide support and comply with any request made of them.

Her gaze is irresistibly drawn back to the couple seated on the edge of the fountain.

"What would he think of you doing such things to me?"

The girl's words come out in a strained whisper as Trystan's grip tightens, each movement sending sharp jolts of pain through her body. She only tolerates his aggressive nature because she finds enjoyment in it, otherwise she would ask him to stop.

He leans into her ear. "I told you I don't want to discuss him."

"But soon he will be king, and we'll have to—"

Trystan abruptly silences her with a forceful grip on the back of her head, entangling his fingers in her thick locks. As he lifts her chin, she lets out a moan of both pleasure and surrender. With her neck now fully exposed, he firmly grips it just under her chin and applies pressure. She squirms as moisture gathers in forbidden places. This is the way they have been from the day he forcefully pushed her down and inserted himself into her mouth. Without complaint, she had accepted his advances, enduring the lingering bruises that took their time to fade.

"And we'll have to what? Tell him? Arrowe Brumah doesn't care what I do anymore than I care who he takes to his bed."

Struggling to find her voice, she attempts to nod, her fingers gently finding his hand. The pressure of his grip intensifies, making it increasingly challenging for her to draw in a full breath.

He grins.

"Put your hand between your legs."

Her eyes widen.

"Do it."

With a gentle movement, she raises her dress, revealing herself to the elements. Visha wants to look away, but she finds herself captivated by their intense and unexpectedly forceful embrace. As her jaw clenches, she slowly lowers herself to the ground, never taking her eyes off the girl.

"Spread your legs," Trystan demands.

She obeys.

He glances downward, licking his bottom lip before biting it.

"Are you wet for me?"

She barely nods.

"Show me how badly you want me."

The girl's hand moves rhythmically, gliding forward and back. Each thrust elicits a sensual moan from her lips. He maintains his grip on her throat while he observes her indulging in her own pleasure.

"Harder," he whispers.

With her legs spread wide, she plunges her fingers into her wetness, her palm now forcefully slamming against her throbbing clit. Silenced by his hand around her throat, she opens her mouth in a futile attempt to scream. As her eyes roll to the back of her head and she starts to slump, he decides to release her. Unconscious, she collapses into his arms. He tilts his head, his eyes filled with a mixture of curiosity and mischief, before gently lifting her hand to his mouth, his tongue darting out to lick her fingers clean. Suddenly, without warning, he smacks her across the face. Gasping, she suddenly comes alive, her current state a result of his actions.

With each kiss on her cheek, she feels herself swaying in response to his tender touch. He firmly grasps her chin and playfully gives it a gentle shake.

"Such a good girl."

Visha is captivated by his endearing title for the girl, a small part of her longing to be praised as well.

The woman with dark, flowing hair and radiant skin gently rubs the side of her head. Trystan pulls her onto her feet, and the world spins around them as he twirls her. It was evident from his beaming smile that he was thoroughly pleased with the liberties she had granted him. Meanwhile, Visha is grappling with an overwhelming surge of unfamiliar emotions, swirling within her like a tempest. Though she knew it was wrong, she couldn't resist the temptation to continue watching them. It was impossible.

Trystan's actions towards the girl had piqued her interest and left her wanting to know more. With a gentle motion, Visha raises her hand towards her throat, delicately exerting some pressure, which sends a delightful sensation coursing through her entire body, gathering and intensifying in the intimate region between her legs. She removes her hand and grins, the memory of their conversation about

Arrowe suddenly flooding back. What role did this boy play in the eyes of their new sovereign? And why would it make any difference if he did? Her thoughts trailed off as she pondered the question.

Visha narrows her pale blue eyes. Wicked thoughts began to gather in her mind, their clarity unsettling. Had Arrowe taken Trystan to his bed? Despite being aware of the rumors, she adamantly refused to give them any credence. As she reminisces, her mind's eye transports her back to the moment when Arrowe gazed at Paxton as he gracefully departed.

In an attempt to calm the nervous flutter in her stomach, she gently places her hand against her abdomen, feeling the sensation akin to the delicate flapping of butterfly wings accumulating within her. A sense of relief floods through her as Trystan breaks the silence.

"Can you stand on your own, or have I finally broken you?"

With her hand raised, the girl gently traces her fingers along the mark that is steadily growing on her throat. Trystan kneels down in front of her, his eyes locked with hers, demanding her attention.

She remains silent, her lips tightly sealed. As Visha leans forward, a sense of curiosity fills her, pondering whether she is upset about what has transpired between them.

"I couldn't breathe, Trystan."

He now rests on his knees. "We've played this game before."

She shakes her head. "Not like this."

Trystan narrows his eyes. "Are you no longer willing to please me?"

With a slight bend in her neck, the girl gazes intensely into his eyes, as if searching for something.

"You frightened me," she whispers.

Visha's level of excitement has risen even higher. The thought of his hand around the girl's throat leaves her breathless, as if she can feel his grip tightening on her own neck. The guilt weighs heavily on her.

Why does she find all of this so appealing?

As the girl gets up, Visha carefully watches her every move. Trystan grips the girl's hand, and she swiftly withdraws it, leaving him kneeling as she hastily makes her way toward the exit. Visha carefully retreats to conceal herself, ensuring she remains unseen.

Her chest rises and falls. The overwhelming excitement of it all left her nearly breathless.

With determination, she pushes herself up and onto her feet, her hands clasped tightly together. In order to find peace, she knows she must let go of it all and seek forgiveness through prayer. Acheron possesses all wisdom. Visha will learn her punishment from his judgment. If she doesn't silently receive word from her Serpent God, then Visha is prepared to confess her sins and feel the weight of her transgressions through a Holy Man speaking for Acheron.

Spying in her direction, Trystan speaks, "Little mouse, I know you're there."

Visha stands frozen, momentarily stunned, but then she straightens her spine, her eyes filled with determination as she recalls who she is and all she has achieved. There was no girl in this kingdom who could match her in terms of manipulating multiple moving parts and reaching the same level of success that she had achieved.

"Must I come—"

Visha emerges from her hiding spot behind the statue of their Queen. Observing her approach, Trystan narrows his eyes. With awe in his eyes, he observes the intricate details of her cloak and the mysterious allure of her Katsumi mask.

"You're the remaining Stone Maiden. The only one who survived the attack."

She nods. "Yes, I am."

Before deciding to encircle her, he snaps his fingers. His eyes roam across her body, taking in every detail. He's fascinated.

"You were poisoned."

She stands tall and unwavering in his presence, refusing to let him intimidate her. As he leans down, his fingers inch closer to her mask, but she quickly retreats, refusing to let him touch it. His hand remains suspended in the air.

A playful glimmer dances in his eyes as a smile of amusement tugs at the corners of his mouth.

"You were bred for Cassius Brumah."

She corrects him. "King Brumah."

Trystan bows his head. "You are correct. Even dead, he is still King until his heir takes the crown."

"You speak of Arrowe as if you know him."

The Stone Maiden's directness captivates Trystan.

"I grew up with the heir. I am the son of a royal."

She tilts her head, "Does that make you his cousin?"

Trystan folds his arms over his chest, "Yes—distant."

Visha looks towards the door before asking, "And the girl —what is she to you?"

She is aware that she can quickly access the door if necessary, but Visha finds it thrilling to speak with the boy in this way. She would never have the courage to do this without first witnessing what she had.

With a deliberate step forward, Trystan's attention remains focused on her lips. He extends his hand, but she withdraws, denying him the satisfaction of physical contact, despite its allure.

"Jealous?" he asks.

She remains silent.

Trystan thumbs at his bottom lip before saying, "You are untouched, meant only for a king, are you not?"

Visha lifts her chin. "We—I mean, I am pure, washed in the blood moon on the day of my birth. Our most wise God, Acheron, chose me to serve my king and bring him an heir. That is my purpose."

"And yet," Trystan moves behind her, leaning in closer to her ear, "you are now a Maiden without a King."

As he positions himself in front of her, Visha turns her head to stare at him.

"I will not be for long."

His eyes widen as he grasps her intentions. Through bursts of laughter, he attempts to utter a few words.

"Oh—you think Arrowe will—"

"I know what he will do. Arrowe is the sole successor to the most illustrious monarch in history. Like his father before him, he will ascend the throne of The Kingdom of Stone and seek a Queen who will be a loyal and devoted companion, ensuring the continuation of the Brumah dynasty."

Trystan rubs his chin. "I'm impressed."

"In what way?"

His eyebrow lifts. "With you, little mouse."

"I wish you would stop calling me that. My name is Visha Aeress, not *little mouse*."

"Visha."

Trystan's voice lingers on her name, the slow pace adding an intimate touch that she savored. Her heart beats erratically. Trystan's malevolent nature is an irresistible temptation, and his allure is strong.

"So, Visha, tell me. How long were you hiding in the shadows?"

Visha's pupils widen as the memory of his hand around the girl's throat floods her thoughts. Despite struggling to breathe, she obeyed Trystan's command to pleasure herself until she passed out. She remained rooted in place because of the powerful hold he had over her. Despite her upbringing emphasizing obedience, she constantly struggles against it. She places the blame on her mother, despite never having met her. Unable to disguise the effect, she alters her stance. Recognizing that a lie would be entirely meaningless in this scenario, she chooses to be truthful.

"Long enough."

"Mmm, and what did you think?"

Visha tilts her head, "I wasn't aware that I would be tested."

A smile plays across Trystan's face, clearly amused. He desires a challenge. His wife's lack of passion can sometimes dull their time together. While she fulfills the role of a model wife, he finds himself longing for something more, seeking it outside their relationship. This is particularly true given that his preferences fall outside the boundaries of what the people within the kingdom consider acceptable. With a dismissive roll of his hand, he ignores the true events that had occurred just minutes ago before he stumbled upon Visha hiding behind the statue.

"I didn't expect to have an audience while I—had a conversation with my friend."

Visha snorts.

"A short one," she mutters.

Trystan is unsure about her answer and finds it puzzling.

"Excuse me?"

Visha's eyebrow cocks behind her mask. "Your conversation was brief."

Trystan's jaw ticks. She's encouraging him to react, and he's finding pleasure in it.

"So, what is it you plan to do, Visha Aeress?" With a sense of ownership, he walks around her for the second time, carefully inspecting every detail, before eventually pausing right in front of her. "Do you expect Arrowe to use you as a vessel to secure his seed? To bury himself deep between your thighs and thrust until he exhausts himself? Is that your plan, little mouse?"

She can feel the heat slowly creeping up her skin. Grateful for her mask, she can hide the flush of embarrassment and the simmering anger on her face. What had initially been a lighthearted game had now taken a sinister turn.

"I don't *plan* on it," she snaps.

Surprised, he opens his mouth in response to her admission. It's possible that the girl was ill-prepared to satisfy his intense desire for these types of games. But before he can mock her, she interrupts with a confident voice.

"I will *make* it happen."

Trystan's bright eyes sweep over her, his index finger tapping against his chin in contemplation.

"The fact that you survived when no one else did is truly miraculous. The night the enemies infiltrated the heart of our kingdom, Acheron's blessings rained down upon you, without a doubt."

"Yes, it was a blessing, although I was also poisoned."

"And yet—you live while the rest rot—including our beloved King."

She is becoming increasingly irritated with his observations.

"Yes, I am alive, but I believe it was *his* will."

Trystan grins. "*His* will—as in our God?"

"Yes, of course. Who else would I mean?"

Trystan looks down upon her. "I can respect your dedication."

"I will always be dedicated to our—"

Interrupting her mid-sentence, he whispers, "No—your dedication to the lie."

His eyes meet hers, and at that moment, she notices a subtle change as they darken with a mixture of desire and longing. Trystan is speaking his truth, as dangerous as it may be.

"Your words could be interpreted as an act of treason."

"And yet I spoke them," he says in a flirtatious tone.

Visha's heart skips a beat. Tension grips her muscles, causing them to tighten, while her mind races with thoughts.

How could he claim to know without any evidence or information? No—no, he doesn't. Quietly, she comforts herself. It's impossible for this cousin, who lacks any restraint over his impulses, to be aware of what she has done. Does he? No. Keep your wits about you, Visha. Remain steadfast and resolute. Admit nothing, or it will be the end of you.

Each passing moment stretches out as if in slow motion,

creating a sense of stillness in the air. Her eyes linger on the boy, captivated by his striking features. His swollen mouth was still glistening from the girl's sweet nectar. Her touch left him with a flushed complexion, a visible sign of their pleasure. His hair, thick and tousled, is styled in a disheveled manner on top of his head. A rebellious blonde curl hides one of his eyes. She is surprised to find him attractive, his charisma and charm captivating her in ways she never anticipated. Lost in her thoughts, she grapples with the weight of each choice, aware of the repercussions they may bring. There is no weapon to wield against him—no means to seemingly injure him without a fight, and she is aware of her own lack of strength to confront him alone. The only option left was to please him, even in ways she had wanted to save for Arrowe. But if it meant keeping Trystan quiet until she could plot his downfall, she would do whatever it took. As she begins to lift her hand, preparing to remove the cloak and entice him with what lies beneath, the sound of Trystan's laughter fills the air. Hoping to suppress his laughter, he places his hand on his stomach, feeling the gentle vibrations.

She feels a mix of relief and confusion wash over her.

Trystan shakes his head. "I apologize, it was simply too easy to tease you."

Once again, Visha is delighted with her choice to wear the Katsumi mask. Its intention is to keep her true feelings hidden.

"I should go."

While she tries to walk away, he swiftly moves in front of her and starts walking backwards. His actions slow her down.

"Wait—wait. I am truly sorry. That was cruel."

In an effort to manipulate him, she carefully selects her words, hoping to sway his thoughts.

"Cruelty is a game for the cold-hearted."

He tilts his head.

"Please don't be angry with me. I—"

"You what?" she deliberately interrupts him, preventing him from speaking.

He rubs the side of his neck. "I've enjoyed talking to you. You are not like the other girls—including my wife."

"Wife?"

Visha asks while glancing behind her.

"Yes—arranged. We don't love each other. She's simply there to host my seed and give me an heir."

"And has she?"

He shakes his head. "Not yet."

"Well, may the blessings of Acheron give you all that you desire."

Moving gracefully around him, she reaches the door, her hand trembling as she struggles to open it. As she slips out into the corridor, he remains oblivious to the profound effect he has had on her.

Visha pauses, her eyes fixated on the vigilant Stone Guardsman stationed outside the protected chamber. Opting to abandon her initial plans, she chooses to focus on what she believes will be the most beneficial for her and redirects her path towards the cathedral. Once there, she plans to ask Acheron for his strength and guidance, just like she has done before.

A gasp escapes her lips as a hand lightly touches the lower part of her back. Trystan has joined her and, unlike anyone else, he dared to touch her.

"Where is it you plan to go?" he asks.

Visha sighs, knowing he won't be so easy to leave behind.

"I'm going to the cathedral."

"May I walk you there?"

With a brief moment of hesitation, she eventually gives in and nods.

Showing his utmost respect, Trystan politely bows to her, extending his arm in a gesture of chivalry. However, she chooses to completely disregard it, opting instead to wait for him to walk ahead of her, adhering to the traditional belief that all men should do so.

"Visha?"

As The Holy Scribe, her father, approaches the two of them, she stands there motionless, unable to react. In his presence, she humbly lowers her head as a sign of respect.

Trystan adjusts his posture, straightening his shoulders. With a fixed stare, the Holy Scribe looks at his daughter and then shifts his gaze towards the boy.

"Go to the cathedral and pray," he demands.

Without uttering a word, Visha swiftly moves down the corridor.

Trystan carefully studies the expression on The Holy Scribe's face, searching for any signs of emotion.

"It's been quite some time since we've spoken."

The Holy Scribe's jaw flexes, the muscles twitching with tension.

"She is a Stone Maiden, meant for Kings."

Trystan's eyebrow cocks, his smooth jawline sporting a light shadow.

With his full lips curved, he asks, "Are you questioning my intentions?"

Chuckling under his breath, the Holy Scribe detects the

delicate aroma of femininity on his breath. But he knows that Visha would never compromise herself in such a way. Her longing for power is directly tied to the crown. Despite everything, The Holy Scribe is well aware that Trystan is still a threat.

"I was only offering to walk her to the cathedral."

The Holy Scribe's lip curls at the edge.

"I would assume you would burst into flames upon entering."

Trystan takes two steps back, extending his arms out in a grand gesture.

"Perhaps I'll chance it someday."

Amused by Trystan's departure, the Holy Scribe chuckles softly, but his smile fades as he turns to join his daughter, a hint of concern in his eyes. The moment is drawing near when they will lay their beloved King to rest and proclaim a successor to the throne. The Holy Scribe hopes to exert the same level of influence on him as he did over his predecessor.

CHAPTER 6

ASHLAND

As the ship approaches the port, Maliah leans over the railing. The academy's grandeur comes into full view. As the building rises higher and higher, it gradually conceals more of the majestic mountain nestled behind it. Its height is nothing short of impressive, measuring no less than seven stories. The imposing façade is made up of meticulously stacked blocks of volcanic rock, chiseled smooth and solid. As the ship moves, its shadow crawls along the dark, polished surface of the stone.

Despite only being for show, Grim has managed to successfully maintain his position at the helm. Tethered by his pride and love for his vessel, he remains rooted in the one place where he felt utmost comfort. Having fulfilled their duty of safely escorting them, the dragons have now scattered and disappeared beneath the waves.

With a gentle twist of the necklace hanging from her neck, Maliah asks, "Do you live there?"

Faeryn looks at her with a light-hearted smile curving her lips.

"Yes, all Dragon Riders live within the walls of Brenna Academy here in Ashland."

With a look of disbelief, Maliah repeats the words again, "Dragon Riders."

Faeryn couldn't help but get lost in the captivating sight of Maliah's soft features and the delicate points of her ears. Once Maliah reached a certain age, she, like any other Fate, adorned her ears with stunning jewelry. This jewelry was given to her by none other than Rowe Efhren. Having conflicting emotions, she both cherished and resented the gesture, knowing that the heir of Fate was unaware of her true role in serving his family. At times, Maliah deeply regrets ever learning the truth. She could have stayed with him and lived in blissful ignorance, but she would never truly be his. It is impossible for a girl with impure blood, who has a stronger connection to the Fae than the Elven, to wed one of the King's sons, as Rowe's father would never allow it. Consequently, her future extends past the kingdom's walls. If she chose to be completely honest with herself, she would admit that the baby dragon had given her a convenient excuse to escape, even though she truly cared for the little creature.

Upon realizing that Faeryn is staring at her, Maliah clears her throat to break the awkward silence. She knows her thoughts were like an open book, ready to be read by anyone who dared to look.

Curiously, she inquires about the name. "Brenna?"

The academy has drawn Faeryn's attention, granting her some relief from the Fate who has captivated her.

"Yes. It means beacon on the hill."

Maliah grins. "I like that—this place feels hopeful."

"It protects those who long for freedom and will fight for it."

A glimmer of excitement fills Maliah's eyes, adding a touch of radiance to her expression. Her mind has been preoccupied with thoughts of freedom for the past few seasons. Her desire to tell Rowe the truth has manifested in countless ways, yet the fear of his disbelief remains a constant obstacle.

With a nod, the purple-haired Witch places her fingers between her lips and lets out a piercing whistle that echoes through the air. High above the academy, her two crimson dragons gracefully plunge through the clouds, their bodies entwined in a mesmerizing dance.

Maliah gasps, gripping the railing.

At the very last moment, they recover from the dangerous dive, with each dragon veering off in their own direction. Faeryn finds amusement and lets out a chuckle.

"I swear they'll be the death of me."

"Why did they do that?"

Faeryn bursts into laughter. "Because they're dragons and rebellious."

Maliah grins. "Like their rider."

They share a moment of silence before Maliah asks, "So, are there more like you?" she juts her chin toward the academy, "studying there?"

Faeryn cocks her brow. "Well, I wouldn't say like me, because I'm the best rider here."

Without wasting any time, Grim moves past them and proceeds to drop the anchor. With incredible speed, it races through the crystal, clear water, gracefully gliding until it finally settles firmly on the sandy floor. The Umbra looks upward, rubbing the side of his head, visibly distraught about the damage that his ship has taken. Faeryn's eyes follow his gaze.

"We will see that your ship is repaired."

Grim sighs. "I appreciate the offer, but all I require is supplies, and I will happily mend her myself." With a gentle touch, he glides his hand along the sleek railing, as if caressing the sensuous contours of a woman's body.

"I will help you," Arren offers.

The two men exchange nods as a sign of mutual under-standing and to acknowledge the shared pact between them. Grim deeply appreciates the friendship with this wolf, just as Arren cherishes the companionship of the scruffy Umbra. As Arren looks at Grim Dashiell, a pang of homesickness washes over him, yearning for the familiar comforts of home. But he made a promise to Arcadia to watch over the tiny dragon and her companions, and he would never break that sacred bond of trust.

A woman's voice pierces the air, cutting through like a sharpened blade.

"Faeryn Zabina!"

With a wince and clenched teeth, Faeryn turns around to confront the woman, who has a striking hairstyle of multi-colored dreadlocks that cascade down her back. She has on a nearly translucent, light blue dress and matching pants that hug her muscular frame. As she walks, the thin fabric trails behind her, fluttering in the breeze like a flowing river. Resting delicately on her collarbone, a sleek bronze pendant catches the light, creating a mesmerizing play of reflections. Her bare feet tread lightly, while the jingle of metal bracelets on her ankles adds a musical rhythm to her every step. Making her way along the side of the ship, she locks eyes with Faeryn and shoots a piercing glare in her direction.

"Hi!" Faeryn nervously waves.

Pausing momentarily, the woman carefully examines the impressive size and length of the foreign vessel. Her lips form a tight line, conveying her deep concern. Despite her attempts to conceal her fear, the unexpected arrival of this ship is greatly disturbing her.

"Faeryn, kindly leave the ship."

Before turning to Maliah, the Witch lets out a heavy sigh.

"This is going to be fun."

"Who is she?"

"Oh, she's the headmistress of the school, and interestingly enough, she is also my mother."

Maliah hisses. "She doesn't look happy."

Faeryn carefully makes her way over to the edge of the ship, her eyes fixed on her mother, whose anger is becoming more evident with each passing moment. With Arren's help, Grim successfully lowers the gangway, establishing a secure bridge between the vessel and the dock. A nod of agreement passes between her and the two men. With a playful wink in Faeryn's direction, Grim elicits a low rumble from Arren, a gesture that is commonly shared among wolves.

"Would you like for me to go with you?" Arren asks.

Faeryn half-grins. "I appreciate the offer, but I can handle this."

Her mother's eyes are fixed on her, filled with eager anticipation, as she slowly descends.

"Mom."

"Faeryn." Hoping to keep her voice down, the woman

glances past her, making sure no one is listening. "Who are these people?"

Faeryn sighs. "Listen, I know you told me to never breach the wall, but—"

Her mother interrupts her. "I realize that you think you can do anything, but this—this," her mother rolls her hand toward the ship now anchored by their dock, "is beyond anything I thought you would ever do. Faeryn."

The purple-haired Witch slumps her shoulders, her deflated expression evident. Suddenly, her mother remembers that Faeryn has always possessed a strong will, unwavering in her convictions.

Gently extending her arm, she reaches out to tenderly cup her daughter's cheek. "I admire your free spirit and fearless nature. I am so grateful for the woman you will become. While I am incredibly proud of you, I cannot ignore the fact that your recklessness has jeopardized the safety of everyone here in Ashland and all that we've accomplished within the walls of Brenna. Do you know what it has taken to establish this place of safety? Many died protecting it and you simply show up with a ship full of strangers after taking your dragons beyond the wall. I thought you—" Her eyes are moist with tears.

"But I had to do it!" Faeryn claims.

As Faeryn's efforts to convince her mother persist, Maliah approaches Arren.

"I feel terrible."

Arren rubs his neck. "Yeah, I wish her luck." He leans against the railing with a more relaxed posture.

"I'm sure it'll be fine," Maliah states, even though she isn't sure.

"I don't know. My mother is still mad about giving birth

to me and my siblings and brings it up every single time she's irritated." He looks over his shoulder. "Faeryn's mom has that look in her eyes." He shakes out his shoulders, remembering how terrifying his own mother can be when angered.

"Should we go down there?" Maliah wonders.

Grim chimes in. "No—no. Absolutely not."

The Umbra nervously smiles while shaking his head.

With calm directness, Maliah places a hand on her hip before speaking, "Is there something else you want to say?"

Grim points at himself. "Me? To them? Nope. I've sailed the most dangerous storms and nearly drown on more than one occasion, but I would never stand in between two females during an argument."

A chuckle escapes from Arren's lips, causing Maliah to snap her head in his direction. Without delay, he hushes himself. Both men are wary of provoking her.

She speaks with a controlled smile. "We are not beasts."

Arren tilts his head. His hesitation elicits the swipe of her hand.

He laughs before redirecting the conversation. "Should we take Rowe ashore? They probably have herbs to help him heal quicker—or food, since we've probably emptied the pantry." Arren glances at Grim. "I can carry him. He's surprisingly light. He may need to eat more."

Just as they turn, a voice chimes in behind them, and they're greeted with a pleasant sight.

"I don't need to be carried by a wolf." Rowe's voice is raspy, but growing stronger. He places a hand on his side.

Despite looking a bit worse for wear, Rowe is still showing his resilience and determination. Maliah rushes in to hug him, feeling a mix of joy and relief wash over her as she holds him.

A moan escapes his lips, but Maliah holds on, unable to let him go. Her fear of losing him was over-shadowed by the fact that the Witch had managed to save him.

"I thought I'd lost you," she whispers, her voice filled with emotion.

"Never," Rowe confidently states, although the pain still lingers in his voice.

She slowly retreats. Before offering a friendly nod, she delicately tucks a strand of her pink hair behind her ear. Typically guarded, she finds herself unable to contain her happiness around him, revealing a side of herself she rarely shows.

Tenderly, he reaches in and cups her cheek, his finger-tips tracing the delicate curve. Tenderly, she wraps her hand around his, establishing a comforting link as their eyes meet in harmony.

"Are you okay?" he half-whispers.

"Yes—I'm good—more than good. I wish you could've seen—"

He interrupts her, his heart burdened with a question he must ask.

"And my brother, Noble. Where is he?" His eyes search the ship.

Maliah glances at Arren as he moves forward.

"The blue dragon made a meal of him."

In a moment of realization, Rowe's eyes widen as he comes to terms with the truth. The fact that Noble had tried to end his life should lessen the emotional burden of his demise. And yet, the weight of the loss rests heavily on his heart. All Fate bear the burden, as blood ties among their people run deep.

Arren places a hand on his shoulder, offering support.

"I want to apologize to all of you for what he's done. I knew Noble was ambitious, but his malicious behavior was inexcusable."

Arren shrugs his shoulder. "There is a saying among my people. Hold on to what is good, even if it's a handful of dirt. Hold on to what you believe, even if it's a tree that stands by itself. Hold on to what you must do, even if it's a long way from here. Hold on to your life, even if it's easier to let go."

Rowe acknowledges Arren's words of support and wisdom with a nod. He is caught in a whirlwind of thoughts. His heart sinks as he realizes that if Noble doesn't return, his father's thirst for revenge will consume him. In the succession order, it was now Rowe Efhren's chance to become the next ruler. The crown was within his grasp unless he made the fateful choice to betray his kingdom.

"Your brother chose his path as you have chosen yours. I know he turned against you—against all of us, but if you want to grieve his loss, I would be happy to build a fire and sit with you as you let his memory go."

Rowe gives Arren a fond look. "I appreciate that, but I don't know if I want to remember my brother anymore."

Maliah looks to him with silent empathy. She understands the deep connections that Fate have with their families. The bond they have with family is as strong and enduring as their bond with the Silver Flame. The fear arises from the realization that Rowe may have to chart his own course, choosing a path that differs from her own.

While taking a massive bite of fruit, Grim can be heard yelling from the pier. "Arren! They have food." A small stream of juice makes its way down, settling into his beard. It's both sticky and sweet.

A small group of women have come with baskets of food and drink to extend a friendly gesture. Looking to their headmistress, they anticipate her wise counsel. Each of them are talented Witches, with deadly casting abilities, and they will not hesitate to attack if instructed.

Arren backs away. "The offer stands anytime."

Rowe places his hand to his heart as a sign of respect before Arren turns and rushes down the gangway. He's met with a side hug from Grim who lets out some hearty laughter.

As Rowe moves forward, Wennie sticks closely by his side, their footsteps synchronized. The argument between Faeryn and her mother abruptly ceases, as all attention shifts to the small blue dragon.

Faeryn leans into her mother's side.

"This is why I breached the wall. She called to us, Mother. The prophecy is true."

The headmistress lowers to one knee and the women who have arrived with baskets of food and drink follow her lead. She lowers her head as Rowe, Maliah and the baby dragon make their way down the gangway and onto the dock before her.

"I am Rowe Efhren, heir of Silver Flame and this is my —" he pauses, "my friend, Maliah Bazzel. That is Grim Dashiell, the Umbra who owns this ship, and my friend, Arren Verrick, wolf protector in the Kingdom of Night."

Wennie cautiously moves forward until she's able to lower her head, tilting it in such a way that she can see the woman's face.

"And that is Wennie," Rowe adds before the headmistress looks up to see that the dragon has taken an interest in her.

She swallows hard and reaches out with a slight tremble in her hand.

"My Queen," she whispers.

Rowe's brow furrows and Maliah looks at him.

The moment her fingers touch the warm blue scales, she can feel the vibrations caused by the dragon's purring. The sight of the small creature fills Shylo Zabina's almond-shaped, pastel pink eyes with wonder. As she marvels at the sight before her, a look of astonishment becomes etched onto her beautifully sculpted features.

"Queen?"

"We need to talk."

He nods.

"I am Headmistress Shylo Zabina, here at Brenna Academy. My daughter, Faeryn, will show you inside. Please, settle into your rooms and we will all meet again later this evening to discuss everything."

While passing her by, Faeryn gives a nod to her mother.

"Make sure they have comfortable accommodations, each equipped with their own private baths."

Headmistress Zabina gazes at the Umbra and his companion, a wolf protector who seems to have transformed into a handsome man adorned with intricate tattoos on his back, neck, and arms.

Having once mated with a wolf, she had developed a deep curiosity and intrigue for these magnificent creatures. The experience left a lasting impression on the Witch, etching itself into her memory. Her fingers delicately trace the curve of her earlobe, catching Arren's attention.

With a forceful nudge, Grim knocks him off balance as

he bumps into him from the side. "That one is finding you worthy."

Arren emits a growl.

Grim chuckles. "Yes, that will get her eager."

"Stop talking." The wolf pushes him forward with a sigh.

The wolf protector acknowledges the beautiful woman with a respectful nod while she takes in the length of his body with her bright eyes.

Once the two men have moved past, the attention of all the women is directed towards them as they make their way towards the entrance of the academy.

Faeryn groans before looking at Maliah.

"After you, my lady," she states with an extended hand.

There is a brief moment of confusion for Rowe as he tries to decipher the meaning behind the look that is shared between them.

As the headmistress reaches down, Wennie feels a sense of security enveloping her as she is lifted into the head-mistress's comforting arms. Tenderly embracing the dragon against her bosom, she reluctantly tears her gaze away from the ominous black ship and joins the others as they venture inside.

Upon entering, each person is captivated by the sheer grandeur and cannot help but marvel at their surroundings. Spread out in front of them is a spacious room, with a towering ceiling that seems to stretch into the sky. It appears that the entrance had been designed to accommodate even the largest dragons, with ample room for them to move around. The black walls of Brenna Academy are brought to life with vibrant paintings of dragons and carefully curated portraits of each student and teacher. If one were to make an educated guess, it would appear that approximately three hundred individuals reside within the walls of the academy. Maliah's chin lifts, her eyes widening in awe, as one of the red dragons gracefully lands on a golden bar. She can't help but notice the shimmering scales, illuminated by the sunlight streaming through the many windows.

Faeryn leans into Maliah's side, feeling the warmth of her presence.

"Although the dragons have access to certain areas within the academy, it is strictly forbidden for them to enter your private quarters. However, they will not let that stop them from entering the classrooms and demonstrating their skills."

"Like what?" Maliah asks.

"Fire-breathing, using their sharpened claws, biting— all the basics for killing things."

With a heavy heart, Maliah swallows hard as she remembers the atrocities her kind had committed against the dragons residing on the desolate island situated to the north of their kingdom. While it is important to note that she would never partake in such actions, it is worth mentioning that she, like many others, voiced no opposition to the way they were treated. Every ounce of her being was burdened by a lingering sense of guilt. As she catches a glimpse of Wennie, now protected in Shylo Zabina's arms, she contemplates whether she, herself, belongs in such a place.

"Come!"

As their hands intertwine, Faeryn effortlessly pulls Maliah towards the center staircase, their footsteps echoing through the great hall. In addition, there are staircases on both the right and left sides of the academy that provide access to different areas.

Rowe finds himself standing alone until Arren and Grim come over to join him. Grim, unable to control his hunger, finishes up a second piece of fruit and chews loudly.

"They seem to be getting along."

Rowe maintains his gaze on the Witch with purple hair, clad in red leather.

"She's in heat," Arren blurts out.

Rowe and Grim both shift their attention towards him.

"What?" Rowe asks.

With a shrug of his shoulder, Arren taps the side of his nose.

"I can smell it. It's pheromones. The Witch likes her."

Rowe's attention is caught by Faeryn and Maliah, who are walking together, laughing and chatting as if they have been the closest of friends forever. As his heart skips a beat, he ponders if Faeryn possesses the power to bring the happiness that Maliah truly deserves.

"She looks—happy," he admits.

Arren and Grim exchange a knowing glance, their eyes filled with unspoken understanding.

"It's beneficial for her to have a friend by her side. While I'm sure you've had wonderful conversations with her, there is a unique energy that emerges when women come together. Together, they become stronger."

Grim shares what he knows to be true, based on the knowledge he gained from his Gen.

Swinging his arm behind Rowe, Grim takes a swipe at Arren, his eyebrows raised and his chin tilted in Rowe's direction.

Arren adjusts his stance. "And I probably misspoke. I

simply meant that Faeryn is exhibiting excitement. That's all."

Faeryn captures the attention of the three men as she momentarily pauses and calls out to them, causing them to look towards the staircase.

"Come on! I'll show you to your rooms!"

"Rooms?" Arren exclaims.

"Have you never had your own room?" Rowe asks.

Arren shakes his head. "I live in a pack. I've never had anything that belonged to me."

Moving swiftly, a visible expression of happiness emerges on his face as he rushes ahead.

Rowe reaches out and gently places a reassuring hand on Grim's arm. "You don't think that Faeryn and Maliah are —you know?"

Grim's head shakes in disbelief, accompanied by a nervous laughter that echoes from the depths of his chest.

"What? No—no. I mean, you're an heir, right?"

His anxious reply doesn't sit right with Rowe Efhren.

Grim places a hand around his shoulder, giving him a firm shake that jolts him back to reality.

"Come, let's take advantage of their hospitality while it still exists."

Rowe reluctantly gives in, and the two men cautiously join the others as the majestic crimson dragon gazes down on the bustling activity below, emitting a thunderous roar before soaring back into the sky.

CHAPTER 7

THE KINGDOM OF STONE

T he sound of the ship creaking echoes through the air as it tilts precariously against the turbulent waves. As The Sorrow ebbs and flows, distant thunder rumbles, foretelling the impending storm.

Gripping onto the railing, Odette Ender tries to steady herself as the vessel abruptly shifts in the opposite direction. As the bow of the ship slices through the ever-growing waves, water spray shoots out to the left and right, creating a misty curtain. In a short while, they will finally reach their intended destination. To conceal Odette's ability to trans-form, the Holy Scribe had insisted on arriving in this manner. Unwanted attention would have been drawn if a large falcon landed anywhere near the Kingdom. The royal household was abuzz with rumors, and a few individuals claimed to have caught sight of the mysterious creature. Odette Ender, unable to use her magickal powers, has to travel like an ordinary mortal.

After what seemed like an eternity, a voice breaks the silence as one of the men calls out from the crow's nest. As the man points, Odette gazes upward and sees a port nestled beyond the churning waves. Built in secrecy, this place was designed to serve as a clandestine route through The Sorrow during the war. The mighty dragons, in their fury, reduced it to ruins during the War of Brumah. But now, thanks to Cassius Brumah's persistence, it has been transformed into a covert outpost where Stone Guardsmen vigilantly monitor the western territories and southern activity. The port is nestled in a secluded cove, concealed by a dense thicket of trees. With a gentle sway, the ship alters its course, setting sail in that direction.

Odette loosens her grip on the railing and descends back below deck. With a sudden jolt, she pulls on the door, her grip slipping as she pushes past two men, who quickly abandon their tasks to aid in the ship's preparations. As the ship tilts the other way, she instinctively lifts a hand and presses her open palm against the wall to steady herself. A heavy sigh escapes her lips. Although flying would have been a simpler option, she understood The Holy Scribe's reasoning for having her arrive in this manner, even though it was inconvenient. Being captured and accused of treason was definitely not what she had in mind when she devised her plan.

As she reaches her quarters, she retrieves a skeleton key from her pocket and effortlessly inserts it into the lock. With all her might, she presses her shoulder against the stubborn door. Once inside, her eyes dart around the room until they land on Talen Freeborn, who is still tightly bound to the bed. Despite the imminent danger of death, Odette remains skeptical that any of these mortals would resist the temptation to deflower the Witch. Talen Freeborn's irresistible appeal was specifically crafted to entice men and maintain a firm grip on their attention, leaving them unable to resist her allure. This phenomenon occurs when there is magick flowing through one's blood. Talen, the second-daughter and heir of the Crystal Garden, is a powerful Witch whose magick radiates with incredible strength.

"Mmm." Talen's groan is stifled by the leather strap tightly secured over her mouth.

Odette approaches the bed and leans in, her fingers delicately tracing the outline of Talen's jaw, feeling the softness of his skin. Shaking her head in anger, Talen forcefully breaks the connection. A flash of anger ignites in her eyes, making them blaze with intensity.

With a graceful movement, the shifter sits down on the edge of the bed.

"Our ship is currently navigating towards the hidden outpost that is known only to a select few."

Her eyes briefly meet Talen's before she releases a sigh.

"I feel it's important to mention that once we arrive at The Kingdom of Stone, I won't be able to ensure your safety. Therefore, it would be wise for you to remain silent and obey instructions. I understand that as a Witch, it may be difficult for you to comprehend, but your aunt successfully accomplished this for many years, so I have confidence that you can also satisfy the mortals' demands."

The ropes dig into Talen's skin as she struggles against their tight grip, her hands and legs bound to each of the four bedposts that are firmly attached to the ceiling.

"I apologize that this is what must be done. I do not hate you, Talen Freeborn. I simply must take advantage of what has presented itself to me."

As she rises, Talen's gaze remains fixed on the shifter, never wavering. Her head pounds and her stomach churns, causing her to grimace in discomfort. She cried an endless stream of tears, her sobs echoing through the room, but now a simmering anger began to replace her sorrow, and the Witch could sense the intensity of her growing hatred. If she found herself free, even for a moment, she would mercilessly seize every opportunity to take countless lives.

The ship's movement grows more serene as it glides past the narrow entrance and enters the harbor, accompanied by the gentle lapping of the water against its hull. Since she departed from the jagged shoreline in the south, the sky has been engulfed in darkness, with menacing clouds and fierce bolts of lightning. In order to ensure her safety, Odette made the decision to seek shelter along the seldom-explored western shores of The Obsideon Veil, where she knew she would be far from prying eyes. The weather in the southern region was still challenging, but not as treacherous as in other areas. She deliberately selected a location hidden from the watchful eyes of wolves on the opposite side.

As the rocking ceases, the ship gradually comes to a gentle halt. Odette's keen senses allow her to discern even the most minute changes in motion. As their time on The Sorrow comes to an end, a sense of relief washes over her, but she knows the second part of the journey will present its own challenges.

Startled by a knock at her door, she opens it while strategically shielding the sight of Talen, who is restrained on the bed. Despite their treacherous mission, she wouldn't hesitate to protect the girl from any men who want to take advantage of her. It wouldn't be difficult for them to assert that she has changed allegiances, opting to launch an offensive, thereby providing them with a pretext to eliminate her and secure the Witch exclusively for themselves.

"The Captain has instructed that you gather your belongings and proceed to the deck. Upon reaching the outpost, we'll rest for the night and depart early, before sunrise, on our way back to The Kingdom of Stone."

"Why not leave now?" Odette asks.

"And tempt the vampires?"

Odette purses her lips.

"True." She glances behind her. "I will be along shortly. I'll bring the Witch."

"I am to take her," the Stone Guardsman claims.

"That will not be happening." Odette stands her ground, uncurling her fingers. "Unless I am to be killed as you try to take her."

The Stone Guardsman's scowl deepens, revealing his disapproval. While moments slip away, the Stone Guardsman finds himself grappling with his own over-whelming hunger and fatigue that have been brought upon by the demanding journey.

"So be it, shifter. You can take it up with my captain once you join us on deck."

Odette exhales, releasing a long-held breath. The fact that the man recognized her fury and made the conscious decision not to engage in a fight is something that she truly appreciates. As she closes the door behind her, she turns to face Talen, who has lifted her head in an attempt to eaves-drop on their conversation.

"It is imperative that we unite with the rest of the group in order to proceed with the next phase of our journey. Should your desire be to stay a virgin, my suggestion is to heed my advice promptly and without delay. Mortal men, particularly those who are uncertain of their survival, are filled with desires that you have yet to come across. Their intention is to maliciously accuse me of turning against them and then brutally assault you until your eyes lose their spark, hence it is imperative that you have faith in me, as I am the sole reason you continue to exist."

Talen's words are barely audible as she mumbles from behind the leather mask, her eyes filled with rage.

"I realize this is not ideal. But I did protect you by placing you here, in my room and standing watch. I hope you will remember this in the future."

It is unfortunate, but Talen recognizes that the shifter is right. Throughout this brief journey, she made sure to place her in the room and keep her safe. Nevertheless, she is not fooled and understands that the situation does not serve her own interests. No. This is for Odette's. Upon their arrival, Talen is uncertain about the challenges she will encounter, however, she is gradually realizing that her ability to survive will be contingent upon the presence and support of Odette.

"I am about to release you from the restraints, but before I do so, I feel compelled to restate my previous warning. I can assure you that no one else on this vessel holds a greater level of care for you than I do. It is within their capability to assert that you somehow managed to escape and then assaulted them, ultimately compelling them to defend themselves by eliminating you. Do you understand?"

Hesitation flickers across Talen's face before she gives a hesitant nod. There is no doubt that she is clearly reluctant.

"I will thank you for eating, although unpleasant. You must continue to do this so you can remain strong. I know you will need it once we arrive."

The words fester in Talen's mind like a poison, growing more toxic with each passing moment. As the thought of what awaits her fills her mind, a sense of dread begins to grow, reminding her of the strength she will have to summon.

Odette once again comes near, releasing the restraints on her arms before heading towards the foot of the bed. With nimble fingers, she carefully unties the knot around Talen's ankle, then moves on to the other. Heeding the shifter's warning, Talen clenches his fists and prepares for a fight. With all her might, she kicks upward and lands a powerful blow below Odette's chin. The shifter is thrown back, crashing onto the hard floor. Talen slips off the bed with a slight thud, and then she quickly darts past her. The shifter's spidery fingers reach out, wrapping around the girl's ankle, causing her to crash onto the floor. Talen winces with pain, feeling a sharp sting in her knees as they bear the full impact of her fall. But she relentlessly kicks with her free leg, landing blow after blow on Odette's nose until it starts bleeding. Scrambling to her feet, she runs out the door, feeling the adrenaline pumping through her veins. With a groan, she removes the gag, revealing a small wooden ball that had been lodged in her mouth. With a heavy thud, she drops the object to the floor and courageously pushes forward, her feet weighed down, her knees showing signs of bruising, and her wrists almost dragging due to the bands tightly encircling them.

Upon hearing voices, she immediately reacts by pressing her back firmly against the wall for safety. As they move into the distance, a sense of relief washes over her. Knowing that Odette will wake and come after her, Talen's mind races as she considers her options, finally settling on a daring plan.

Her eyes dart around, taking in every detail as she moves forward, determined to find a way out. Finally, she reaches a door and struggles to grasp the handle. The handle is pulled downward as she permits the weight of the metal encasing her wrists to take effect. As soon as the door is open, she eagerly steps outside. As the gentle touch of the cool breeze caresses her skin, her light-green hair gracefully dances behind her shoulders.

Her heart swells with a sense of freedom as she looks up at the boundless expanse of the sky, even if just for a moment. As the light quickly fades, the flame inside her grows stronger. She can do this. She must.

Hiding against the wall, Talen can hear the rhythmic sounds of the men's footsteps and the commands they shout to each other as they work together to bring the ship into port. Her eyes fixate on the sturdy railing, and a rush of determination fills her as she contemplates making a break for it. She hopes to scale over the edge and escape in one of the smaller boats typically used for rowing to shore.

Limping along, she struggles to bear the weight of her metal restraints, her every movement hindered. Out of nowhere, a man donning the crest of The Kingdom of Stone on his chest emerges, catching her off guard.

"Kneel," he demands.

Talen lifts her chin. "I kneel for no man."

The Stone Guardsman scowls, his face twisted with anger, and delivers a forceful backhanded blow across her face. Despite stumbling, she refuses to back down.

"Kneel!" he yells.

Her drying lips curl into a crooked grin, and with a fierce war cry, she spins in a circle, her weighted hands swinging out at her sides. Not wasting a moment, she strikes the Stone Guardsman twice - one blow lands on his arm, causing him to wince, and the other hits him squarely in the back, catching him off guard.

With a swift movement, she finds herself on the opposite side of him, her back pressed against the railing.

The man's anger boils over as he delivers a forceful kick to her stomach, propelling her over the railing. The back of her head collides with the unforgiving hardwood of the hull. As the Witch falls backward, away from the ship, time seems to stretch out, every second feeling like an eternity. Just moments before Talen hits the water, the man leans over the side and watches in horror as she vanishes beneath the surface, her weighted wrists dragging her deeper into the depths of The Sorrow.

As she descends into the dark water, the echoing sound of her little sister's sweet voice fills her ears, accompanied by a flood of memories flashing through the Witch's mind like a vivid picture book.

The garden.

Her bedroom.

Sunlight on her skin.

Crystal flowers bursting with color.

The spell bottle in her hand.

The expression on Cullen Moore's face when she left him in The Kingdom of Shadow.

She parts her lips. Her lungs feel starved for oxygen, and the intense pressure makes her body feel as if it is engulfed in white-hot flames. As the water floods her mouth, causing her to flinch, she suddenly feels a strong arm wrapping around her waist, pulling her towards the surface. However, in that critical moment, she can't help but close her eyes as life slowly slips away from her. The last thing she can hear is the desperate voice of the vampire, pleading for her to come back to him.

But knowing she has failed.

Talen abruptly wakes up from her slumber, her senses immediately alert to the sounds of men engaged in conversation and the distinct clanking of their swords against their sturdy metal armor. With an intention to speak, she makes an attempt to open her mouth but winces in discomfort upon realizing that her lips are seemingly fused together. With a trembling hand, she bends over and brings her mouth closer to her index finger, carefully examining it for any abnormalities. It appears as though someone has sewn her lips together. As the horrors of her captivity begin to take form, she can't help but let out a soft, pained moan.

"It is a spell."

Startled, Talen flinches, her senses heightened as she becomes aware of another presence nearby.

In the shadows of the wooden box where Talen Freeborn is being held captive, Odette leans forward, her eyes fixed on her. The bruising that resulted from Talen's attack is gradually fading away beneath her eyes. Despite the situation, the shifter does not hold any anger towards the Witch. She is well aware of the level of tenacity that their kind possesses. The thought of this being an effortless endeavor never crossed Odette's mind. The only way she could take Talen was by catching her off guard. Had Talen known about Odette's plan to bring her to The Holy Scribe as payment, it is likely that both the shifter and the Witch would have perished. Despite her ability to conceal her true intentions, it had ultimately worked out in her favor.

"Since we will be arriving soon, I feel it's important to be honest with you."

The box is swaying back and forth. They are currently

being transported through the dense forest, following a well-established path that was constructed many years ago and meanders alongside the northern banks of The River Wilde.

"Please understand that I did not intend for this to be my final plan and I do not want you to think otherwise. I had hoped against all odds that it wouldn't come to this, but as soon as we crossed the threshold into The Kingdom of Stone, I knew deep down that achieving my personal goal was an impossible feat." In a moment of reflection, she pauses, as if contemplating the past. "Ideally, we would have all benefited that day, but instead, our actions only led to the demise of an old monarch and his Witch."

Leaning back, Talen feels the rough texture of the wood against her shoulders, providing a comforting support. Her body throbs with pain, her wrists sear with a burning sensation, and her soul feels almost shattered. She fears that her only chance to escape has slipped through her fingers. She swallows hard, feeling a lump form in her throat. Due to her drowning, her throat has become raw and her lungs are feeling ragged. Her exhaustion is gradually increasing, moment by moment. Maybe she should consider submitting, if only for the purpose of safeguarding herself against further trauma. This behavior goes against the principles of a Witch. With their freedom at stake, a true Witch will summon all their strength and fight with an intensity that cannot be matched. The thought of being imprisoned is so unbearable to them that they would choose death instead. Understanding this, Talen holds the belief that her Aunt Naya did whatever was necessary to safeguard them. There is no other possible explanation for why such a powerful Witch would remain in the Kingdom of Stone, indicating that there must be a significant reason for her choice. However, Talen ponders if this will be her destiny as well. Will she have no choice but to combine the power of both books, their ancient knowledge intertwining, in order to grant mortals eternal life? Undoubtedly, she will come across different opportunities that could provide her with an escape route from the nightmarish existence Odette has forced upon her. The union of Moonrise and Starfall poses a challenge for her, as the two books have always been under the control of a queen - or in some cases, even two, like the twin sisters.

With the party coming to a stop, the dark wooden box is brought to a standstill as well. Talen, feeling a mix of anticipation and apprehension, takes a slow breath, fully aware that the moment she has been waiting for is about to arrive - the moment she will come face to face with the individuals who assisted Odette in executing this audacious scheme to abduct her.

As Odette looks over at the girl, a sense of regret seems to wash over her, while at the same time, Talen's feelings towards the shifter have turned to hatred, despite her awareness that it was most likely the shifter who rescued her from drowning in The Sorrow. The Witch wonders if she would have been better off had the shifter permitted her spirit to pass from this realm to the next. Despite everything, she must remain firm in her resolve. The fate of her people now rests on her shoulders, making her own survival a matter of utmost importance. Perhaps all of Ellian. If she can appease these men, then maybe other women will escape the same fate. If not, she will do whatever it takes to gain their trust, eliminating as many as possible before succumbing. It seems that is the only viable path to take.

Anger flickers in her pupils as her eyes narrow, their blue hue shifting like a mood ring.

"I will remind you once more to be mindful of your manners. They do value you, but that doesn't guarantee they won't hurt you."

As the door on the end of the box opens, a stream of light floods in, illuminating Talen's face. Her lips shimmer with the sparkle of translucent thread, running smoothly along their fullness.

Before she exits, Odette turns back. "Rest assured, there won't be any scarring. By casting a spell, I effectively bound your lips together to prevent you from speaking. I am aware that none of this is comfortable for you, but I can promise you that the discomfort will be short-lived. It would be best if you simply comply with the request." Despite the closed door and extinguished light, Talen's mind is desperately seeking strategies for survival.

As Odette rises to her feet, her back emits a series of creaking sounds, indicating the effort it takes for her spine to straighten. Her choice was to remain with the girl, making sure that she was safe and would not pose a danger to herself.

With a stern expression, the commander of the Stone Guardsman confidently strides towards her, his presence commanding attention.

"The Holy Scribe has specifically instructed us to rendezvous at the south gate, ensuring our privacy and avoiding any unwanted attention. We will then escort you to see him, and the Witch will be confined to the dungeon."

"No." Odette is quick to refuse.

With a slight tilt of his head, the leader casts a glance at his men. A woman saying no is disrespectful.

"These are my instructions."

"I ask that we both see him together. I ensured the safe delivery of the Witch and will follow through to the end."

His jaw muscles tighten and flex.

"Are you making the assumption that I lack the ability to protect her?"

With a swift motion, Odette contorts her neck, resulting in a series of bone-cracking sounds. The exhaustion from traveling all night in the box with Talen is finally alleviated as she finds solace in stretching her fatigued muscles.

"Although I have faith in your skills, it is worth mentioning that the Witch's life was put in danger on your vessel when one of your own crew members succumbed to anger. I am aware of the challenge of closely supervising a multitude of individuals, so I humbly suggest that the Witch remains in my company until I have finished dealing with the King's emissary."

The commander subtly shifts his weight, observing his men once again. He is well aware of the difficulties that come with managing them. In addition, Odette has carefully selected her words and has even given him a compliment.

With a slight lean, Odette positions herself closer to his ear, suggesting a desire to convey a message confidentially. "Rest assured, I will personally inform them about your outstanding performance in bringing us to this point and explain that the girl accidentally fell overboard while trying to escape."

With a slight lift of his chin and a nod, he signals his agreement to the shifter's terms.

Odette's gut feeling was unwavering - she knew with absolute certainty that Talen Freeborn would find the greatest protection under her wing. Having spent a considerable amount of time dealing with mortals in this world, she knows this fact all too well. They have a tendency to change their minds without warning, as long as it suits their needs. Nevertheless, she can be confident that she will receive her payment as promised.

"Very well," he replied, his voice laced with resignation. "However, if questioned, I will inform them that you were insistent on this being the plan."

Odette grins, her teeth gleaming as she reveals their subtle, sharpened edges. The commander's face contorts into a grimace of displeasure.

A sudden snap fills the air as he effortlessly snaps his fingers. "You are all relieved, except for the four of you. Proceed with the shifter. Take the hidden passageway that will lead you straight to the chamber where the inquisitors conduct their investigations."

The very mention of that place causes Odette to recoil, as if she can still feel its haunting presence. It has been a long time since she sat within those walls, feeling the cold stone against her back as she was interrogated about her connections to the Witch Queen and her formidable magick. It was at that moment when Odette became bound to The Holy Men in The Kingdom of Stone. She paid a hefty price for it. However, her determination to gain her freedom burned brighter than ever.

The men carefully lift the box, its weight straining against the two thick poles, while Talen shifts uncomfortably within. Despite her best efforts, she struggles to hear any of the words being spoken in the conversation occurring just outside her prison.

Odette takes the lead, guiding them towards the southern entrance where a magnificent golden gate is raised, and then two towering doors swing open, granting them passage into the majestic kingdom walls. As soon as they step inside, the doors close with a loud thud and the gate is immediately lowered.

Moving swiftly through the small courtyard, the shifter steadily advances towards yet another door that is heavily guarded. Before she can enter, the man opens the door revealing a corridor illuminated by torches spaced a few feet apart. The light dances across her black feathers, casting an ethereal glow on her neck, corset, and flowing dress. Upon reaching the elaborately decorated doors, she pauses to take in the intricate etchings of the great snake, symbolizing their God, Acheron, amidst the entwining vines and blooming roses. Behind these doors, the echoes of past trials and the weight of lives lost during The War of Brumah lingers. In order to erase any trace of their existence, they were ruthlessly dismembered and scattered throughout the dense forest, leaving no discernible markers. The bodies taken to the forest had been carefully placed to nourish the blood roses. Once fully grown, the roses were plucked and carefully arranged for the vampires residing in the northern region. This is the reason behind their deliciously sweet flavor.

With a deliberate motion, Odette inhales deeply, preparing herself as the doors are swung open by two vigilant Stone Guardsmen. These Guardsman, who have been specifically assigned to protect the Holy Scribe, grant them access to the oval-shaped room. A stunning stained glass ceiling looms over them, capturing the image of their deity, the serpent God Acheron, elegantly entwined around the feet of Cassius Brumah, the ruler of this kingdom, who proudly wears his crown and other regal attire as a symbol of his sovereignty. The walls are constructed in a way that completely isolates any sound from escaping the room. The room is adorned with pictures, hanging every few feet throughout the entire space. These portraits depict each and every Holy Scribe who has faithfully served this kingdom. Niam Jazine's portrait is positioned next to the tall bench, on the right side.

Odette's gaze is fixed on the towering bench in front of her. It is customary for the Holy Scribe, the Vested Cardinal, and the Archbishop to be seated in the three chairs. These three men in power rendered judgments on numerous individuals, swiftly punishing them and breaking their spirits.

The box is gently lowered to the floor, and the men quietly step back. With a nod, the Stone Guardsman exits the scene, leaving the Witch and the shifter in a tense silence. Odette directs her attention towards the center of the room. In the center of the floor, there is a sleek black circle with chains connected to the sturdy loops embedded in the stone. This place had held many captive. The black stone was a merciless conductor of heat, causing a burning sensation on any flesh that touched it. Most of the people who were chained here were scantily clad, or sometimes not clothed at all, which served as a means to coerce false confessions during interrogations. The majority of individuals gave in, but Witches were a rare exception, renowned for their refusal to capitulate, often enduring far longer than others in Ellian.

Out of nowhere, a small beam of light shines from behind the tall bench, illuminating it. As Odette discreetly clears her throat to the side of her hand, she is taken aback when a cloaked figure suddenly emerges from behind the tall bench and positions themselves directly in front of her.

With a deliberate motion, the mysterious stranger lifts their hands and proceeds to unveil their face by removing the hood on their cloak. As Odette observes this act, her brow furrows, perplexed by the unexpected sight of a young man with a pale complexion and petite features.

"My name is Paxton. The Holy Scribe has asked me to pass on the message that he will be joining us shortly. As you are aware, there is a funeral approaching in the near future, and he is diligently taking care of every aspect of the arrangements in the cathedral. He has graciously provided you with exclusive access to a private bathhouse, where you can relax and unwind. Additionally, he has arranged for a delicious spread of food and drink to satisfy your appetite."

Odette's eyes flicker toward the wooden box, where Talen Freeborn is held captive.

"And what of the girl?"

Paxton's eyebrow cocks. "I am to watch over her until he arrives."

The shifter purses her lips. "I believe I shall remain here."

Paxton clasps his hands together, intertwining his fingers to show his readiness.

"I give you my word that she will be kept out of harm's way, there is no need to worry."

"Yes, well," she says, trailing off as she searches for the right words. "I am committed to remaining here until we have the chance to talk. Then I will gladly take him up on his offer."

"The Holy Scribe." Paxton corrects her use of words when referring to his holiness.

She nods. "Of course, The Holy Scribe."

"Is there anything I can bring you while you wait?"

"Chairs, a table, some hot tea, and cushions would be nice."

Paxton quickly bows to her and hastily walks around the tall bench, disappearing from view.

She looks intently at the wooden box. "Their clear intention is to separate us, but rest assured that I will not allow them to cause any harm to you while you are with me, just as I vowed to you previously."

With determination, Talen manages to maneuver herself to the front of the box, where she finds solace in leaning against the solid wood. Her sewn lips can't hide the faint hum that escapes from deep within her.

"Mmm—mmm," she murmurs.

With a graceful movement, Odette leans in and waves her hand, causing a shimmering line to manifest in the air. Slowly, the line transforms into a perfect square, outlining the form of a door. As it opens, Talen tumbles forward, her hands slapping against the frigid stone floor. With great determination, she fights to push herself up just enough to catch a glimpse of Odette standing just a few feet away. Her bright eyes meticulously scan the oval room, taking in the intricate details of each portrait, the grandeur of the high bench, and the vibrant hues of the stained glass ceiling. As she lays eyes on Cassius Brumah, her gaze becomes sharp and piercing. The man she considers her sworn enemy.

With a quick, fluid motion, Odette pivots to face her, her expression steely and focused. "Behave, and I will undo the stitch spell that has silenced you. If not," she threatens, "I won't hesitate to have real stitches placed to keep you from insulting anyone," her words laced with a dangerous edge.

Talen pauses to take a measured breath before consenting with a nod.

Odette advances towards her, contorting her elongated fingers while observing the gradual unwinding of the translucent threads. The stitching gradually disintegrates and evaporates into nothingness. Talen herself knows the spell, which she often uses to delicately bind together herbs and fragrant flowers, allowing their scents to mingle as they dry. This particular spell had never been utilized for the purpose of silencing someone before. The Witch's lips moved in sync with her jaw, her muscles flexing and relaxing. While searching for a comfortable position on the floor, she gazes up at the shifter. The weight on her wrists has become so overwhelming that she lacks confidence in her ability to walk.

"Why did you save me?" Talen asks.

Odette's brow cocks with confusion. "I cannot allow you to perish. I explained this to you before."

"I will refuse whatever is asked of me," Talen states without fear.

"Mmm. I know your stubborn nature, so I have prepared for this."

With a heavy heart, Talen gazes at her wrists and yearns for the weight that binds her to vanish.

"I don't respect you, Odette Ender. Not one thing you've done. You attacked us near the cave, knowing I would not be prepared to fight you. You hurt my friend, deceived us, and have bound me in these archaic weapons of war."

Odette stands tall, allowing the Witch to insult her. "I told you what was done to our people."

Talen interrupts her. "And I guess that because you suffered, I must suffer the same?"

Odette adjusts her stance, a rare departure from the usual stillness of shifters. Their emotions were always kept hidden, but Talen has somehow unearthed a sensation within her that had been dormant for years. Does she feel pity? Without question, it has to be.

"I regret you are the one who must carry the weight of this."

"Tell me, Odette. How did you get Moonrise from my mother's tower? What have you done to my family?"

With a graceful motion, the shifter brings her hands together, a faint tingling sensation coursing through her fingertips. With her hands cupped, she skillfully massages the webbing between her index finger and thumb. Due to the extended duration of holding this form, her muscles are starting to ache, as she has surpassed her usual limit, refraining from transforming into either the majestic falcon or an unkindness of ravens.

"Your mother was once much different than she became."

Talen's eyes follow Odette's every movement as she paces back and forth, her nervous energy palpable.

"She is unwell."

"Was," Odette corrects her.

"What do you mean?"

Behind the benches, a door creaks open, and Paxton emerges, leading a procession of several girls who gracefully follow him into the room. Each and every one of them is blindfolded, unable to see their surroundings. The sight of their undernourished frames and tattered clothing is a heartbreaking reminder of their desperate circumstances. Their arms and legs are marked with bruises, indicating that they have endured some form of physical trauma. Before Odette, the girls arrange two chairs, a table, cushions, a tray with a steaming teapot, and cups. They link hands as Paxton guides them out of the room. Then he returns.

"They are mute."

"By natural causes, no doubt."

Odette jabs before taking a seat at the table.

"The only options are either that or taking extreme measures against others because they saw you and the girl. Which would you prefer I do in order to fulfill your request for tea?"

Just as Paxton is about to take a seat, Odette shakes her head to signal her disagreement. Her eyes briefly shift towards Talon.

"Lift her into the chair."

Before approaching her, Paxton shows some hesitation.

Talen looks up at him and hisses. "I'll crush your heart in my hands if you dare touch me."

He moves away. Odette finds it amusing and chuckles.

"Perhaps you should leave now."

Inquisitively, Paxton's eyes are fixed on the shifter.

"I was told to remain here until The Holy Scribe arrives."

Odette leans her body against the back of the chair, taking a moment to adjust her position on the soft cushion beneath her.

"And what is it you think I will do young Acolyte? Do you think I traveled all this way so that I could ask for some substandard tea and then escape with that secret? Perhaps you think I long to own one of these portraits painted by a shifter who I know was once imprisoned here until his death? Or maybe I just put my life in danger so that the Witch could crush your heart in her hands?"

Paxton let out a sigh, clearly unimpressed by the sarcastic remark.

"Very well, but I'll be right outside the door if you need anything, Odette Ender."

She looks away, tired of the boy. "Thank you."

Paxton hesitates but does as the shifter asks. Picking up a cup and sipping from the edge of it. Odette leans in, studying his face for any traces of discomfort.

"Okay, you may go." She waves her hand.

After Paxton's departure, the shifter's attention turns to the Witch, who maintains her position on the chilly stone.

"Join me, Talen Freeborn."

Talen narrows her eyes.

"Do you wish for me to lift you up?"

The Witch feels the urge to summon all her strength and fights her way back up onto her feet. With a gradual pace, she approaches the table and settles herself into the chair, resting her hands in her lap. Her gaze falls upon the blood-stains marking the edges of the metal bands. She is grateful that the pain has reached a point of numbness. While Odette is busy preparing two cups of tea, her eyes gradually start to lift.

"What if it's poisoned?" Talen asks.

"Then I guess we will meet our end together—but I know they would not be so foolish."

Showing her kindness and concern, Odette carefully brings the teacup towards Talon, making sure to position it near her lips, which are in desperate need of moisture. The Witch eagerly consumes the contents. The sensation of warmth permeates her body, providing much-needed relief.

Odette tilts the cup until Talen coughs, promptly taking it away.

"I'm happy to see that you're no longer refusing drink or food."

"I suppose I should gather my strength for whatever comes next before I burn this place to the ground."

Odette snickers. "Always so determined."

Talen cocks her head. "Not determined—truthful."

The shifter takes a sip of her tea, wrinkling her nose before placing the cup on the saucer.

Talen shakes her head, to move some of her hair away from her face. It's been days since she brushed it, leaving her looking disheveled.

"You will be bathed and dressed in fine silks," Odette speaks while eyeing the walls.

"I don't care to wear their silks or bathe in this terrible place."

Odette's black eyes lock on her. "You will bathe and look presentable when you meet their new king."

Talen's nostrils flare and her eyes dilate. "I don't wish to meet their king."

Odette leans forward, lowering her chin.

"You will."

"I will tell him everything," Talen defiantly blurts out.

Odette clicks her tongue. "Don't make me do this."

"Do what?" Talen laughs, her voice rising above them. "What more can you do?"

Odette forcefully strikes her hand against the table, causing the cups, saucers, and teapot to tremble. Anticipating the shifter's eventual outburst, Talen leans against the back of the chair, ready to witness her temper. Odette's neck is surrounded by rising feathers, which suggests that the dress is an integral part of her. Until now, Talen was completely unaware of this fact.

"You asked me how I got the book from the tower."

Nervously, Talen fidgets and adjusts herself on the chair, causing it to emit an audible creaking sound.

"Yes. Tell me."

Before speaking, Odette crooks her neck one more time. "Your mother didn't give me a warm welcome when I arrived. Instead, I was ensnared in a tormenting spell that mercilessly tugged at my bones. Despite the pain, I endured it because I loved her."

"Loved—you keep referring to my mother in the past tense. Don't think I haven't noticed, Odette, and how do you have magickal abilities?! I wasn't aware that you knew how to cast. I see no bottles!"

Odette runs her tongue across her teeth, savoring the metallic tang of blood. Her blood, a vibrant red, marks them as a grim reminder. When trying to shift her focus away from anger, she often does this. With a grin, she reveals her crimson-stained teeth to Talen.

"I am not frightened by you—tell me, what have you done?"

"I took her magick, Talen Freeborn. I stripped it from her soul like mortals used to do in these lands. And then I watched as she turned to dust before me."

Tears well up in Talen's eyes. The anger towards her mother was so intense that she had not even considered the possibility of losing her, but rather focused solely on compelling her to alter her behavior.

"No—no," Talen chokes out.

"Yes. I am the reason your mother no longer holds sway over The Kingdom of the Crystal Garden. Which was once a beautiful place before her obsession twisted her mind."

"I will take my revenge on you, Odette Ender."

"It seems you are the only one left who can."

Talen's eyes widen as she contemplates the vivid images of her little sister, Sage, playing in her mind. She shakes her head.

"Tell me that Sage is safe—tell me now!" Talen screams.

Odette stands up, causing Talen to raise her chin to maintain eye contact. Talen Freeborn's tears flow freely, as if they could somehow fill The Sorrow.

With a swift motion, Odette seizes Talen's chin, prying her mouth open, and swiftly moves towards her face.

"You are now a Queen—act like it."

Talen, consumed by fury, vigorously shakes her head in an attempt to break free from Odette's grasp, but Odette remains resolute, refusing to release her hold.

"And as far as telling their king about me, well you will do no such thing, for I will take that memory from you."

As Odette kisses Talen with an open mouth, a rush of memories floods her mind - the sight of the majestic Kingdom of Stone, the scent of earth and moss, and the sound of their footsteps echoing through the ancient halls. Talen's memories of their initial meeting flood her mind, causing Odette's form to disintegrate like black smoke. When they reach the kingdom and break through the walls, the same thing occurs. Odette's presence in each memory fades away in the form of black smoke, leaving only Cullen, Koa, and the Witch to carry on together. Her escape takes a different turn as she now rides on the back of a wolf, fleeing the Kingdom with Cullen and Everleigh. Odette has been removed from all aspects of their plans and the daring escape. Black mist surrounds the shifter's lips as she stumbles backward, causing the Witch's eyes to glaze over as her mind replays the sequence of events that resulted in Starfall's capture and Everleigh's return to The Kingdom of Shadow. None of which includes Odette Ender.

After a few blinks, Talen finally looks up and sees Odette standing before her.

"Wh—who are you?" she asks.

Odette nods.

"Your only friend within these walls."

CHAPTER 8

THE KINGDOM OF SHADOW

With keen interest, Cullen observes Everleigh as she takes a bite of bread and proceeds to chew while using the side of her hand to shield his view. Despite her refined mannerisms that suggest she was meticulously trained to behave around men, she surprised him by dancing on his dining room table, wielding a knife, and pressing it against his throat as she demanded to know the whereabouts of Talen Freeborn. Cullen couldn't help but admire her courage. Everleigh Aeress, fully aware of the vampire's lethal power, fearlessly allowed the sharp blade to graze his throat, seemingly unaffected by the potential consequences for her own life.

She swallows hard, her fingers nervously tracing the texture of the bread as she nods in agreement.

"This is delicious."

"All thanks go to those who once worked here."

With a pensive expression, Everleigh pauses, her mind racing.

"Are they dead?"

Her emerald-green eyes brim with empathy as she asks.

Cullen moves away from the doorway and ventures further into the kitchen, taking his place opposite her. Opting to utilize the high table as a barrier between them is likely a wise choice. It's best for them to have as much room between them as possible.

"I believe they're with my father," he says, his voice filled with a mix of worry and fear.

"Where is he now?"

As Cullen settles into his seat, his stoic demeanor belies the heavy burden of his father's absence. As he ponders, small wrinkles appear on his brow, hinting at his growing concern.

"He's taken one of our ships and sailed out onto The Sorrow."

"Should we go find him?"

Cullen's jaw ticks. "I cannot leave."

"Your loyalty to Koa is admirable, but I know there are things outside these walls that worry you."

He swallows the bitter venom, feeling its acidic burn as it slides down his throat. As his desire for Everleigh grows, he finds himself salivating more frequently, a tangible reminder of his increasing hunger for her. With a worried expression, he gently rubs his arm, aware of the spreading disease beneath his skin. This reason further contributes to his reluctance to venture beyond the Kingdom's borders. The realization that his time is slipping away weighs heavily on Cullen Moore, leaving him with the inevitable decision to pursue a cure. In spite of all odds, the vampire holds onto the hope that Everleigh has the potential to restore his health. Nevertheless, he is concerned that it could lead to her own destruction.

The vampire prince chooses to reveal only a fraction of the truth.

"I promised the Witch I would look after you."

Everleigh corrects him.

"You mean Talen."

He shifts in his seat on the tall chair, trying to find the perfect balance. The use of Talen's name still stirs up unsettling emotions within him. He is concerned about her in numerous ways that he does not want to acknowledge, but if he departs, Koa will certainly perish. Talen Freeborn had made him swear to look after Everleigh, emphasizing that she possesses more power than any other witch in Ellian.

"Yes."

"Why do you find it difficult to use her name?"

In her innocent curiosity, she asks, suspecting that there must be a valid explanation. It is hard for Everleigh to deny her fear that the Heir of Shadow has developed feelings for Talen Freeborn, especially when she saw the way they gravitated towards each other. She dreams of the vampire's love, a love so intense and forbidden that it haunts her every waking moment.

While waiting for his answer, the girl's mind starts to wander.

Everleigh Aerres remains unwavering in her determination to overcome the ever-growing wave of longing. Occasionally, it appears to be an insurmountable challenge, as her visions seamlessly merge with her perception of reality.

For countless nights, she had dreamed of this blond-haired boy, often finding herself writing about him in her journal, her hand occasionally trembling with excitement. Despite her inability to articulate it, she has a profound sense of loving him for what feels like an eternity, even prior to the moment she locked her gaze with his captivating crimson eyes, admired his irresistibly kissable lips, and found herself irresistibly drawn to his enigmatic and mysterious nature.

How intoxicating it would be to feel his fangs sink deeply into her flesh, draining the poisonous love from her being. She couldn't help but question her identity without it —without him—uncertainty clouding her thoughts. The heat rises on her skin, causing a prickling sensation. As time goes on, the embarrassment of her increasing need for him becomes harder to ignore.

Cullen becomes aware of a subtle change in the Stone Maiden's demeanor. As her heartbeat quickens, a surge of heat spreads throughout her body, causing her emerald-green eyes to dilate, betraying the fact that her thoughts were wandering into forbidden territory.

Recognizing her emotional intensity, he clears his throat in order to rescue her from it.

"It's the magick in her blood, nothing more, nothing less. Vampires are drawn to it, much like moths to the flame. But we are also endangering ourselves because a Witch is built to appear as perfect prey. It's been this way as far back as I can remember."

Everleigh slowly opens her mouth, and a faint gasp slips past her parted lips. Now, she can't help but wonder if this is the very thing that torments her. Were her charms intentionally crafted to captivate him, oblivious to the artificiality of these emotions? Could she, like Cullen Moore, become a victim of this as well? The mere thought of it brings such sorrow to her that it feels as though her heart is on the verge of breaking. The unimaginable cruelty of the situation is difficult to bear.

With knowledge of her intended purpose within the walls of The Kingdom of Stone, she can't help but wonder if surprise is even justified. Her upbringing revolved around serving a king, her body destined to carry his legacy. The entirety of her worth was contingent upon this single, undeniable fact. Now residing in this foreign place, a world apart from the lands she had once called her own, she had begun to dream of a different destiny, yet it seemed that all roads ultimately led to Cullen Moore.

Although she longs to share this with the Heir of Shadow, she finds herself stating the obvious instead.

"The same magick I possess now?"

With a casual gesture, Cullen brings his elbows onto the table and carefully intertwines his fingers.

"In some ways, yes—in others, you are completely different. But witches are enticing to my kind. Your scent— well." During a brief pause, Everleigh's attention is drawn to his elongated fangs, clearly visible behind his full lips. The mere thought of him sinking his teeth into her flesh is now causing a gentle vibration to spread between her legs, a sensation she desperately wishes to suppress. Despite everything, her yearning for him shows no signs of diminishing; in fact, it seems to be getting stronger.

The vampire prince finishes his thought. "It is, at times, most distracting."

Trying not to offend him, Everleigh conceals a smile, fully aware of his sentiments. It can be said that Everleigh shares some striking similarities with a vampire. In the most unexpected of ways, she finds herself irresistibly drawn to Cullen Moore, with no sense of control over her emotions. Reflecting on the memory of how she hastily made her way down the table and leapt onto his lap, she continuously replays the scene in her mind, not as an act of defiance, but rather as a form of seductive foreplay. Playing this dangerous game only fuels her attraction towards him.

Clearing her throat, Everleigh tries to suppress the memory of their encounter in the dining hall. As she tries to hide her emotions, her body inadvertently reveals the truth to Cullen, who can feel the rapid beat of her heart behind the soft contour of her breasts. If only the vampire prince could see her as more than just a conquest, someone to love and cherish. Perhaps then he wouldn't constantly be filled with anxiety. As he swallows more venom, his stomach churns in protest. Everleigh can hear the faint sound, but she refrains from teasing him. There is no need.

Without thinking, she taps the edge of the plate, feeling the smoothness of the ceramic under her fingers.

"I know that in most instances, I would be the meal."

Cullen's attention is caught and he becomes more animated.

"No—I would never—"

Everleigh instantly regrets her words when he denies it without hesitation.

"I'm sorry. I was only trying to lighten the mood. You know, tease you."

Cullen finds it amusing and chuckles.

"Your presence alone is enough to tease."

A tense stillness fills the space between them, punctuated by Cullen's nervous gesture of rubbing the side of his neck and Everleigh's soothing motion of running her hand along her arm. Both are at a loss for words, feeling as though they are tangled in a complex puzzle, a result of a grand scheme set in motion by unknown forces.

As Everleigh lifts her hand, she can't help but fixate on

the sight of the dirt embedded beneath her fingernails. Her thoughts transport her back to the day in the garden, where she remembers Talen's patient guidance on harnessing the crackling electricity of magickal power that now pulses beneath her skin. While she yearns for a relaxing bath, she is aware that approaching Cullen for such a favor might only exacerbate the already mounting tension between them. However, the Heir of Shadow is keenly observant and notices even the slightest of movements. In this instance, he directs his attention towards her hand and detects the presence of dirt. The deepening shade of crimson in his eyes signals a growing intensity. Cullen cannot help but feel regret for not offering sooner. It goes against his nature to be rude and inattentive. In his early vampire days, he possessed an unexpected tenderness towards those he would eventually feed on. He was well aware of the deadly poison coursing through Everleigh Aeress's veins, but that didn't stop him from being drawn to her.

Without thinking, he blurts out his question.

"Would you like to take a bath?"

Unaware of the implications, Everleigh asks for clarification.

"With you?"

The girl had never taken a bath by herself. Like most activities, the Stone Maidens took baths together. The strict schedule was a part of their daily routine that they diligently followed. Except when Everleigh would sneak off to the library, where the scent of old books would fill her senses, or when she would wander in the Forest of Blood Roses, hearing the crunch of fallen petals beneath her feet. Scared to admit it, she cherished those moments of quiet reflection, relishing in the absence of prying eyes.

It seemed as if she had always craved freedom, not only in her choices, but also in her dreams. Despite her Mother Ward's wishes and Everleigh's intended purpose of giving birth to an heir, she continued to work against it. The young Stone Maiden couldn't help but question why she had been cursed this way. It was clear that she had never truly fit in with them, leading to the unsettling possibility that she had been a Witch from the start.

As he grins, his captivating smile sends a shiver down her spine, adding to his already irresistible charm. Everleigh despises the idea, but surely he has been with countless girls before.

"I—we—well, there is a heated spring that those like you can visit, offering a soothing escape from the outside world."

Everleigh feels her emotions being pulled at by his nervous nature. The harmful effects of spending time with this vampire has taken a toll on both of them, resulting in their shared suffering.

"That sounds wonderful." Her voice is now soft with affection.

Cullen rises, and Everleigh follows his lead, mirroring his every move. He waits for her to start walking, but his attention is fixed on how close they are to each other. The fear of potentially harming her weighs heavily on him, as he knows the sickness is still spreading throughout his body. The curse has already taken hold, evident in his permanently locked and elongated fangs, and the venom that now pools heavily on his tongue. He hoped this would be the worst of it before he could find a solution, but Everleigh may get her wish if Cullen is forced to leave her for fear of endangering the young maiden's life.

Everleigh steps out into the corridor, feeling the coolness of the polished marble floor beneath her feet. In an attempt to catch his attention, she repeatedly glances over her shoulder, locking her eyes with his despite his desire for her not to do so. There is no denying the sheer beauty she possesses, and the intoxicatingly sweet fragrance that emanates from her only intensifies the tension building in his muscles with each passing moment. A tight vest is concealed beneath his form-fitting coat. It would help to hide his quickened breath if only he were in need of breathing. With a high-collared shirt and well-fitted pants, his outfit enhances both his style and physique. Over his slim pant legs, his boots are tightly laced up. A ring on his right hand catches Everleigh's eye, its intricate design demanding her attention. Cullen's eyes briefly drift to the ring, his fingers absentmindedly turning it, before he looks back at Everleigh.

"It was a gift from my father, so I believed."

The Stone Maiden narrows her eyes. "Are you not certain now?"

Cullen lifts his hand, gesturing towards a side hallway that appears narrower than the main corridor. As they walk side by side, their shoulders brush against each other, creating an unavoidable closeness.

"I am uncertain of many things." The words escape his lips with a dryness that is hard to ignore.

With a limited reach into the past, he struggles to recall his life as a mortal, let alone his significant roles as Cassius Brumah's brother and the designated Heir of Stone. The fragments that Talen collected for him are now inside the charm bottle she left behind, and that's all he has. The thought crosses his mind - if he were to release them, would he gain a deeper insight into his past? However, he decides against it, considering his current state. The thought of his sickness spreading faster haunts him, especially when he experiences intense emotions. His increasing infatuation with Everleigh only serves to heighten the level of danger.

The aroma of pure, fresh water wafts through the air, drawing Everleigh's attention to the radiant mist seeping out from under the formidable black door. The door, seemingly made of metal, is easily opened by Cullen without any resistance. It is truly impressive how strong he is.

"It's right through here."

As he speaks softly, their bodies move closer to each other, a proximity that exceeds what is considered appropriate. However, Everleigh interrupts the momentary connection between them by stepping inside. Before her, she is met with a sight that takes her breath away. The room is bathed in a soft glow as the clear water gently churns, creating subtle ripples on the surface, all thanks to the heated spring beneath the chamber. A captivating display of artistry can be found throughout the space, as the floor, walls, and ceiling are all meticulously tiled with a breathtaking mosaic portraying a vibrant sunrise on one side and a tranquil moon on the other. Overhead, the two scenes seamlessly transition into one another through a fading effect. The parallel between the scenes of a sunrise and a full moon and the books Starfall and Moonrise is striking, as both the scenes and the books can merge harmoniously into one captivating experience if given the proper consideration.

Everleigh softly whispers her thoughts. "It's so beautiful."

The sunlight reflects off the water's surface, creating a mesmerizing dance of light on her smooth, velvety skin.

With a deep focus on the girl, Cullen breathes his response in a whisper, "Yes."

The room fades into the background as his thoughts become consumed by her. Cullen's hand hovers inches away from her face, but he quickly retreats, his movements a blur, ensuring she remains unaware of his near touch.

Everleigh steps forward, feeling the tightness of her corset against her breasts and waist. Frustrated, she attempts to reach the lace running up her spine, but it remains just out of her grasp.

Cullen lets out a resigned sigh.

"I would have someone assist you if I could."

As Everleigh pulls her ebony locks to one side, her dainty shoulders and the back of her neck become visible to him. Her eyes briefly flicker to the side as she glances over her shoulder, sensing his presence behind her. It would not be truthful of her to deny that it set her senses ablaze.

"If you loosen the lace, I should be able to get it off on my own. Please."

Moving closer, he raises his trembling hand. To soothe his muscles, he must press his thumb firmly in the center of his palm. The Stone Maiden remains motionless, her unflinching stance revealing a misplaced trust in him. Unbeknownst to her, the vampire prince conceals a terrifying secret—a sinister creature that lurks beneath his charming facade. He fantasizes about taking her in ways that would leave even the most experienced of lovers speechless.

With careful precision, Cullen lifts his hands and delicately unties the white lace at the bottom of her corset, surprising her with his uncommon tenderness. In any other moment, he would have eagerly removed this corset from her and passionately pressed her against the wall or even indulged in the warmth of the rectangular reflective pool located in the center of this bathhouse.

His eyes slowly trace the contours of her back, lingering on every graceful curve. With gentle precision, he delicately spreads the bottom of the corset, repeating the motion meticulously until he reaches the base of her shoulders. With each breath, Everleigh feels her ribs and lungs expand, a sensation that brings her a newfound sense of freedom as she holds the corset in place. A passing desire consumes her as she wishes, if only for a second, that Cullen Moore, the Heir of Shadow, the prince of darkness, would lay his hands on her. She longs for his fingers to explore her body as deftly as they undid her corset. Though possibly with a tad more forcefulness.

With a graceful movement, the Stone Maiden effort-lessly pushes the garment over her beautifully curved hips and then glides it down her rounded thighs before finally stepping out of it. She pauses for a moment, delicately lifting it up to inspect for any signs of damage. The edges still bear traces of blood, and it is unclear whether it is her own, from the vampire, or possibly from a fallen Stone Maiden who perished in the Cathedral. Her mind drifts to those final moments, replaying the image of her family's faces as they were abruptly torn away from her.

"Are you injured?"

Lit up with worry, Cullen's eyes, a deep crimson hue, reveal his genuine concern. While she is absorbed in exam-ining the corset she holds, he takes a step forward and posi-tions himself directly in front of her.

"No—well except for being poisoned, dying, and then having you resurrect me."

Even at this moment, the vampire finds her morbid

sense of humor amusing. Everleigh places the corset in Cullen's outstretched hands, feeling the smooth fabric against her fingertips. Each Stone Maiden was forbidden to wear anything other than the white corset and dress, meticulously crafted by their Mother Ward.

"I rarely removed this from my body. It was required that we wear this corset throughout the day, from morning until we went to sleep at night. It was designed to be a symbol of our purity. But I—"

The girl is spared from sharing more as Cullen intervenes. The vampire has no need for a reminder of her innocence. Every inch of him is sensitive to it.

"It looks to be damaged. I should have provided an opportunity for you to change your clothes earlier than this. Please accept my apologies. I'm sorry if I've made you feel like a prisoner during your stay. It was not my intention to be a terrible host."

As she reaches out, her fingers brush against his hand, sending a tingling sensation up her arm. Before he's able to control it, Cullen emits a low, menacing growl.

As Everleigh observes his pained expression, her eyebrows knit together, causing her to retract her hand from his. It has, in certain ways, inflicted injury upon him. It is a haunting reminder for the vampire, of the warmth and tenderness that the girl possesses.

"There is no need to apologize. I'm grateful to be out of that golden cage. Hopefully, you will trust me to remain free of it. Besides, I have no intention of leaving you, Cullen Moore."

Everleigh cunningly brings up the cage, aiming to exploit his vulnerability for her.

"I would think you would want to be rid of me."

With a serene look on her face, she gazes at him.

"Where would I go?" she asks, ignoring his assertion. "I have to confess that I am more skilled at drowning than swimming, and I am not properly dressed to explore an unfamiliar forest."

Like a star in the night, she wishes that the vampire prince will always desire her presence, never wanting to let her go.

He nods, but his guilt weighs heavily on him for treating her as if she were a caged animal, confined in a golden prison, only providing sustenance to keep her alive while he contemplates his next move. Despite his efforts, the vampire prince couldn't fully realize his plan. The growing sickness in his blood is causing his once sharp mind to falter. Instead, he allowed himself to be overwhelmed by his yearning for this girl.

Cullen vanishes momentarily and reappears with a new dress. The thread used to make it is a vibrant shade of red, carefully woven to create a fabric that is so light it almost seems weightless. In a gesture of tribute, Cullen lifts it up before Everleigh. Despite being tempted, she resists touching the exquisite blood-colored fabric that perfectly complements Cullen's eyes, due to her soiled hands.

"One moment. I almost forgot."

In a blur, he disappears once more, only to reappear holding a red corset that perfectly matches the rest of the outfit.

The Stone Maiden's eyes light up as she sees it. The red corset appears to have a glossy finish, smooth to the touch, almost shimmering like it's been coated in a thin layer of moisture. This garment is designed to lift and support her breasts while still providing freedom of movement.

With a delicate touch, she reaches in and feels the smoothness of the bottom edge.

"It is stunning."

"It is my mother's. I suppose she has no use for it at the moment."

His pleasant expression is a welcomed change.

"Will she care?" Everleigh asks.

Cullen clenches his teeth, his gaze shifting downward.

"I'm certain she would be glad to know that you appreciate its beauty. Her daughters frequently received such things from her, including jewelry. She would carefully style their outfits, transforming them into living dolls."

He chuckles, as though the memory brought him joy. To be truthful, his mother's obsession with outfitting her servants could be quite unsettling. However, he decides to keep this information from the Stone Maiden.

"You have sisters?" Everleigh asks, scanning the room.

"Oh—she would refer to them as daughters before biting them once too often."

Everleigh takes a step back, refusing to touch the corset he is holding.

As Cullen's crimson eyes lift, he notices her expression and realizes that his previous statement may have disturbed her.

"I'll place this over here."

Moving as if on ice, he effortlessly makes his way towards the table before elegantly turning back, offering a subtle bow to her.

"I will leave you to enjoy your bath."

Everleigh's lips part as he walks towards the door.

"Please stay."

She says in a small voice. The sound echoes within him,

delving into the deepest recesses of his soul. As if she's hurt him, he hunches his shoulders, creating a protective barrier.

"I don't want to be alone," Everleigh admits.

The power of her presence is too strong for Cullen to ignore, so he turns back. Despite his efforts, the vampire can't help but notice how her erect nipples stand out against the white fabric of her dress.

"I don't think I should—"

She delicately raises her hand, her fingers grazing the fabric of her dress as she pushes it off her shoulder, causing him to turn away, his eyes widening and his mouth starting to ache. With unwavering determination, Everleigh continues until the dress lies in a heap around her delicate ankles. Stepping out of the dress, she reaches for the smooth railing that runs alongside the stairs, guiding her descent into the shimmering water. With a gasp, she feels the sensation of warm water lapping at her toes, gradually submerging them as she takes each step. The soothing embrace of the spring water envelops her entire body, enabling her to gracefully navigate the reflective pool's underwater terrain. In her quest to find the perfect spot in the calming waters, she reaches a depth where swimming becomes necessary. With grace, she turns her body and waves her arms with gentle movements to stay centered.

With his back still turned, Cullen avoids the risk of seeing her in such a vulnerable position.

"This feels incredible!" She laughs through her words. "Bathing at home was never this relaxing. The water is simply incredible. Every ache in my body is melting away. You should join me!"

Cullen closes his eyes.

"That would be a terrible idea," he mutters.

"Cullen—it's beautiful." She stares upward.

As she leans back, Everleigh's body floats effortlessly on the surface, her attention focused on the ceiling above. With a grin on her face, she finally feels her body start to relax, as if the weight of years of stress and worry has been lifted off her shoulders.

"Would you like to listen to some music?" Cullen's voice cracks.

"Music? You have no one left to play in the kingdom." Everleigh states.

"I have this musical box." Cullen rushes toward the wall and winds the side of a gramophone. A vinyl disc sits under the needle.

"What is that?" Everleigh asks.

Cullen glances toward her, but quickly looks away, almost forgetting that she's naked.

"A relic from an ancient time, this object existed long before we were even born. Over the centuries, my father has amassed a vast collection of various items. But this—" His eyes are focused on the spinning record player. "This is something that he has refused to let go of. According to him, this world used to be filled with things like this to entertain mortals. Better times, I would assume."

With a careful hand, he places the needle on the spinning record, and the room fills with the warm crackle of music. The delightful interaction between violins and cellos fills the room, creating a sense of joy and enchantment. With a subtle retreat, Cullen gracefully raises his hand and begins to rhythmically move his fingers.

"I love it!"

Everleigh squeals with delight, her giggles echoing through the air as she continues to float on her back. She breathes in deeply, feeling the tension melt away. This is the most relaxed she has been in what felt like an eternity. With a sigh, she relishes the sensation of the warm water rushing between her fingers and lapping at her sides.

Cullen surrenders to his love for music and starts swaying, gracefully twirling with his arms elegantly poised as if he is engaged in a dance with an unseen companion.

As the vampire is preoccupied, his elongated shadow slowly creeps towards the edge of the reflective pool, until it finally slips beneath the surface. Moving with the grace of flowing fabric, it slowly approaches the maiden, delicately entwining around her ankles before dragging her beneath the surface without a chance to call for aid. As she kicks her feet, she glances downwards and notices with growing fear that something dark and ominous has latched onto her ankles, gradually creeping higher and winding itself around her calves and thighs, effectively trapping her beneath the water's surface. Her hand descends, reaching out, but as she tries to seize it, her fingers pass right through, reminiscent of the graceful motion of waving her hand through an elusive black mist.

The burning sensation intensifies in her lungs, causing her to cry out in agony and release the small amount of air remaining in her lungs. As she continues to fight the shadow, hoping to break free, the air bubble floats gracefully above her. Gradually, her movements become slower. As her eyes begin to close, a vision starts to take shape.

In her line of sight, a gigantic ship comes into view, making its way towards the water's edge before ultimately tumbling over. Overwhelmed by the sensation of her body descending, she lets out another cry. As she gazes upwards, her eyes focused on the vast expanse above her, she stretches her arm out in anticipation. Suddenly, like a majestic creature emerging from a dream, a magnificent blue dragon materializes before her, seemingly in slow motion. The creature gracefully wraps itself around her, its ethereal presence encasing her body, and as the ship continues its tumultuous descent towards the clear water below, she is lifted effortlessly into the air.

Safely cradled in the grip of the dragon's claw, Everleigh tilts her head, causing her ink-black hair to dance in the wind. She then catches sight of land in the distance, featuring a majestic structure that rises above all else. Positioned behind the object, there is a towering mountain, and beneath her, the water sparkles with a clarity that she has never witnessed before. As the dragon descends, she catches her reflection along the surface and is startled to see a girl with pale skin and crimson eyes staring back at her. Her lips part, revealing a set of long, pointed fangs that glint in the light.

Without warning, Everleigh hits the hard floor. Cullen had bravely dived in to save her, but the menacing shadow clung to him like a coiled serpent. Rolling to her side, Everleigh gasps as water pours out of her mouth and lungs. As she inhales deeply, the air burns her lungs, but she can't help but feel a sense of gratitude for no longer having to fight for her life underwater.

In an instant, Cullen shoots up from the center of the reflective pool, causing a violent spray of water in every direction as he extends his arms and unleashes a powerful cry. With his shadow held in front of him, he swiftly tears it apart as if slicing through a piece of fabric. As he is violently thrown backward, the force of the impact against the tiles causes them to crack under the weight of his shoulders.

With a quick slide down the wall, he lands on his side, still and motionless. The shadow twists and turns, emitting shrill cries of agony as it reassembles itself, before slipping under the door and evading any further wrath of the vampire.

Despite her exhaustion, Everleigh manages to push herself up and stumbles towards Cullen, who shows no signs of movement. With a gentle movement, she descends and settles down right beside him.

Despite the strain and raspiness in her voice caused by the water she had swallowed during her fight with his shadow, she still manages to call out to him.

"Cullen?! Cullen—can you hear me?"

Overwhelmed with sorrow, Everleigh's tears cascade down her face, convinced that the vampire prince has met his end. However, in a sudden twist of fate, he begins to show signs of life, slowly raising himself up and leaning his head back against the wall.

"Cullen!"

She holds on to him, her arms wrapping tightly around his neck, never wanting to let go.

As Cullen Moore reaches up, his fingertips graze the smoothness of her bare back.

"I'm alive," he chokes out.

The maiden releases her grip and remains close to his face, their lips almost touching.

His eyes barely lower, meeting hers with a shy, lingering gaze.

"You are not wearing anything."

"It seems I am not."

"I think you should get dressed," he urges.

"I think you should tell your shadow to stop trying to

kill us."

"Duly noted."

"We could have died, Cullen—you could have died."

Her hand inches closer to his face, finally touching his cold flesh, leaving a shiver down his spine. Her hand radiates an intense heat, almost scorching him, but he craves the sensation, hoping it will linger forever.

"Everleigh," he whispers.

"I don't want you to die," she whispers.

His crimson eyes shimmer, capturing the ethereal beauty of the Stone Maiden's reflection. Cullen is so captivated that he cannot tear his eyes away.

As she leans in, studying his lips intently, he gently interrupts her before their mouths meet.

Upset with his rejection, she asks him. "Have I done something to offend you?"

His head shakes as he stares deeply into her eyes.

"I wish you could offend me, maybe then I wouldn't feel so—"

The Shadow Heir hesitates, his silence revealing the heavy burden weighing on his heart.

"Feel what?" she urges.

"Weakened by you."

"You could never be weak, Lord Cullen Moore, Vampire Prince—Heir of Shadow. You are immortal."

His crimson eyes lock onto her mouth.

"But you are not." He softly whispers, gently placing his hand to the side of her head and cradling it. "And for this reason, I am compelled to protect you—even, as it seems, to my own demise."

His eyes search the room.

"Your disagreeable shadow has fled. It reassembled itself and slid beneath the door."

"I would kill it, but unfortunately, it's my soul, which makes it quite tricky."

He grins, exposing his sharpened fangs.

As she extends her hand towards his mouth, he swiftly grabs her wrist to avoid making things harder for both of them.

"Please," he begs.

Tears fill her eyes, and her cheeks glisten with moisture. He longs to reach out and brush away her tears, to protect her tender heart, but he is unable to do so.

"I couldn't care less about my identity, or that you exist without a pulse."

"Everleigh—we face more than that."

"What is it then—do you love her? Is this why you refuse to be with me?"

Cullen's brows knit. "Talen?"

"It must be that. I—I should've known."

Despite her efforts to retract her hand, he refuses to let go, keeping her uncomfortably close. As their eyes meet, she scans his face for the answers she desperately seeks. Despite his inner conflict, the vampire realizes that he must make this decision, as he recognizes the injustice it would bring upon the young maiden.

"Everleigh—Talen was able to show me a memory during the War of Brumah, and it was a truth I both despise and wish was not true."

With great anticipation, the Stone Maiden eagerly waits for Cullen to reveal the news to her. "What is it, Cullen? Please tell me."

He grimaces as he feels the bitter taste of venom sliding down his throat.

"You may be the daughter of Cassius Brumah, Everleigh —unknown to him, but a daughter, just the same. Naya hid you within the kingdom—even from herself, it seems, or by some other form of dark magick placed upon her."

The wrinkle between her brow deepens, a sign of her growing realization—if she were the King's daughter, that would mean Arrowe is her half-brother. She forcefully pushes that thought to the back of her mind, trying to banish it completely.

"I'm so sorry to tell you this—now."

Everleigh shakes her head. "You must know that if I am his daughter—if I am a Brumah, as much as I hope it isn't true—I will never be like him. I don't hate you, Cullen Moore, or any other like you." She leans forward, wanting to kiss him, but he stops her once again.

"Everleigh—if it is true, if you are Cassius Brumah's daughter, then that would make me—"

He pauses, nearly unable to speak his truth.

Everleigh searches his eyes for more. "You are not my enemy!"

He shakes his head before speaking. "Everleigh—I am his brother!"

A gasp escapes the Stone Maiden's lips.

"I am Cullen Brumah, the firstborn son and rightful Heir of Stone. This awful truth has tainted my blood. I bear the burden of a merciless heritage, woven into the fabric of time. These men are driven solely by the pursuit of power. It is the thread that ties me to my ancestors, flowing through my bloodline. Everleigh, I see myself in them, a glimpse of my former self. If my heart had not stopped beating in my chest or if my blood had not ceased flowing in my veins, I would still be the same as I was then."

Everleigh shakes her head. "I see good in you, Cullen. I see light beyond the darkness."

Cullen's eyes narrow.

"I was sacrificed to Lord Raiden by my own brother, by Cassius—given to the King of Shadows to replace a son he lost in the war. Cassius did this so that he could rule in my place."

The Stone Maiden searches his eyes, forcing him to look at her.

She whispers with hopeful intent. "You are not your brother. I believe you would have ruled with kindness and compassion."

A low growl rumbles from the back of his throat.

"Everleigh."

"Cullen—please, you must—"

"No—listen to me."

"Cullen—"

Interrupting her pleas, he lightly shakes her. His voice rises, carrying a mixture of frustration and determination.

"If I hadn't been robbed of this, if my memories hadn't been stolen from me with the poison that silenced my heart —I would have been the ruler, and I can't guarantee that if I had been given the same opportunity, like my brother was, that I—"

"No—please don't say this—please."

She softly begs, her voice filled with desperation, wishing he would stop.

"Had I known that eliminating the only threat to the crown was an option, it is not impossible to imagine that I would have followed in Cassius' footsteps, turning against my own brother and delivering him to the vampire."

As the truth settles around them like a heavy burial shroud, they find themselves trapped in the moment, feeling the weight of their words hanging in the air. Despite his hope for her to distance herself from him in every possible manner, deep down he knows that he would go to the ends of the world to protect her.

"I—"

As she pauses, he tilts his head curiously, trying to read her expression.

"I don't care."

In a fiery moment of passion, their lips collide, igniting a rush of desire. Cullen's hands gently explore her sides, one settling at the small of her back while the other finds its place at the nape of her neck, ensuring her stability as their tongues intertwine. The sound of Everleigh's moan makes his back go rigid. In a moment of carelessness, his sharpened fangs nicked her bottom lip, leaving a thin trail of blood. With a sudden jolt, he breaks free from her embrace and rushes to the opposite side of the room, his body quivering.

With caution, he reaches up and gently wipes away the blood, making sure not to consume any, even though the taste is beyond his wildest imagination. With his back turned to her, he is teetering on the edge of ecstasy.

As he recites the poem, the borrowed verses blend seamlessly with the heartfelt words he penned during his long, loveless years.

"Yes, I will be thy priest and build an altar to you in some untrodden region of my mind, where branched thoughts are new and grown with pleasant pain and yet can be claimed as mine. A curse I bear, to be granted sight and hear your song. To be tempted by fate, in such a way is simply wrong. And in the midst of this wide quietness, a rosy sanctuary will I dress, with buds, and bells, and stars without a name, who breeding flowers, will never breed the same. And there shall be for thee all soft delight, that shadowy thoughts can win, a bright torch, in my endless sea of night, if only I could let love in."

Everleigh turns, her mouth stained with blood.

"Cullen? I said I do not care."

As his soul begins to fracture, he musters the strength to speak.

"Yet, I do—more than you'll ever know. This is why you cannot be mine."

The door closes, and as Everleigh places her face in her hands, she can hear the faint echo of the music coming to an end.

CHAPTER 9

THE KINGDOM OF STONE

Visha gazes up at the imposing statue of a serpent, its eyes seemingly watching her every move. She has devoted numerous days of her life confined within the walls of this room in her quest for the blessings of Acheron. With her hands tightly clasped together, she softly whispers her prayer, her voice barely breaking the silence. The moment The Holy Scribe enters, a powerful energy fills the space. As he walks, his black robes billow behind him, trailing along the ground like the remnants of a forgotten soul.

With his right hand waving, he yells, his voice echoing through the space.

"Out—out—out!"

There's no doubt that he's upset, and it's completely justified. Everyone has been dealing with Trystan's troublesome behavior for quite a while, and it has become a constant source of frustration. Years ago, Arrowe had extended an invitation to the boy to share his bed, and their scandalous affair had become the subject of much delightful gossip among the servants in the royal house, a topic that Niam had grown weary of over time. Due to his status as the king's son and the sole heir, Arrowe Brumah received a unique form of protection that no other male in The Kingdom of Stone could have obtained. Cassius had made it abundantly clear, on numerous occasions, that he was displeased with his son. However, he harbored a deep affection for his queen, Arrowe's mother, and as long as she was alive, Arrowe was off-limits. Niam was aware that if the plan succeeded and a worthy heir was produced, Cassius would finally have the means to rid himself of his son, whose habit of wearing his mother's clothes and painting his face had been a lifelong source of shame and irritation.

With the intention of paving the way for a suitable successor to his throne, Cassius had initially planned to kill the boy. However, those plans have now been thwarted, leaving The Holy Scribe with no other option but to work with the sole blood heir of their late king. Undoubtedly, The Holy Scribe has the power to unite Visha and the boy, resulting in the birth of an heir who could eventually take his place. He is determined to follow through with his plans until the very end.

"Now!" Niam's voice booms with frustration, his patience wearing thin like a frayed rope.

Like insects, the acolytes scatter in every direction, desperately searching for their escape routes.

Niam reaches the front of the room, his footsteps echoing in the silence as he paces back and forth, lost in thought. He absentmindedly rubs his chin and then nervously fidgets with his hands. He pauses, shooting a piercing glare at Visha, who remains deep in prayer with her eyes shut. Her dedication is so strong that she won't acknowledge his presence until she finishes, as her faith teaches her that not even her father should come before their God. As it should be.

Getting off her knees, she catches his eye, and he can't help but stop and stare. Each pew has a padded bar for praying, providing a welcome relief from the discomfort of kneeling on the chamber's cold stone floor. Visha's mask remains firmly in place as she stands, her hands clasped in front of her. In solidarity with the entire kingdom, she has chosen to keep wearing her black cloak as they mourn the loss of their sovereign.

"What was the reason behind your interaction with that boy?" He inquires, tilting his head.

Despite her calm demeanor, Visha displays hesitation when answering. With a sudden burst of speed, Niam charges towards her, tearing off her mask and sending her cloak's hood flying. Backing away, he tries to steady himself, the rhythmic tapping of the mask against his fingers providing a sense of comfort.

As Visha swallows the anxiety, she can feel it coalescing into a tight ball at the back of her throat. But then, she recalls her true self, and the fear melts away.

With her pale blue eyes fixed on her father, she waits for his response. She reaches up, feeling the softness of her amber hair against her fingertips, and carefully tucks it behind her ear. Her skin seems to radiate a soft glow in the subdued lighting of the room. Her mother's memory lives on through the striking resemblance they share. Something The Holy Scribe despises.

"Being polite," she lies.

"Mmm. Were you alone with him, out of sight?"

Visha's father fails to notice her nostrils flaring.

Clenching her fists, she presses her nail into her skin as she prepares to tell another falsehood.

"No—I was passing by the atrium and he was coming out."

Narrowing his eyes, Niam intensifies his gaze. "Did you see anyone with him?"

Visha makes a clicking sound with her tongue. "Not with him, but a girl exited the room before he emerged. I don't know what happened, but she looked—disheveled."

Niam sighs. "Surely up to no good."

"Is this boy someone you know?" Visha asks.

As the Holy Scribe takes a step forward, he extends his hand towards Visha, granting her permission to retrieve her mask. As she lifts the mask to her face, her father steps around behind her and tightens the ribbon, his words dripping with disapproval. "Trystan has always had a reputation for being quite promiscuous. He has lured many into his bed, using promises of affection to deceive and betray them, but he is incapable of love."

"He is a non-believer," Visha says, fully aware it will upset her father.

While tying a bow, Niam accidentally pulls Visha's hair and she lets out a hiss. Dropping the ribbon, he walks past the pew and gazes at the towering statue symbolizing their serpent deity. He fights the lingering chill in the cathedral by holding onto his wrists inside his bell sleeves.

Visha moves closer to him, positioning herself beside him. Taking a moment to look up at the statue, she finds herself lost in thoughts about her position within the kingdom and the desires that lie within her. Her belief is rooted in the idea that Acheron has graciously bestowed his blessings upon her, leading her to believe that every action she has taken is in accordance with his divine will.

"Did he tell you this?" The Holy Scribe questions, his voice remaining steady.

Her lips form a tight line. "No—I just feel it."

Niam faces her.

"I am assisting in the preparations for the funeral of our dear king, Cassius Brumah. As you are aware, it will occur when the sun sets tomorrow evening. You only have this night and one more day to show your worth to his successor. You should prioritize taking care of Arrowe Brumah instead of wandering in forbidden areas of the kingdom."

Visha slowly parts her lips, revealing a hint of anticipation on her face. His steady tone belies his underlying suspicion towards her.

"I was only walking to clear my mind and—"

As Niam strikes her upside the head, she loses her footing and struggles to maintain her balance, almost tripping and falling down. With a swift movement, he extends his arm and firmly grasps the fabric of her cloak, clenching it tightly just below her chin, exerting enough force to almost lift her off the ground. He leans into her face, forcing her to stand on her tiptoes. The scent of strong teas and wild berries lingers in his breath, which he delights in each afternoon.

"Unholy adulteress."

"I am sorry for angering you, father."

"Do you think I did all of this—let you live, sheltered you —placed you in a position to receive such power, only to have it all thrown away for a boy who is undeserving?"

Struggling to shake her head, she can feel his fist pressing against her chin, making it nearly impossible to move. Niam has a pattern of losing his temper and lashing out at her. Despite her awareness that lying to him would result in consequences, she strangely derives enjoyment from the outcome. Maybe she enjoyed watching Trystan manipulate the girl's every move just as much. Although she is not attracted to her own father, the impact of his abuse has deeply ingrained itself within her, causing her to develop a twisted desire for it, as it often serves as a substitute for any semblance of affection he would occasionally display towards her.

This is how Visha defines love. In its rarest form, danger became visceral, raw, and undeniably dangerous. It is an ache deep within her, a longing that never ceases. It makes her feel alive.

Niam's eyes remain fixed on her face, his gaze penetrating deeply into her soul. Killing the girl would be pointless. His goal is for The Kingdom of Stone to be the center of the world, and he spent years grooming her to become empress.

He releases his grip and gently sets her down on the ground, allowing her feet to rest firmly on the stone. In a tender gesture, the Holy Scribe adjusts the front of her cloak, softly brushing the fabric with his hand.

"The day has been challenging. I am sorry for my anger. I'll seek assistance from Acheron to redirect my passion. My only desire is for your well-being and the prosperity of our kingdom. You do understand, do you not?"

"Yes, father."

"Good." He places his hands on her shoulders.

"Arrowe will deem you worthy, I know it. Demonstrate to him that you are attentive to his every need. Remember, everything you do is for our God. He speaks through me now."

Visha inhales deeply, embracing her blessing.

"Thank you," she whispers.

"Now, go to him. He's waiting for me in his chamber, but I'll send you in my stead. Approach him and comply with his wishes without hesitation. Offer your support. When he takes the crown, we want his focus solely on you, ensuring that no other distractions come into play. If you make him trust you, he will do this without hesitation."

Visha nods.

"Go now," he whispers urgently, the sound barely audible over the distant rumble of thunder. Visha doesn't linger, instead rushing down the center of the aisle, her footsteps echoing against the wooden floor. She reaches the doors and pushes through, her heart pounding in her chest as she pauses to catch her breath against the wall. Her hand trembles as she reaches up to cradle the side of her head, feeling the pain pulsating through her temples. The ache is beginning to dull, but she can still feel the residual sting from the force of his blow. After lowering her hand, she gently presses it against her chest. Her heart is pounding, the rhythmic thumping echoing in her ears. Visha understands the importance of calming her nerves before entering Arrowe's chamber, so she takes a moment to collect herself. She takes a few more breaths, allowing her lungs to fill with air, until she feels assured that her voice will sound steady and composed. Following her father's instructions, she turns and walks down the corridor.

Visha's cloak trails behind her, mirroring the flowing movements of her father's. There are multiple ways in which she mirrors him. She is fully committed to her faith, willing to go to any lengths to safeguard their way of life, regardless of the personal toll it may take.

The door leading into his chamber looms before her, and as she gets closer, she notices the intricate carvings etched into its surface. Standing tall and vigilant, a single Stone Guardsman keeps watch. Visha wishes she could avoid speaking to the man, though it is customary.

Standing before him, she lifts her hand.

"I come at The Holy Scribe's request."

The Stone Guardsman takes his time to respond, examining her carefully.

"I speak in his absence," Visha adds.

"Do you have a scroll stating this?"

Visha lets out a sigh. "I do not, but he is in the cathedral now if you would like to ask him."

The Stone Guardsman gazes down the corridor, carefully considering his options, but ultimately decides to turn around and proceeds to knock on the door instead. The door barely opens.

"I told you I didn't want to be bothered," Arrowe says, his voice filled with annoyance.

"I'm sorry, my Lord. However, this young woman claims to have arrived at the behest of The Holy Scribe."

With measured caution, Arrowe opens the door slightly, revealing Visha standing on the other side. His eyes narrow in recognition, before a smile gently spreads across his lips.

"Please come," he says, graciously opening the door wide enough for her to enter, while keeping his body concealed from her sight. Upon entering, she promptly comprehends the reason. Arrowe is dressed in nothing but a pair of pants, with the top half unbuttoned, revealing a trail of black hair that starts from below his belly button and disappears beneath the fabric.

Visha rubs the side of her neck, feeling the warmth spreading across her face and neck.

As he snaps his fingers, Visha's attention is drawn to movement coming from behind the fabric that hangs over his grand canopy bed. The sound of giggling can be heard. It appears that he was keeping someone entertained.

"I can go."

Just as Visha starts to leave, Arrowe steps in her way and uses his arms to block her.

"I hope you're not intending to depart without informing me about The Holy Scribe's message. It seems to hold such significance that he entrusts you to deliver it on his behalf."

Visha strains her neck. The scent of ale reaches her nose. It is true that Arrowe has been drinking, but given the circumstances, it appears only fair for him to do something to ease the burden.

"The burial ceremony is scheduled for tomorrow evening at sunset."

While nearly stumbling, Arrowe asks, "And?"

"And he bestows Acheron's blessings upon you during these most difficult times—as do I."

Visha hears laughter coming from behind the fabric and straightens her posture. Whoever is occupying his bed is becoming a source of irritation for her. She clenches her jaw.

Arrowe's laughter subsides as he realizes Visha is not amused.

With a deep breath, he rests his hand on his chest, feeling the rise and fall of his breath, before letting it glide down until his fingers find their way inside the top of his pants. For a brief moment, he tilts his head back, stretching his neck. Her eyes are drawn to his chin, but soon enough, she finds herself savoring every detail of his body. Smooth chest, chiseled abs. Despite his current condition, he remains beautiful, maybe even more so. He emits a moan, gradually moving his hand beneath the fabric of his pants, while simultaneously lowering his chin, a mischievous glint apparent in his eyes.

"Arrowe," a girl's voice calls out from the bed, "could you come back to bed? You can either send her away or bring her with you."

There is a noticeable change in his expression.

"Will you take it off for me?" With a gesture, he lifts his free hand and points at her mask, making his statement more clear.

"Tell me," Visha says.

Tilting his head, Arrowe shows curiosity.

"Tell me to take it off for you," she clarifies.

He inhales slowly, withdrawing his hand from his pants.

"Take it off, now," Arrowe demands.

Visha lifts her hand and takes off her hood, letting it drape over her back. The tips of her fingers gently graze the ribbon's edge. She reminisces about the day that altered everything. As soon as this plan materialized, everything seemed to align perfectly. She had dreamed of elevating her status in the kingdom, but now, with Cassius gone, as well as her competition, perhaps she would finally ascend to the title of empress, just like her father had claimed.

Arrowe takes a few steps, positioning himself behind her. As Visha grasps onto the mask, he takes the initiative to untie it for her. The unexpected release of it brings a liber-ating feeling she didn't foresee. Her hand dangles by her side, the weight of the mask pressing against her fingertips, until Arrowe gently takes it from her and raises it to his face. Tilting his head, a mischievous grin replaces his once charming smile.

As Visha peers up at him, his shoulders shake with laughter.

"Perhaps you should wear it, my Lord," she suggests without taking her eyes off him.

A girl calls from the bed. "I'm getting lonely."

Visha inhales slowly. The moment would be absolutely perfect if this girl didn't dampen the mood with her drunken laughter.

Arrowe snaps his fingers. The room falls silent as the sharp sound resonates, extinguishing the laughter. It is evident that Arrowe and the mysterious whore in his bed share a silent understanding. Although Visha wishes Arrowe had been alone, she resigns herself to dealing with the current circumstances. The Stone Maiden will continue to make do, just as she always has.

"Come to me."

Visha prepares to follow the instructions, but Arrowe gestures for her to remain in place.

"Not you—little mouse," he whispers.

In that moment, her breath catches in her throat, a mixture of surprise and anticipation. Just like Trystan, he affectionately referred to her by the same endearing term. But she wonders which of them had been the first to use it, and whether it was directed at each other or part of a twisted game they played with the girls in the royal house.

Behind the thinning fabric draped over Arrowe's bed, a pale figure silently emerges. Standing just a couple of inches taller than Visha, there is a girl with jet-black hair and eyes that resemble those of a doe. In some ways, she reminds her of Everleigh - a fact that she can't deny bothers her. Visha Aeress ponders if Everleigh's ghost will remain here forever.

Arrowe removes the mask and sets eyes on the girl. She is completely bare, with no clothing to cover her. Despite Visha's attempts to disregard her rounded hips, thick thighs, and small waist, they become impossible to ignore as Arrowe seizes her hand and whirls her around to face Visha. With a quick flick of her tongue, the girl leaves behind a shimmering line of moisture on her lower lip. Visha can only imagine the source of the swelling in her mouth, as it appears red and noticeably larger. Her nose has a slight rosy hue, possibly due to the ale. The sight of empty bottles scattered throughout the space indicates that Arrowe had been drowning his sorrows in his chamber for a considerable amount of time, possibly a full day.

Smiling, the girl reaches out and takes Visha's hand. Visha is slowly coming to the realization that a gentle touch isn't her preferred form of affection. While she tends to blame her father's controlling behavior, the Stone Maiden suspects that there is a darker force at play. She can't deny the presence of a forbidden desire within her. The image of Trystan pleasuring the girl and giving her intense pleasure remained with Visha, creating a sensual sensation between her legs. While she prayed for forgiveness, her desire remained palpable, and she chose to stay on her knees, determined not to leave any noticeable mark on the wooden pew. If she had, surely her father's suspicions would have been confirmed.

As Arrowe carefully lowers the mask in front of her face and ties it securely, the girl intertwines her fingers with Visha's, their hands tightly connected. Her pupils expand upon seeing it. Visha finds herself grappling with the unexpected pull she feels towards her. Her jaw tenses and her grip on the girl's hand tightens, betraying her anxiety. As she squeezes her fingers, the naked girl, who is wearing her Katsumi mask, hisses in response, but surprisingly, she doesn't pull away. Maybe she prefers a firmer touch?

From behind, Arrowe embraces the naked girl, applying pressure against her body. With one hand, he cups and caresses her breast, skillfully massaging it. Simultaneously, he lifts her slightly, causing her toes to gracefully point towards the solid stone floor. As his grip becomes firmer, the girl can't help but let out a moan. At the same time, his chin rests gently on her smooth shoulder and he stares deeply into Visha's eyes, displaying a desire filled with such intense lust.

Overcoming her discomfort, Visha bravely keeps her eyes fixed on Arrowe as he delicately pinches the girl's nipples, which are a beautiful shade of pale pink and perfectly rounded. Using her free hand, the girl reaches behind her back and slides her fingers over Arrowe's growing bulge, causing him to growl in response. As he continues to apply more pressure, causing waves of pleasurable pain to course through her body, she instinctively begins to stroke him, feeling his size gradually increase in her hand until her fingers can barely make contact with him. Arrowe has always possessed an impressive combination of girth and length, a test for those who shared his bed. However, this girl has surrendered to his desire, feeling him bury himself inside her from behind. Her demeanor suggests that she is made to fulfill his wishes, accommodating them with either a gentle compliance or, more frequently, a hostile animosity.

The girl's grip tightens on Visha's hand, urging her closer, but just before Visha reaches them, she abruptly recoils, choosing instead to observe as he persists in tormenting her.

"Remove your mourning cloak," he says, his voice stern and commanding.

As the girl maintains a steady rhythm, it has made him grow harder. She notices that the tip of his cock is now wet, prompting her to run her thumb across it. She then proceeds to pull it out of his pants and brings it to her lips. In a display of dominance, he forcefully seizes her wrist and inserts her thumb into his mouth, proceeding to seductively lick it until it is clean. With the anticipation of a serpent entwining its prey, she sensually wraps her body around him, eagerly yearning for the sensation of his cock in her hand, mouth, or even better, as he stretches her wide while her legs rest gracefully on his shoulders.

In a seductive manner, Visha bends down, her fingers gliding along the fabric of her cloak as she slowly lifts it up, gradually revealing the smooth skin of her calves and the enticing curves of her thighs, until her black panties come into view, tightly clinging to her swollen lips, nestled enticingly between her legs.

With a sigh, Arrowe watches as Visha gracefully lifts the black cloak up and over her head. As her stomach muscles flex, he is taken aback by the sight of her perfectly round and firm breasts. She releases her grip, the black cloak glides down and settles on the floor, creating a soft rustling sound.

"Are you untouched?" he inquires, fully aware of her response, yet longing to hear her verbalize it.

Visha nods. "I am by all but one."

He narrows his eyes.

"There was an incident earlier where a boy named Trystan forcefully took hold of my hand, and the unsettling gaze in his eyes left me concerned about his intentions."

Crooking his neck, Arrowe is visibly bothered by it.

"Did he kiss your lips?"

Visha nervously bites her lips while his captivating blue eyes remain fixated on her mouth.

"No, but I believe he might have wanted to do such a thing—perhaps more."

Arrowe's gaze wanders around her, carefully examining every inch of her body, savoring the sight of her alluring curves. Engrossed in the moment, he lifts his hand and delicately grazes his thumb across his lower lip, his focus then shifting to the mesmerizing small of her back and the alluring curvature of her perfectly rounded ass.

"Did he know who you were?"

She briefly looks over at him before returning her attention to the girl who is engaging in self-pleasure by fondling her own breasts, all while Arrowe remains fixated on Visha.

"I was wearing my mask—so yes, he knew. In fact, he asked me if I was untouched, just as you have."

Arrowe positions himself between her and the naked girl, casting a stern gaze upon Visha.

"And did you tell him?"

As Visha locks eyes with him, she is entranced by the untamed intensity in his piercing blue gaze.

"I did."

"And what else did you tell him?"

Taking a brief pause, she makes the choice to offer him further details. "That I was bred to serve a king—to bring forth a worthy heir to the throne."

As Arrowe leans into her, she can feel the warmth of his

breath and the gentle touch of his hand in hers. The pressure of his thumb against her palm sends tingles of pleasure up her arm. His full lips gently caress the edge of her ear, creating a tantalizing sensation. With determination in his voice, he proclaims, "I will be king."

As he retreats, he keeps a tight grip on her hand, his movements deliberate and measured. His grip is like a vice, firm and unyielding.

"Yes—a worthy king and sovereign."

"Am I deserving of your precious gift?" As he asks the question, his eyes linger on her black panties.

"It depends," she says.

His eyebrow arches, adding a hint of intrigue to his expression. He finds her spirited attitude exhilarating. Arrowe has the power to choose anyone he wants in the kingdom and has done so multiple times, but he finds pleasure in pursuing challenges, something that Trystan has presented in the past, including their last encounter in the Great Library with Everleigh Aeress observing discreetly from behind a bookshelf.

"On what?"

"On how well you instruct me, my Lord," she whispers.

Arrowe's nostrils flare, capturing the tantalizing scent of his prey. A flicker of emotion crosses his face, causing his eyes to darken and take on a more piercing shade of blue. Lowering his chin, he gently guides her hand to rest on her flat stomach, feeling the warmth radiating beneath his touch. With each breath, her chest rises and falls rapidly, betraying her heightened state of excitement.

"Have you pleasured yourself in such a way?"

Visha shakes her head. Even though she had vowed to resist such sinful behavior, she couldn't help but dream about this day, with or without a crown adorning her head.

With a firm touch, he guides her hand into her panties and encourages her to explore the wetness between her lips. The sensation of pressure gliding over her clit makes her gasp with delight. Arrowe brings her hand back up, teasing her clit with a gentle touch, causing her to quiver with pleasure. His body responds, his arousal evident as his cock stirs against the fabric of his pants, begging for release.

Reaching behind, he gently pulls the unclothed girl closer to his side.

"Get on the floor."

Her grin widens, her thighs now slick and glistening with her intense craving for him.

Arrowe intervenes and stops Visha from stimulating her clit by pulling her fingers away. As the girl kneels before him, she rubs her fingers together and feels the wetness. While maintaining eye contact with Visha, he reaches down and reveals his swollen cock, pulling it out of his pants. At first, she hesitates to look down, but eventually succumbs to the temptation. He firmly grasps the girl's chin and directs the tip of his strength into her mouth. With a gradual motion, her head begins to move forward and back, gradually gaining momentum as Arrowe diligently keeps a watchful eye on Visha. The Stone Maiden watches with intent, eager to learn a skill that will sustain her. If providing this pleasure is what he desires, she will gladly fulfill his wishes.

Demonstrating his dominance, Arrowe seizes the girl by the back of her head, intertwining his fingers in her hair, and forcefully urges her to move forward. With each thrust, he buries himself deeper inside her, causing her to moan in pleasure as she feels him reaching the back of her throat. Despite her resistance, he firmly holds her in place while he withdraws, causing a shimmering trail of saliva to stretch from her mouth to the tip of his cock. Despite her gagging, she still desires more.

Always more.

Despite the girl's attempts to move forward, Arrowe refuses to let her proceed, instead teasing her by keeping the tip of his cock just out of her reach. Visha's pulse is steady. The rhythmic sensation that mirrors the throbbing between her thighs.

By exerting pressure, Arrowe coerces the girl to change her position, causing her to kneel and then forcefully pushing her onto her back. Reaching out, he grasps Visha's hand and guides her over the girl's body. Visha can feel the firm grip of the girl's hands tightly wrapped around her ankles, keeping her rooted in place.

Arrowe places his hands on Visha's shoulder and applies pressure, directing her over the girl's face. On her knees, Visha could feel the other girl's arms encircling her legs, exerting pressure to separate them. The girl slowly pulls down Visha's panties, revealing her bare skin.

Arrowe moves a few steps aside before coming back with a blade that gleams in his hand. He lowers himself onto his knees and skillfully cuts away her panties. Visha gasps once again, her breath catching in her throat as Arrowe tears the rest away. He lifts them to his lips, savoring her sweet scent before discarding them to the side.

As Arrowe rises above her, the girl beneath Visha tightens her grip on her thighs, ensuring her legs stay spread. With a commanding presence, he holds her chin while his thumb delicately spreads her lips, creating space for him to slide his cock into her mouth. He takes his time, relishing the feeling of Visha's tongue caressing him, not wanting to rush the moment. Arrowe moans, feeling the strain, but Visha remains calm and unyielding. Instead, she resigns herself to the fact that her mouth will have to stretch even further to accommodate his remarkable size. A clear expression of satisfaction adorns his face, his mouth slightly ajar as he maintains unwavering eye contact with her.

"Look at me," he says.

Visha's eyes lift to watch him as he moves in and out of her mouth. She takes great care to open her mouth wide, ensuring her teeth don't graze against him.

As the girl beneath her rises up, she extends her rigid tongue, tracing it slowly along the length of her slit, occasionally pausing to make small circular motions. Visha's moans reverberate, sending a pulsating sensation through Arrowe's core. He pushes forward, and she willingly accepts half of his length, opening her mouth eagerly. Biting into his bottom lip, he lets out a low moan and grasps the back of her head, keeping it still as he finds his rhythm. As he thrusts deeper, the girl beneath her reaches up and seductively sucks on her finger. With a firm grip, she slides her fingers into Visha's ass, eliciting a reflexive tightening of her muscles. With each stroke of her tongue, the girl can taste her, eliciting a low, sensual moan.

With both hands, Arrowe firmly holds Visha's head, using her mouth to fulfill his every whim. A mixture of their passion clung to her chin, leaving it moist and flushed. She grabs his hand, guiding it to her throat, urging him to apply pressure. He brings her fantasy to life and Visha's eyes spark with desire.

The girl's ferocious pace matches the rhythm of her

finger, which was now deeply buried inside Visha. The sound of Visha's moans filled the air, growing louder with each passing moment.

Arrowe buries himself inside her mouth, holding her head steady as she grinds against the girl's mouth, both of them lost in the moment. The pleasure between her legs grows, fueled by a fiery heat akin to that of a dragon's breath. The girl beneath her grips Visha's thighs, her fingernails digging in, causing a mixture of pain and pleasure to surge through her body like a torrent.

With a quickening pace, Arrowe cries out and drives his cock all the way to the back of Visha's throat, forcefully emptying his seed in her mouth. As Visha reaches up, her fingertips graze against his side, drawing blood and marking the beginning of her first taste of liberation. With each swallow, she relishes the taste of every precious drop, savoring the moment.

With a swift motion, Arrowe removes himself, leaving a trail of glistening saliva connecting his cock to her lips, as the naked girl on the floor slips away.

"Is it my turn?" she asks, rising to her feet and approaching him.

Arrowe forcefully grabs her, positioning her over the side of the bed. He enters her with intensity, pressing her face into the comforter, making it difficult for her to breathe. Her arms flail wildly, striking the bed with a loud thud.

Visha rises up, observing as he hastens his pace once more. Arrowe looks to Visha, who seems unmoved. He slows, withdrawing from the girl. She whines, twisting her ass, wishing he would return.

With each cautious step, Visha inches closer to him, causing him to retreat in a desperate attempt to regain his breath. Finally, she reaches the bed and crawls onto it, fidgeting with her hair. Effectively taking the place of the whore who had held his attention until Visha had arrived.

Arrowe narrows his eyes, a glint of determination in his gaze, and then snaps his fingers.

"Get dressed and go," he commands. "Now."

The girl rises, silently gathering her clothing and dressing herself, while Arrowe watches Visha with curious eyes. Rushing to the door, the girl slips out, careful not to make a sound as the Stone Guardsman stands sentinel over the heir's chamber.

"Are you lacking entertainment?" Arrowe asks, his gaze unwavering as he waits for her response, never breaking eye contact.

Visha drops one of her curls, her fingers brushing against the soft strands, and looks up to him.

Her eyes lock with his, and she utters the words, "Make me your queen," as she brushes her hand against the soft fabric.

Arrowe's bright blue eyes track the movement of her hand, his vision momentarily blurring before he regains focus. The ale has caused him to almost lose his sense of self.

"Make you my queen?" He scoffs at her demands. "And why should I—"

Looking up at him, Visha brazenly interrupts him, disregarding any social niceties.

"Make me your queen," she pleads, her words hanging in the air as the scent of blooming flowers filled the night. "Offer me a crown, and I will conveniently overlook any misbehavior you may engage in."

Arrowe's laughter echoes in the air, filling the space between them.

"There is no limit to who I can have whenever I please."

"Now—in this moment, yes. But in the coming days, your life will become intertwined with the lives of the people, with the destiny of this kingdom, and with the duties associated with the crown. The things you relished as an heir will prove challenging to maintain once you ascend to the throne. However, I won't prevent you from indulging in such pleasures. In fact, I will be happy to join you when you ask."

"When I demand," he growls.

Showing her eagerness, Visha starts crawling towards him just as he reaches the edge of the bed. As she rocks back on her knees, she slowly begins to open her legs, revealing the intimate treasure nestled between them. Her pleasure still glistens, leaving a radiant glow.

"Yes," she says with a sinister grin, "and tightly grip my throat."

He sighs.

"Make me your queen."

Placing her hand against his bare chest, she rises up on her knees, feeling his heartbeat against her palm.

"And I will never complain—nor stop you, even if a man were to slip into this chamber, seeking companionship."

She leans in, her lips barely touching his chest, before tracing circles around his nipple with her tongue, leaving a lingering sensation.

"Pledge your allegiance to me as queen, in front of everyone at your father's burial ceremony, and I will prove to be your strongest ally and unwavering defender."

"And what will you offer me, Stone Maiden?"

"Other than carrying your secrets?"

"Yes."

"I will also carry your seed. For I am born to be bred."

As she reaches down, her fingers make contact with the front of his pants, sensing the slight warmth emanating from the fabric. He tightly clutches her wrist, his fingers digging into her skin. Her lips curl into a small, satisfied smirk.

"I will bury my seed as deeply as it will go inside of you, but not until my father is buried, and the crown sits upon my head."

While holding her in place, Visha lets out a deep sigh.

"But there are other ways we can indulge ourselves."

She leans back as he slowly climbs on top of her.

Arrowe's eyes sparkle with anticipation, for he has finally found another whose intensity matches his own.

CHAPTER 10

BRENNA ACADEMY

Standing on the seventh floor, Maliah directs her gaze out the window, her attention captivated by the towering wall of water that the ship had tumbled over. However, no matter how high she looks, its top remains hidden from her sight. The wall seems to rise into the sky, disappearing beyond the clouds. The fact that they are still alive fills her with a deep sense of gratitude. If it wasn't for the majestic blue dragon, they would have plummeted to their deaths. The ship's damage was minor in comparison.

"It's truly remarkable. This place is like nothing I've ever seen before. It's truly beyond my wildest imagination."

Faeryn carefully arranges two soft blankets on Maliah's new bed, her long, purple braid gently brushing against the side. She catches herself staring at Maliah, captivated by her radiant smile. The room is bathed in a soft, golden light from the large window, illuminating the young Fate's skin with a radiant glow. Faeryn joins her, standing side by side to fully appreciate the magnificent view.

"I often take it for granted, forgetting that I was born here when the mountain still rumbled from the depths and spewed a river of fire. The mountain is responsible for creating everything that you see. It gave us the fertile lands to grow food and allowed the forest to grow thick and tall. The water is both sweet to the taste and believed to possess healing properties. We use it to soothe aching muscles and create our spells. Ashland is like a paradise. A home that is perfect for both us and the dragons."

Maliah briefly looks at the Witch, who has her arms folded. She continues to wear the red leather that complements the color of her dragons. The young Fate catches a quick glimpse of the patch on Faeryn's upper arm just before the Witch realizes she is examining it.

While touching the patch, she says. "I am a Cleric."

"You mentioned that before, but what does it mean?"

"Well," Faeryn, feeling restless, decides to unfold her arms and starts fidgeting with the end of her braid in an attempt to fix the binding that holds it together. "Brenna Academy is a place where we learn to cast, heal, ride our dragons, and—" she pauses.

"And what else?"

Faeryn's face lights up as she breaks into a grin.

"Practice diplomacy."

"Mmm, do you mean aggressive negotiations?" Maliah asks.

Faeryn, seemingly reluctant to provide more details, declines to elaborate any further. "Do you like your room?"

As she takes a moment to look around, Maliah's lips curl into a smirk, clearly pleased with her new accommodations.

"I love it. Who else will be staying here?"

A puzzled expression crosses Faeryn's face as her brows knit together. "No one—this is only for you."

"All of this?"

Maliah approaches the large chest at the end of the bed and unlocks it, only to find it empty. Rushing towards another door, she quickly opens it up wide and discovers her private bath. Positioned in the center of the floor, there is a tub made of chiseled black stone that is raised a few feet above the ground. It is designed with steps leading up from all directions, ensuring convenient access. With a smile on her face, she gracefully brings her hands together and rests them beneath her chin.

"Have you never slept alone?" Faeryn asks.

Maliah turns to face her, her cheeks flushed and a hint of embarrassment in her eyes. It is clear that the question isn't meant to be inappropriate, but there is still a subtle discomfort that lingers in the air.

"I slept with my mother. We shared a room with three others. That is how servants—" she pauses.

Shedding the thought of being a servant was difficult for her, especially after years of being told that serving the royal house was her duty. The only reason for her existence.

"Well, there are no servants in Brenna. We are assigned duties that are equally shared among the students. Some days we cook, others we clean—sometimes we help tend to the dragons, but this is not done with force. We all carry this weight for the good of the academy—for each other."

"It sounds—fair," Maliah confesses, just moments before she spots her own reflection in the mirror that is placed above the water basin. Moving closer, she extends her hand towards her face, but retreats when she catches sight of Faeryn approaching from behind.

Maliah finds it difficult to look at herself, which prompts Faeryn to inquire about the reason behind it. "Have you never seen your own reflection?"

As Maliah turns her body, she stretches out her arms to both sides, using the black countertop surrounding the water basin to stabilize herself.

"We were explicitly forbidden from having mirrors in our possession. There was a belief that the experience might trigger some dormant memories from our pasts. Until now, I've only seen my reflection in moving water."

Confused, Faeryn moves nearer, unable to comprehend why those who ruled her kingdom would be so paranoid and cruel.

While reaching around, she gently lifts Maliah's chin and whispers.

"Look. You are beautiful."

Maliah whispers back. "I am not like those in the royal house."

Unable to withstand the intensity of her emotions, Maliah is compelled to break eye contact with her own reflection after a prolonged stare. Swallowing hard, she locks eyes with the dragon rider, her heart pounding in her chest.

She weaves her fingers together, creating a tangled pattern.

"A Fate is neither Fae nor Elven, but a blend of both."

After examining her hands, Faeryn refocuses on her pale pink eyes.

"I don't see why this is a problem."

"It was not uncommon for our monarch, King Elio Efhren, to openly express his disapproval of individuals whose bloodlines were considered impure. Despite this, he entered into a marriage with a Fate to unite our two peoples. However, our queen, like him, wasted no time in dismissing her Fae ancestry."

Extending her arm, Faeryn reaches in and places a comforting hand on Maliah's shoulder. In an effort to prevent Maliah from lowering her chin again, she leans in closer.

"No offense, but it sounds like your King and Queen are quite ignorant."

Maliah's shoulders shake with laughter. "Oh, I would have loved to see someone say that to them."

"Here in Ashland, everyone is treated as equals. There is no one who serves and no one who is judged. Every single one of us owns a mirror. Although I still think I'm the best rider here."

In an effort to brighten the mood, she can't help but let out a small chuckle.

As Maliah tilts her head, a hushed connection forms between them, heightened by the gentle movement of Faeryn's thumb against Maliah's collarbone.

"This room is perfect for you, Maliah."

As soon as she hears Rowe Efhren's voice coming from the doorway, a wave of tension runs through her body.

Faeryn pivots her body as Maliah walks by.

"Isn't it beautiful?" she asks.

"Yes—it is."

His gaze shifts away from her and settles upon Faeryn, who stands nearby, her arms crossed over her crimson flying leathers, once again displaying a guarded stance.

"Rowe, this is Faeryn—she was the one who saved you on the ship. She is a—"

He completes her sentence for her. "Witch."

The room falls silent. In an attempt not to be rude, he touches his side, yet Faeryn's intense interest in Maliah still manages to irritate him.

"And thank you for healing me." He nonchalantly mentions it as an afterthought, even though it should be his main focus.

Faeryn can't help but smirk, a sly grin playing on her face.

"I am a Cleric—but I guess the term Witch will do. I can cast, but it's for healing purposes."

"And you ride dragons," he adds.

"Yes, I do. Students at Brenna have the ability to ride dragons in various environments, including the air, water, and land."

He gestures towards her arm. "It appears that you have a high level of organization here, resembling that of a military outpost."

Her eyes flicker towards her arm, where she runs her fingertips along the edge of the patch.

"Well, I can't take credit for Brenna," she says, staring at Rowe momentarily before inquiring, "Have you been shown your room yet?"

He nods, his chin jutting forward with determination.

"It's just down the hallway, in very close proximity to this one. So close. Practically on the other side of the wall."

His intention is to stress the fact.

"Good! I hope you were pleased with it."

His eyes linger on Maliah for a moment before returning to the girl with the purple hair.

"I am."

"I mean, it isn't a royal house, built for a King."

Rowe's jaw tightens momentarily before he consciously

forces himself to relax.

Unamused by her jab, he asks with a touch of sarcasm. "Where is Wennie?"

Faeryn lifts a hand. "There's no need to worry. She's with my mother."

"I don't know your mother." Rowe is quick to emphasize.

Faeryn wastes no time responding to him.

"Well, she won't take her wings."

Rowe's eyes turn a shade darker as anger surges through him. His hand tightens into a fist, the veins bulging with tension.

Desperate to diffuse the situation, Maliah springs into action. "Will we get a full tour of the school?"

Maliah manages to capture Faeryn's attention once again, causing her glare to soften.

"I would be glad to show you around, and later tonight, we will have a meeting with the Founder, following a delicious meal."

"The Founder?" Maliah asks.

"The first of us—the one who discovered this place and created the school."

Rowe and Maliah make eye contact before she says, "We look forward to it and thank you—for everything."

A lingering silence fills the space between them, growing more awkward with each passing second. Maliah, feeling the need to fill the void, takes it upon herself to speak up.

"It would be a good idea for me to get settled in first, and then I definitely need to make time to take a bath." As she sniffs her arm, a look of disgust crosses her face. "I'm starting to smell like Grim."

With a shake of her head, Faeryn says, "Umbras."

Faeryn, with a slight bow, proceeds towards the doorway, but her pace slows down as she crosses paths with Rowe. Their eyes meet, conveying a tense exchange of emotions, before she finally leaves the room.

Exhausted, Rowe sighs deeply and relies on the doorway to bear some of his weight. He is still not fully recovered from the actions of his brother.

"Rowe," Maliah grumbles.

His eyebrow cocks. "What?"

"Faeryn saved your life."

"Just to remind me of my father's actions."

Maliah nervously bites her bottom lip before finally letting it go. "Okay, it's true," she admits, "she was a little aggressive, but so were you."

Feeling defeated, he lets out a sigh and focuses on his palm, gently massaging it.

"I know what my father did was wrong," he whispers, his voice filled with guilt. "My presence here is proof that I don't support it."

She finds herself entranced by the way his lilac eyes appear to sink into her, creating an intense connection.

"But," Maliah adds.

"But, what, Maliah? I don't know what more you want me to say."

As she observes him closely, her attention is drawn to the intricate white tattoos that extend across the bridge of his nose and continue beneath his bottom lip. The love that Maliah has for Rowe had evolved over time, bringing both joy and disdain to her heart. Without realizing it, he was her captor. While she was aware that he would never hold her against her wishes, there was still a lingering sense of uncertainty. His father's blood ran through Rowe Efhren's veins. There was no way he could deny or escape it.

Regret lacing her tone, she admits her mistake. "We all knew."

Rowe presses his body against the doorframe, feeling the sturdy wood against his side. "Maliah."

Despite the hesitation in her voice, she gathers her courage and firmly states, "No—I need to say this. We all knew that your father took the dragon's wings." Her eyes grow larger.

He pushes off the doorframe, using his strength to stand. "Does that make us guilty?"

Fidgeting with her nails, she glances around anxiously, until her hands drop and her eyes instantly connect with his.

"It makes us complacent. Which, in some ways, is worse. We stood by, Rowe, and did nothing. How often did you have the chance to visit Dragon's Keep? Your journeys to the dragon's lair were not motivated by a need to liberate them, but rather by a sense of curiosity and a misguided need to impress a brother who was not worthy of your admiration."

As Rowe approaches her, he can see the sadness in her eyes, wishing he could offer solace but understanding that she is correct.

"I didn't know that Noble was so cruel."

"Well, he was always that way. He tormented me when were younger, angry that I was given to you and not him."

As he approaches her, he gently places his hand on the side of her face, tenderly cradling her cheek. She closes her eyes for a moment, savoring the warmth of his touch against her skin.

Softly murmuring, his words barely reach her ears. "Why didn't you tell me?"

As she opens her eyes and looks up at him, she can't help but wish for a different outcome, but she feels the weight of change settling in, beyond her control.

"Because, in The Kingdom of Silver Flame, I was no one."

As she attempts to look away, he shakes his head and leans in closer. His fingers softly graze her chin, guiding her eyes to lock with his.

"You were never no one to me, Maliah Bazzel."

"You are going to be King. The Silver Flame will call out to you as well as the crown," she whispers.

His eyes narrow. The mere idea of it causing a lump in his throat. Despite his reluctance to become king, he is now faced with the question of what to do in the wake of his brother's death. When Noble does not return, there is no doubt that his father will demand an explanation.

"All that I care about stands before me now."

With a gentle sweep of his hand, he lovingly brushes a stray strand of her pastel-pink hair away from her face, his heart yearning for more than anything to feel the soft touch of her lips against his own. But the tranquility of the moment is shattered by the echoing voices of Grim and Arren, calling out in the hallway, searching for their companions.

Grim raises his hands to his mouth in order to shout.

"Rowe—Maliah!"

The Fate Heir lets out a sigh of frustration. Realizing that the Umbra will persist until he reveals himself, he takes a step back. He reaches the doorway to Maliah's room, and he can sense her presence right behind him.

With a swift turn, the Umbra claps his hands together,

the sound echoing through the room, as a wide smile lights up his face. The man is unable to conceal his emotions, whether through animated hand gestures or the mischievous sparkle in his light blue eyes. Engrossed in thought, he runs his fingers through his untidy beard. Close behind, Arren Verrick cranes his neck to study the tall corridor lined with oval windows. The mountain spreads across the horizon, framed by each window. Its breathtaking beauty stops him in his tracks, causing him to run his fingers through his shaggy black hair. He is still without a shirt, allowing everyone to witness the impressive display of his flexing muscles and the intricate tattoos that seem to ripple like a wave across his skin. Mesmerized by his strikingly chiseled features and towering height, Maliah finds it difficult to look away. Arren, like all wolves, emits pheromones that can easily seduce others, similar to the vampires in the north. Whispering softly to one another, a small group of dragon riders make their way past him, their eyes lingering on him. Clad in leather similar to Faeryn's outfit, two of them are dressed in bronze, one in black, and the remaining two wear blue. He looks in their direction, giving them a playful wink, and the girls excitedly rush down the hallway, their giggles filling the air.

Maliah takes a step forward to observe their hasty departure. "Why are these outfits different colors?"

Rowe follows her gaze. "Maybe they specialize in different things?"

Faeryn approaches, tapping a blade against her palm. With a flick of her wrist, she flips it and seamlessly slides it into its sheath, securing it at her side. A smile spreads across Maliah's face, revealing her happiness at the sight of the purple-haired Witch.

"Among the dragons that inhabit this realm are ones of fiery red, as well as sleek black, shimmering bronze, and majestic blue. Our clothing is the same color as the dragons, so that we blend in while riding. Some came to help us move toward the shore, under the water. All but mine. They don't like to swim. And the largest and oldest of the blue dragons, known as Hiro, is the reason the ship made it to the bottom of the wall."

"Your dragons?" Rowe asks.

"Yes—the twins. They seem to like me best. No one else can ride with them—or I should say, want to. They can be quite feral. But I like wild things." Faeryn's attention is drawn to Maliah.

Before Rowe can inquire any further, the Umbra firmly grips his shoulders and gives him a vigorous shake. It is proceeded by a hug and a hearty slap on Rowe Efhren's back. He pulls the Fate Heir away from Maliah and Faeryn, who are now chatting by the window.

"Friend, words cannot express the joy I feel seeing you up and moving," Grim speaks his truth, relieved that the Fate had survived his brother's blade.

Rowe nods to him, a silent gesture of acknowledgement, before Arren joins the two of them.

"So, we're meeting with someone known as the Founder?" he asks, in a quieter tone, raising an eyebrow.

With a confident stance, Grim places his hands firmly on his hips. "Expect to be scolded for showing up here."

Arren shifts his position and leans in, emphasizing, "It was Faeryn who guided us to this place. She led us across the abyss. It's true that when your brother and his guards attacked, the blue dragon saved us not once, but twice."

As Rowe reflects on the incident, a noticeable change

occurs in his expression, triggered by the memory of his brother's face just moments before he attempted to take his life. He forcefully pushes the intrusive thoughts out of his mind.

"I don't think it was for our benefit," he mutters under his breath, his tone tinged with suspicion.

"Then why?"

"For Wennie." Rowe clarifies, while keeping his voice down. "Didn't you see how Faeryn's mother reacted to her? I think they want her to stay here."

When Grim looks at him, there is a sense of intensity in the air. "Well," he says, lifting his hand to rub the side of his neck.

A frown forms on Rowe's face as his eyebrows knit together. "Doesn't this concern you? He looks to Arren, his eyes pleading for support. "They mean to steal her from us."

"Rowe—Wennie is..."

"She's a Queen," Arren blurts out.

"A what?" Rowe asks, looking from one man to the other.

Maliah's voice breaks into their conversation. "It's true. Faeryn said the prophecy has come true. They have waited three hundred years for her to arrive."

She quickly looks back to find Faeryn still standing by one of the large windows, as Maliah confirms the information. The Witch understands that it will be simpler if she avoids getting involved, considering Rowe's combative nature towards her.

Rowe's mind drifts back to the cave on Dragon's Keep, recalling the mystical pull Mara had on him. She had instilled in him a strong desire to protect Wennie. He had felt a heaviness in his heart as he watched her energy swirl above him and leave the cave that day. The weight of his worries vanished as soon as he found Wennie nestled in the dragon's nest. Maybe Mara had chosen him not just for protection, but because she believed he had the skills to safely bring her to Ashland.

While another group of dragon riders passes by them, Grim lowers his tone and rubs the side of his neck. "But for what reason?"

All eyes are fixed on the Umbra.

"What do you mean?" Maliah asks.

"From what I've learned, a prophecy holds significant meaning. With the arrival of a new ruler, change inevitably follows."

While lost in thought, staring toward the mountain, Arren casually remarks, "Or war."

Maliah cautiously backs into her dimly lit room, gesturing for the three men to follow her inside. Rowe shuts the door behind him, pivots, and locks eyes with her.

"Do you think this school is designed to train them for battle?" With a quick, anxious movement, her eyes flicked back and forth between the men, trying to gauge their reactions.

As Arren crooks his neck, he hears a satisfying crack, finally easing the stiffness. "The existence of many dragons and those trained to ride them indicates another motive."

"Faeryn's mother was furious with her for daring to breach the wall of water." Maliah reminds them.

Before he speaks, Grim narrows his eyes. "Perhaps their intention is to stay unnoticed, keeping their existence a secret from the rest of the world until the moment is right?"

"Well, we will get answers tonight when we speak to

this Founder," Rowe insists. "I will be direct when I ask my questions."

"Okay, but for now, let's avoid any further discussion on this matter." Suspiciously, he scans the room, taking note of every detail. "You never know who is listening—so can we agree?"

A silent understanding passes between them as they exchange looks, and they all nod in agreement.

"It might be a good idea for everyone to go back to their rooms and enjoy a relaxing bath." Rowe looks at Maliah and adds, "Surely, it'll look less suspicious than this."

"I agree," he whispers, his voice filled with anticipation. "Just act as if everything is normal, and tonight we'll get our answers tonight."

AFTER TAKING A HOT BATH, Maliah gazes at herself in the long mirror, admiring the steamy glow on her skin. Her body glistens with beads of moisture. Turning to the side, she admires the detailed white tattoos that crawl over her hip and elegantly wrap around her side. This trait often serves as a distinctive identifier for those with more Fae blood than Elven. Unlike Rowe Efhren and his father, the king, their tattoos stand out with distinct patterns. During the War of Brumah, Fae emerged as a valuable ally to the Elves, their strategic minds and flawless execution of war plans turning the tide of battle. Fae are notorious for their ruthless fighting skills and lack of mercy towards their opponents. As the war raged on, Elio Efhren had also adopted this merci-less attitude. It is, in many ways, his lack of empathy that empowered him to carry out the most despicable actions, like brutally cutting off the wings of the dragons who had faithfully served his people in the war. This disloyal act had hardened his heart toward the creatures, and as time passed, he became indifferent to their presence.

As her fingers glide over the white tattoo, she can feel a slight tingling sensation spread across her side and stomach. With a deep breath, she turns her attention towards her reflection, seeing herself with fresh eyes. It was something Maliah had never been given permission to do, a rule that felt unnecessary and unkind. She softly explores her flat stomach with her hand, glides it across her collarbone, and finally pauses at the nape of her neck. In her mind, she has always seen herself as anything but beautiful, instead perceiving her appearance as flawed in numerous ways. At one point in time, she had a deep aversion to her Fae blood, but has her perspective changed? Her understanding and appreciation for her heritage is slowly growing. It is not the Elves, but rather the Fae who grant her the skill to handle a blade with such remarkable precision. Contemplating her identity, she ponders whether it is time to let go of the term "Fate" and fully embrace her inherent connection to the Fae blood flowing within her.

The faint sound of a door opening, followed by a soft click, reaches her ears. She moves swiftly and soundlessly towards the partially open door, which divides her bedroom from the bath. Her eyes immediately catch sight of a package that had been left on her bed. Taking a quick look around to ensure that the person who visited her has left, she cautiously walks towards the bed and notices a black box adorned with a vibrant blue ribbon. With anticipation, she reaches out and feels the smoothness of the ribbon between her fingers, giving it a slight tug to release it before she opens the box. When she peers inside, her eyes widen at the sight of the sleek, black leather. Soft to the touch, she gently runs her hand over the supple leather. Maliah pulls the long-sleeve shirt from the box, examining the fine stitching and the slight scent of lavender that lingers on it. She then retrieves the pants and wristlets, their smooth texture reminding her of the ones Faeryn wears. With a slow breath, Maliah decides to get dressed, accepting the clothes that were offered to her. As she slips the shirt on, she can't help but notice how comfortable it feels against her skin. She effortlessly slides into the leather pants, feeling their tight embrace against her calves, thighs, and hips. The waistband rests snugly below her belly button, hugging her curves. She moves her legs, and the sensation is almost surreal, as if she's walking completely naked. The broken-in leather feels as smooth as silk and weighs next to nothing. As she strokes her arm, she could swear it was her own skin. With precision, she slides one wristlet onto her wrist, then carefully repeats the process with the other, ensuring that the loop comfortably rests over both of her middle fingers. She places her hands on her stomach, feeling a mix of excitement and nervousness, and rushes back to the long mirror to get a glimpse of her reflection.

What Maliah discovers leaves her in complete disbelief. Never before had she worn anything that made her look as fierce—or fit as well. With a sideways turn, she breaks into a grin. The black leather material tightly adheres to the contours of her back, smoothly draping over her curves and cascading down to accentuate her ass.

With a nod, she takes a moment to brush out her pale pink hair before skillfully braiding it down the center. As she moves, the braid lightly taps against the center of her back.

Her burnt-orange eyes caught sight of the patch on her arm, shaped like an arrowhead, drawing her attention. There are two gold keys, crossed over each other, against a black background. The patch is adorned with gold and green leaves, giving it an elegant touch. Additionally, it features gracefully curved words written in gold along both the top and bottom edges.

With a look of scrutiny, she narrows her eyes.

The curved inscription reads Libertatem Omnibus. Along the bottom of the patch, the words Scout Division are clearly displayed. But she has no idea what any of it means or why she's been given clothing that would make others think that she is a student at Brenna Academy.

Backing away, her concern fades into a warm smile, but her movement abruptly ceases as she hears a knock at her door. She rushes to the door, swinging it wide open. Standing there are Rowe, Arren, and Grim, all dressed in matching outfits. Rowe's is a vibrant shade of blue, while both Arren and Grim are donning bronze attire. With a graceful movement, she raises her arms and spins on her heel. The three men, overwhelmed by what they see, stand in complete silence.

Arren clears his throat.

"Holy shit."

Grim's words prompt Rowe to swiftly shift his position, almost as if he's tempted to obstruct their sight of her.

Despite Maliah's hopeful look, Rowe's face remains impassive, showing no sign of reaction. His new outfit, which fits him as snugly as the one he wore in the Kingdom of Silver Flame, only enhances his handsome features. Yet, in numerous ways, much more pleasant. Refusing to acknowledge it, the Fate Heir's hand lingers on the patch on his arm.

"Mine says, Flyer Division—what does yours say, Maliah?" Rowe asks.

"Scout—and yours?" She looks to Arren.

"Blade."

"Same," Grim responds, casting a quick glance down his body. He shakes his leg. "It really gets up there, doesn't it?" As he reaches behind himself to pick at the material, Maliah can't help but burst into laughter.

She brushes her fingers against the patch on her arm. "Can someone decipher the meaning of the words along the top?"

"It's an old language," Faeryn offers as she approaches the group, her voice filled with a sense of reverence. "It means Liberty for All."

Her eyes sweep across Arren and then Grim, seemingly ignoring Rowe. She steps up next to the Fate Heir and is instantly mesmerized by the sight of Maliah Bazzel. Her hand unconsciously moves up, twisting the bottom of her purple braid, which has been tamed and now radiates a glossy sheen. Like the rest of them, she has bathed.

In a moment of calm, Rowe takes a slow breath, gathering his thoughts. "The new clothing is a nice gesture, but it raises suspicions we might be getting recruited for an unknown purpose."

"The same outfits are worn by everyone here. Even though they come in various colors. It plays a role in establishing a sense of belonging. Except the headmistress. My mother dresses in whatever she pleases."

"Mmm," he mutters, expressing disbelief.

"I thought it would be nice to give you a tour of the school before we eat."

A shadow falls over Rowe's face. "I thought we were going to meet the Founder?"

"Trust me, you will. Of course, that will happen after we complete the tour and enjoy our meal. Unless you don't want to eat?"

Grim speaks quickly on behalf of everyone. "Um—no. We want food."

"Besides, the Founder is not here. They decided to take their dragon to the mountain to check on the storm."

Rowe looks toward the window, noticing blue sky. "It appears to be fair weather."

"No, The Storm is the family of dragons that live on the mountain. Besides, they must be eager to meet their new queen."

"Wennie is with the Founder?" Rowe asks, his jaw tensing.

Faeryn squares her shoulders to match his aggressive posture.

"I assure you that no one could protect her more than the Founder and The Storm."

Hoping to provide comfort, Maliah places her hand on Rowe's arm. She has a calming effect on him.

"Come this way," Faeryn says, passing by him and shooting him a quick look. "If you don't mind, Lord Efhren."

He corrects her by saying, "I'm not a Lord, I am an Heir." but Faeryn doesn't react. When he looks over to Maliah, she shakes her head as if to say *let it go* and urges him to move on.

The five of them proceed down the corridor together, eventually coming to a set of large black doors that seem to have no means of entry. With a serene expression, Faeryn extends her arms and shuts her eyes, as if entering a state of deep meditation. With each word she utters, her chant takes on a magickal quality, the unfamiliar language harmonizing into a captivating melody that hangs in the air like an enchanting song.

A mesmerizing portrait of a dragon slowly emerges on the surface, radiating a luminous white glow. With a wave of her hands, the metal locks click from within the heavy doors, and they slowly start to open.

Within the chamber, rows upon rows of books fill the space from floor to ceiling, creating a labyrinth of knowledge. The room is beautifully set with long black tables positioned down the center, each one complemented by a collection of matching chairs. Above them, an awe-inspiring floating chandelier hangs in the air, seemingly unaffected by the absence of any support from the lofty ceiling. The air around it shimmers with tiny sparks of light, creating a radiant glow. The object is undeniably under the influence of magick.

At the end of the room, their eyes are drawn to a round window that protrudes outwards, inviting them to sit on the cushioned ledge beneath it. Beyond it, there stretches a land of abundance, with fertile green fields and vast forests teeming with unfamiliar trees, known as 'green pine' in Ashland. Beyond the trees, where the land lifts, sections of the dense forest are adorned with a delicate white mist. Its beauty is so mesmerizing that it leaves everyone in a state of wonderment.

"This," Faeryn announces, her arms raised, "is the Great Library of Brenna. It is filled with more knowledge than is known in all of Ellian."

Rowe disagrees by shaking his head. "Our library has an extensive collection that spans the entirety of our existence," his gaze becomes fixed on the dragon rider with purple hair.

"Hmm," Faeryn's gaze shifts from Maliah to the Heir of Fate, her light purple eyes settling on him, "You see, this library extends far beyond that, reaching back to the very beginning of recorded history in our world."

"Wait—are you saying before Fae and Elves?" Maliah asks.

"Was it even before the wolves?" Arren inquires.

"Well, we all existed in different ways. For instance, you, Arren Verrick. Your people owned lands that were taken by foreigners long ago, and over time, as you and your kin were continually challenged, you changed—or evolved, as we like to say. Your bodies responding to the added dangers until you became what you are today—able to shift from this form to the mighty wolf."

Hanging on her every word, Arren is left in a state of utter disbelief, completely taken aback by the depth of her knowledge.

"And you—" Faeryn's eyes shift towards Maliah, "Your ancestors were fierce warriors, once known as Vikings. You sailed The Sorrow, that was called the sea in those times. You were fierce warriors and no one could stand against you. Women, such as yourself, led them into battle to claim territory and expanding your growing empire. But tragically, with war comes loss, and to survive your people also evolved into what you became—the mighty Fae."

With a hint of anticipation, Rowe inquires, "So, what kind of stories have you heard about me?"

"Long ago, your people were what they referred to as

scientists, using their intellect to explore the wonders of the natural world. Although highly intelligent, your kind's creation of devastating weapons sparked fear among the people in this world. I am sorry to say that your kind played a significant role in the eventual destruction of the world as it once existed, along with your close ancestor, mortal men."

While Maliah leans into Rowe's side, he quietly utters the word, "Lies."

"And me?" Grim asks.

"In those days, the term "Ronin" was the designated name for you. These fierce warriors possessed the unique ability to fight both on land and water, but unfortunately, they lost popularity over time and found themselves aimlessly wandering, unless someone hired them for their services, as they were often sought after for their exceptional protection skills."

"And what about you?" Maliah asks Faeryn.

Faeryn falls into a sudden silence, only to break it by clearing her throat. "In this world, witches have always been present, however, their existence has been marred by recurring instances of persecution driven by ignorance and the unwillingness of certain individuals to let go of their pride and religious convictions. It is truly shocking that any of us survived, given that they relentlessly hunted us down, inflicting torture upon many, and ultimately resorting to burning us alive in an attempt to cleanse the world. Similar to all of you, we too have evolved, which in turn has granted us unnaturally long lives, much like the Fate."

This truth visibly unsettles everyone.

Faeryn persists in her narrative. "Mortals were afraid of us, just like they were afraid of all of you. Healing was a unique gift bestowed upon my kind. These mortals couldn't grasp its complexity. To escape death, a number of us concealed our identities within the masses, adopting the profession of healers, commonly referred to as doctors during that period."

"And all of this is right here? These truths you claim about each of us?" Rowe asks.

"Yes, the entire history. These books have been around since before any of us can even imagine, connecting us to a distant past. Through the use of potent magick, these artifacts are safeguarded here, ensuring their survival against those who sought to bury them."

Unable to contain her curiosity, Maliah asks, "Are you suggesting that there are people in Ellian who know about this?" Fully aware that the truth might be painful.

With a slight hesitation, Faeryn bites her lip, steeling herself before she turns to face the group.

"Every ruler, from Kings to Queens, throughout history, made a deliberate pact to conceal it from the people of Ellian."

The room grows colder, matching the growing sense of confusion and disbelief as they try to process what has been shared with them.

In a fluid movement, Faeryn raises her hand and points towards the table positioned on the right side. "A selection of books has been gathered with the intention of aiding each of you in connecting with your origins and gaining a deeper understanding of your place in this world."

Grim takes a step forward, his heavy boots thudding against the ground. He glances at the rest of them, trying to read their expressions. "What? I think we should know."

A grin spreads across Faeryn's face. "However, I would like to complete the tour before anything else. The books will be delivered to your rooms so that you can read them later."

With a calm expression, she turns towards the group.

"Come—let me show you where we learn to fight."

Arren emits a low growl, prompting Grim to eagerly rub his hands together. "Now we're talking."

With a wave of her hand, she guides them out of the room. With a soft click, the doors close behind them, and the once vivid image of the majestic dragon slowly dissolves into nothingness. The doors now appear seamlessly fused together once more.

Slowly, she descends the grand staircase, and as she does, the others in her company follow closely behind. However, their attention is immediately captivated by the sight of a majestic black dragon gracefully soaring through the air above them. The dragon then gracefully lands on a magnificent golden bar, its sharp talons effortlessly gripping onto it. The strangers are feeling the weight of the dragon's gaze, as its attention bears down heavily upon them. With a mighty shake of its head and a graceful lift of its wing, the creature affectionately nuzzles its elongated nose against the underside of its majestic wing. Upon discovering the discomfort, the dragon extends its wings, feeling the muscles stretch and flex. It is impossible to ignore its immense size, a sight that demands attention.

While staring at the large creature, Arren can't help but ask, "So, do they have rooms here?"

A deep-rooted unease stirs within him whenever he spots something in the sky, a result of the traumatic history his kind endured, hunted and killed from above.

With her chin lifted, Faeryn looks directly at the black dragon and shakes her head.

"No, they all call the mountain their home, where they can easily find food and enjoy refreshing baths in the waterfalls. Here, they are given the liberty to come and go as they please, and we ensure they are treated with the respect they deserve."

Upon reaching the bottom, Faeryn leads them through another corridor carved into the black stone. They stop in front of a pair of metal doors, adorned with handles. The thick brackets firmly anchor it to the rugged volcanic rock. It seems this room is not as well guarded as the library on the floor above them, but it's understandable, given that it houses the history of the world—the true history, with ancient manuscripts filling every shelf.

As Arren, Rowe, and Grim enter the room, Maliah remains behind, taking a brief pause. Faeryn's curious gaze is fixed on her.

"He cares for her—for Wennie, very deeply."

Faeryn folds her arms over her chest, creating a protective barrier.

Maliah sighs, her breath escaping in a soft, resigned exhale. "Could you please at least refrain from constantly reminding him about his father's actions towards the dragons?"

The witch raises her eyebrow. "The truth is deeply ingrained in the teachings at Brenna, and the deeds committed by Elio Efhren against the dragons on that accursed island, leading to the ultimate extermination of their entire population, are common knowledge here."

With a hint of confusion, Maliah draws nearer and questions, "I'm a bit confused. The dragons were not killed by Elio. To ensure compliance with the treaty, he clipped their wings, but still granted them permission to reside there.

That is where Wennie came from. Her mother was a blue dragon named Mara that lived at the furthest reaches on the island, deep in a cave, on a small patch of land beneath sunlight."

"Are you certain?"

Maliah nods, "Yes. Rowe told me that is where he found her."

"So have you been to this island called Dragon's Keep?"

"Well, no, but—"

Irritated, Faeryn sighs and starts to turn away, only to be halted by Maliah's touch on her arm. "What I'm saying is true. Listen, you may hate Rowe Efhren and his father, but he gave up everything to save Wennie—he left all of it behind to protect her, almost dying on that ship when his brother came to abduct me and kill him. He stood in between us, protecting me and Wennie and sacrificed his life, so I ask that you give him a break—please. I mean, why save him if you only planned to make him suffer?"

Maliah's departure leaves Faeryn standing there with a softened expression. Despite acknowledging Maliah's trust-worthiness, her hatred for the Fate Heir poses a challenge. She's questioning if it's due to his background or his connection to Maliah Bazzel.

Following Maliah, The Witch enters the room. The air is heavy with the combined scents of sweat and determination, creating an atmosphere charged with energy. Three large circles formed with students gathered closely around each, their voices echoing excitedly. The walls of the room are adorned with shimmering rows of blades, ranging from short to medium and long in length. Attached to the slender wooden handle is the longest blade. Without hesitation, Arren pushes through the students congregated around the middle circle. Looking upwards, Rowe spots a window made of opaque glass, concealing the view from this side. He has a suspicion that there are onlookers as the students train in this room, practicing their combat skills. Yet, what is the purpose of their preparations and who is occupying the other side of the glass?

With no ceiling to confine it, the room opens up to reveal nothing but endless sky above.

Along the edge of the sparing circle, the five of them reunite just in time to witness two girls facing off. The two girls face each other, one brandishing a pair of short blades while the other grips a single, menacingly long blade. In their matching bronze leather outfits, both girls seamlessly blend in with the rest of the crowd. When Maliah looks around the circle, she observes a diverse group of students wearing various colors including black, red, bronze, and blue. In the group, there is an equal number of girls and boys, creating a balanced mix.

As Faeryn leans into her side, she can hear the steady rhythm of her breathing. "At Brenna, we have a total of four divisions. Scout, Cleric, Blade and Flyer."

"What are they?" Maliah asks.

"The two girls are both members of Blade. They are prepared to engage in battles both on water and on land. Their dragons are built like tanks, burdened by their weight and hindered by their undersized wings. They reserve flight for the most critical situations."

Maliah's eyes are fixed on her patch.

With a quick shake of her head, Faeryn's pink braid bounces playfully against her shoulder. "You are not meant for much flying or sparring."

Maliah touches the edge of the patch. "What is a Scout?"

"Information, mostly—strategy."

"But I am skilled with my blades," she confidently declares.

Rowe listens in on the conversation and then interrupts by saying, "I have to say, Maliah is truly one of the best."

With excitement in their eyes, the girls in the center of the circle rush toward each other, their footsteps echoing on the ground.

Maliah, feeling bothered by their assumptions about her, takes a deep breath and steps into the ring. As she moves toward the two girls, the students all fall silent, holding their breath. Maliah's eyes dart to the wall, and she tilts her head up to stare at the tinted glass. Like Rowe, she believes someone is watching behind the glass and aims to prove she shouldn't be wearing black.

"Maliah!" Faeryn calls out.

As she takes a step, Rowe swiftly raises his hand, signaling her to stop.

"Watch," he calmly tells her.

Maliah clenches her fists at her sides, her knuckles turning white with tension. "I challenge both of you to a match," she announces, her eyes locked on her opponents.

"Both?" Faeryn asks. "Does she have a death wish?"

Rowe bursts into laughter. "No, that's just Maliah being herself. She's always been this way. A huge pain in the ass."

Confusion etches their brows as the two girls exchange bewildered glances, then shift their focus to her.

"And who the hell are you?" The girl, who has white-blonde hair and sun-kissed skin, demands with authority. Her eyes are a familiar shade of amber, not so unlike Arren's.

As Arren sniffs the air, he detects a familiar scent, indicating the presence of others like him in the room.

"There are wolves here—juveniles."

"Yes—quite a few," Faeryn answers, never taking her eyes off the two girls who now stand opposite Maliah in the center of the sparring ring. "These are the children of the wolves who followed the Founder here. The council consists of not only Witches and Fae but also some of their parents, who also happen to be wolves."

"Fae? Pure blood?" Rowe asks.

"You mean devoid of any trace of Elven lineage? Yes. They also came here at the end of the war."

"I don't detect the scent of any mortals or vampires. Not a one."

Faeryn's jaw ticks. "As of *yet*, Ashland remains off-limits to both vampires and mortals. We will see if that ever changes."

"In that case, it is not inclusive for everyone."

As Faeryn grits her teeth, a low growl escapes from between her clenched jaws.

"I am not in charge of Ashland."

Her focus returns to the center ring.

"I think it's time for me to intervene before things escalate."

Glancing sideways, Rowe says, "Just wait—unless you want Maliah to hate you forever. I mean, it's up to you."

Maliah gently tilts her chin downwards. A playful smile spreads across her face, accentuating her full lips.

"My name is Maliah," she states, her voice filled with a hint of pride.

"Okay, Maliah. You do realize that you have no weapons, right?" The girl rolls her eyes in disbelief.

Maliah responds with a nonchalant "Uh huh," lifting her hands and flexing her fingers.

"So how do you plan on—"

Without warning, Maliah rushes forward, the sound of her footsteps echoing through the air as she pushes off the ground and takes flight, soaring above the blonde-haired girl. Maliah swiftly swings her leg forward, making contact with the girl's shoulder, and sends her spinning to the left. With impressive agility, the young Fate uses the girl's shoulder as a pivot to somersault over her. As Maliah lands on the other side, she skillfully catches the blade mid-air. But as she rises, she begins to spin the blade effortlessly, the metal glinting in the light, before turning to face her opponent.

The blonde-haired girl's war cry echoes through the air as she lunges forward, swinging her blade with such force that Maliah has to arch her back to avoid it. The tip of the blade comes dangerously close to her face, but Maliah smiles, feeling the rush of adrenaline as she drops down to the floor and spins on her knee. Sweeping her leg, it collides with the girl's foot, causing her to stumble sideways. With lightning speed, Maliah reaches out and snatches her other blade, skillfully twirling both weapons in her hands as she rises above the falling girl.

Slapping the floor in frustration, the girl growls fiercely, her teeth on full display.

"Yield!"

Faeryn shakes her head. "She's—amazing."

Rowe doesn't respond but notices how the purple-haired Witch is unable to take her eyes off Maliah. This festers inside him and starts to take the form of something he's never known before—jealousy.

With a quick glance, Maliah's attention is drawn to the girl who now wields the long blade.

"Let's go!" she exclaims, feeling a surge of energy.

With a fluid motion, Maliah extends her blades outward, showcasing her precision and control, before tightly clutching them, bringing them to an immediate halt. Her gaze sweeps across the circle, landing on Faeryn, whose wide eyes are fixed on her. The thought of proving her abilities to Faeryn is a powerful motivator that she can't ignore.

The second girl skillfully spins her long blade in front of her, creating a whirling wheel of steel before gracefully sheathing it by her side and extending her other hand in a gesture of acceptance.

As the red-haired girl lowers her chin, shadows dance across her face, accentuating her features before making her intentions clear.

"Show me what you got," she demands.

Maliah and the girl cautiously sidestep, their eyes locked on each other, searching for the ideal moment to strike. Each of them cries out in excitement, their footsteps echoing through the room. But their anticipation quickly turns to fear as the deafening roar of a dragon fills the air. All heads turn towards the sky as the majestic blue dragon gracefully descends. They collectively step back and make space for the dragon's arrival. The figure on the dragon's back is clad in blue leather, perfectly matching the majestic creature. As the dragon lowers its body, the rider skillfully dismounts, relishing the feel of their fingers gliding along the creature's smooth scales. With a surefooted landing, the rider rises and squares their shoulders, exuding confidence.

"It's the Founder," Faeryn whispers.

Excitement spreads throughout the room, accompanied by a rising chorus of whispers from the students. The Founder rarely makes an appearance in the sparring rings.

Gripping her blades tightly, Maliah holds them out at her sides, her heart pounding with anticipation as the figure draws near. A blue, form-fitting helmet adorns the dragon rider's head, seamlessly blending with their leather attire and the dragon they command.

The Founder reaches up and delicately removes it, revealing a cascade of pale pink hair flowing over her shoulders. The woman lifts her chin, locking eyes with Maliah and half-grins.

A scar cuts across her face, starting above her right eye and extending halfway down her cheek.

Maliah is so struck by the resemblance between herself and this woman that she drops her blades.

Their eyes, hair, and lips are identical, making them look remarkably similar.

Maliah struggles to speak and is unable to get the words out.

As the woman rushes in, she immediately wraps her arms around her in the tightest embrace, creating a sense of warmth and safety.

Her voice is barely a whisper in her ear. "My name is Zimora."

As the woman lets go, her eyes are drawn to the necklace nestled against Maliah's chest, and she lifts it with curiosity. Tears well up in her eyes, glistening with emotion.

"After all this time," she says, her voice filled with surprise, "you kept it."

Confusion flashes across Maliah's face, evident in her furrowed eyebrows and questioning eyes.

"Who are you?"

With affection, the woman touches her cheek and whispers, "Oh, my dearest one. I'm your mother."

CHAPTER 11

THE SERPENT, THE WITCH, AND THE CRONE

A s Odette awakes, the gentle rays of sunlight filter through the curtains, casting a warm glow in the room. Startled, she sits up, realizing that she has been away from Talen for much longer than she had planned. She rushes from her chamber, the sound of her hurried footsteps echoing through the long corridor. She is feeling the weight of guilt tugging at her conscience.

She comes to a full stop upon witnessing a nightmare.

As they exit the room, the four Stone Guardsmen can be seen adjusting their pants. Odette clenches her teeth, her jaw muscles tensing. The moment of realization hits her, and she begins to understand that what lies beyond the door is even more horrifying than anything she could have ever imagined. Stepping out, the Holy Scribe's face is flushed and covered in a shimmering layer of sweat. With vacant eyes, he looks towards the shifter but then proceeds to crook his neck, stretching his muscles.

"What have you done?" Odette demands an answer.

"Do not dare to question me," he says sternly, his voice laced with authority.

As a sign of dissent, Odette firmly reminds him. "We had an agreement, did we not? I deliver the Witch, along with the books, and you give me what I—"

As the Holy Scribe steps closer, the pungent odor of his sweat overwhelms her senses. Just as she had suspected, the man reveals himself to be nothing but filth.

"It would be a shame for you to come all this way and leave empty-handed, would it not?" he asks.

Although Odette contemplates attacking him, the sight of more Stone Guardsmen standing watch on either side reminds her of the impossible odds she would face.

"She will be no use to you this way." Odette warns.

"Oh, but that is where you will help me. Heal her body and take the memories, as you did before."

The rush of adrenaline flowing through her veins causes her breathing to hasten. Unfortunately, this man has chosen to prioritize his sick fantasy over the needs of Talen Freeborn, causing unnecessary harm.

"The act of taking memories is not something that can be done without risk."

The Holy Scribe's brows furrow, forming a deep wrinkle.

"You erased your presence in her mind, did you not?"

"Yes, as you instructed, so she will not mention me to anyone and what we—"

As the Holy Scribe's eyes shift down the wall, they catch the flickering light of the torches, casting dancing shadows on the faded murals and other Stone Guardsmen.

"Leave us!" He demands, before agreeing to discuss it any further with Odette.

Without sparing a glance at the shifter, the Stone

Guardsmen march past, the sound of their disciplined foot-steps filling the air. She harbors a deep desire to eliminate each and every one of them in retribution for the sinister task they have been called upon to carry out. One cannot fathom how these men could stand idly by, with the knowl-edge that Talen was being assaulted behind that door, and not take any action to stop the heinous crime.

Now that the hallway is empty, the Holy Scribe's atten-tion returns to the shifter, his eyes narrowing in scrutiny.

"Throughout these many cycles of the moon, your service, Odette Ender, has been invaluable to me. Your ability to erase memories from people like Naya Freeborn is a highly prized skill that I greatly appreciate. I assure you that your efforts will be generously rewarded."

"I was asked to do this once with each, not multiple times. I have already done this with Talen Freeborn to hide my involvement when we entered this kingdom and took the book."

The Holy Scribe taps his chin. "So, are you unable to clear this girl's mind?"

Odette pauses, "I can—yes, but no more. This may strip her of things you want to know, including how to control the book that will soon call out to her with her family gone."

Letting out a sigh of defeat, The Holy Scribe expresses his frustration. His desire to see the Witch suffer and plead for mercy was so strong that he wanted to inflict even more torture upon her. However, in light of the impending war against formidable foes like the Fate, vampires, and wolves, he must recognize her true value and understand the impor-tance of possessing such a weapon. While their fighting abilities are commendable, it is the mastery of magick that holds the key to triumph in this war. With grand aspirations, his ultimate goal is to see Arrowe Brumah crowned as emperor and his daughter as empress. His plan is to establish this, and then remove Arrowe from power, replacing him with his own heir. But first, he needs the potent sorcery of a Witch to aid him.

A Witch such as Talen Freeborn.

"While erasing the events of today involving the Witch, I ask that you work diligently and exercise caution. My goal is to make her docile in order to exert control over her actions. She is—spirited."

"She is strong, as all women are," Odette says, her words sinking into the man's pride like an insidious parasite.

"Yes, well," he mutters under his breath, his words carrying a touch of annoyance. "I guess it is time to give your reward, but not before you do this last thing for me—a small task standing between you and your well-deserved prize. I will honor our agreement and grant you what you seek."

Odette's heart pounds with nervousness. This is why she had done so many terrible deeds, causing pain to those around her. She chose to ignore the suffering of others, hoping that by doing so, the man would grant her the chance to see her love once more. Within these walls, a man she would willingly give her life for had been confined for far longer than she cared to acknowledge. Together, they could forge a future untouched by the bloodshed and chaos that men had unleashed upon the world, finding solace and contentment in each other's company. Perhaps they could bring a child into the world, ensuring that the legacy of shifters would not fade away with Odette.

The Holy Scribe steps aside, his hand raised toward the

door, and Odette braces herself for the unknown sights awaiting her on the other side.

Odette's hand lingers on the doorknob before she finally pushes open the door, revealing a dimly lit room. Her gaze lands on Talen, who is huddled in the corner, her body tense as she sought solace in the protective embrace of the shadows. Sensing movement, the Witch quickly presses her hands against the wall, feeling the rough texture of the stone as she uses it to push herself upright. They can try to break her and inflict pain, but she will not surrender without a fierce struggle. Taking a moment to steady herself, she feels her chest rise and fall, a physical manifestation of her resolve, as she prepares for the worst - the return of more men and the horrors they may bring.

Moments that are permanently imprinted in her memory and stripped away every layer of her being.

With each step she takes, she wobbles slightly, struggling to maintain her balance. Blood coats her hands, the result of the wristlets tightly constricting her magickal powers and the bits of flesh she collected while trying to fight off the men. If only she could remove them, she would unleash her fury upon these mortal men, tearing them limb from limb for stealing her innocence.

Upon seeing her, Odette's emotions are clearly visible. She raises her hand to her mouth, trying to stifle her gasp. Talen's lips are visibly bruised and cut in two spots, evidence of a forceful strike. Upon closer inspection, one can see the haunting marks of abuse scattered across her body. Signs of a desperate struggle are evident on her neck, arms, and legs. Unfortunately, the most concerning aspect is the blood between her legs, which has stained her bare thighs.

"I can erase the memory of what they did to you," she says, her voice trembling with sincerity.

"You can erase it, but the scars will remain," Talen admits, refusing to cry.

When Odette turns around, she is surprised to find Talen standing right in front of her, struggling through the pain. She is uncertain about how the girl managed to find the strength to continue standing, not to mention walk towards her. It is a testament to the strength of women and how men can never truly break them.

She lifts up her hands. The space between her fingers now emits a soft light, illuminating both of their faces. As Odette pulls them apart, the light immediately returns to each hand, but her fingers retain their radiant glow. She raises them to Talen's temples as the Witch speaks, keeping her eyes fixed on the shifter.

"Is this why I do not remember you?" she asks.

Odette clears her throat. "Permit me to alleviate your suffering by doing this for you."

"As long as I am held here against my will, in the company of men, I will suffer."

Odette's voice carries a hint of sadness as she confesses, "I wish I could grant you freedom."

"Tell me, did you bring me here?" Talen asks. "Were you a friend who betrayed me?"

"This will be the last time I see you. I offer this final gift. Tell me what you wish to forget."

With a visible effort, Talen forces herself to swallow. The taste of blood still lingers on her tongue. She flinches as the memories of hands touching her all over and the intense pain between her legs flood back.

"What they did to me in this room and nothing more. I

want to remember my life as it is—for the Witch that I am. I know he will come for me. I will survive this to see his face once again."

"Who do you speak of? The vampire?"

Talen nods. "Cullen Moore, he is a prince you know, who prefers to be called Lord Cullen."

Her broken lips curve into a meek smile, revealing a hint of vulnerability. The mere thought of him is her sole motivation to keep fighting and stay alive.

"Talen—I—"

"Yes?" the Witch asks, curious what Odette wishes to share with her.

With a solemn vow, she declares, "I will leave his memory intact." A pledge she intends to honor with every fiber of her being.

As Odette ponders the Heir of Shadow, she could not help but recall the sickness that she had unleashed upon his kind, using a poisoned mortal that Raiden Moore found so tantalizing. The scent of the girl was irresistibly enticing to the vampire king, prompting him to consume her flesh and bones, a long-forgotten pleasure from centuries past. Once he was infected, the disease quickly made its way through their royal house. It is another successful task completed by the shifter in order to please The Holy Scribe, just like the rest.

Odette Ender should take pride in her successful endeavor of driving the Witch queen to madness, spreading sickness throughout The Kingdom of Shadow, and deceiving everyone to bring Talen Freeborn to this very place as instructed. Yet, there was no cause for celebration as she met the gaze of the young Witch who had trusted her.

Odette had sentenced herself to eternal damnation, with no chance of escape or salvation.

With a gentle touch, she places her hands on each side of Talen's head, feeling the warmth of her skin. As Odette draws the horrible memories of her assault from her mind, the sorrow that had settled into the Witch's bones begins to melt away. As Odette's fingers darken and she emits a hiss, she persists until she drains every trace of it from Talen's mind, akin to removing a poison.

Lowering her hands, she catches Talen's eye. With a wince, she touches her lip before placing her hand across her stomach. Odette allows the horrific memory to slip inside a bottle that she quickly conceals. Her plan is to let it sink to the bottom of The Sorrow. Never to be discovered—especially by the Witch.

"You were injured in a fall." Odette lies, giving Talen something that will help her accept her current state. "It was severe, so you must rest."

Despite the Holy Scribe's request for her to heal the Witch, she decides against it and opts to let her remain in her current state as a means to dissuade the man from causing additional harm. The Witch would be no good to him dead.

Talen wraps her arms around Odette's waist, pulling her close and finding comfort in the warmth of their embrace. Slowly, Odette places her hands on the girl's back, relishing the soothing silence that envelops them both. With a tear streaming down her cheek and collecting on her chin, Odette summons her strength and deftly maneuvers her arms to coerce Talen into granting her freedom.

"I want you to have this," Odette says, as she pulls a small vial from her pocket and gently places it in Talen's open palm. "All you must do is drink and then you will sleep so deeply and awake in the lonely forest. There you shall be free."

Talen nods, understanding the gravity of Odette's offer. She knows that, if necessary, she may have to rely on it to end her life. However, she remains determined to hold out as long as possible, patiently waiting for the prince of shadows.

"I appreciate your kindness," Talen whispers.

Odette nods solemnly and, with a heavy heart, finally turns her back on the Witch. She hesitates, her hand gripping the door handle tightly, before making the difficult choice to leave her behind forever.

The moment the door closes behind her, she instinctively flinches and turns her attention towards The Holy Scribe.

"Have you done as I requested?"

Odette nods. "Although I managed to capture the memories, I am afraid that her injuries are too severe to ignore. My attempts to heal her body were unsuccessful. You must leave her alone to heal, or you will kill her, and I know that is not your intention. In fact, I would suggest that you never allow her to be touched again. I fear she will not survive it."

The Holy Scribe's eyes narrow as he looks towards the door. "Very well."

Odette feels a wave of relief wash over her, knowing that she has allowed Talen the necessary time to heal and the option to escape by drinking the poison. It is merciful. The only mercy the shifter can offer the girl is a swift, painless death.

"I have done as you have asked, and I would like our

dealings to end—never to see you again or this wretched place you call home."

The Holy Scribe purses his lips before nodding.

"This way," he says, leading her away from the chamber of horrors.

Odette's hands clasp together so tightly that her knuckles turn pale. She trails behind him until they finally reach a nondescript door, lacking any distinguishable markings. The Holy Scribe lifts a skeleton key and unlocks it, the hinges creaking as it swings open to reveal another door behind it. As they enter the cramped space, he takes out yet another key and proceeds to unlock the second door. With a momentary pause, he gathers his strength and grunts as he presses his shoulder against it.

Odette peeks inside and observes that there are metal bars and a sturdy lock fastening it to the stone wall. With a determined look on his face, the Holy Scribe steps past her and begins to unlock the thick chain, the metallic clinking sound filling the room. Once loosened, he is able to open the barred door, revealing a dimly lit corridor that smells of dampness and decay.

With a hint of hesitation, she takes a deep breath before embarking on the journey down the curving stairs. The path is illuminated by bright torches, securely fastened to the curved stone walls every few feet. While descending the stairs, the air grows colder until her breath becomes visible. With The Holy Scribe close by, she reaches the bottom at last.

Concerned with the biting cold, she voices her discomfort to The Holy Scribe.

"Is there no fire to warm the air?"

As the Holy Scribe moves past her, she can't help but

notice the vast open space stretching out before them. It takes him some time to reach the next door, which is three times his height and intricately carved with a large serpent. Excitement causes her pupils to dilate. Many moons have passed since her heart had last been filled with such eager anticipation. As she stands there, her excitement grows, making her skin feel alive with energy.

Every horrible thing she had done was for this moment.

With a swift motion, Niam raises his hand and gently rests it on what looks like a dial, before proceeding to do the same with a second dial. As he turns the one on the right three times, Odette can hear the distinct sound of mechanisms clicking within the door. He then turns the dial on the left in the opposite direction, feeling the resistance as he twists it twice. Turning the dials towards each other, the Holy Scribe completes the task of opening the door, resulting in a sudden release of air from underneath. Odette notices the dust gathering at her feet but focuses her attention on The Holy Scribe as he starts to push on the door. It's sluggish, as if no one has moved it in a long time. With a pause, he surveys the barely lit space in front of him, where thin rays of light cascade down from above. Odette hesitates briefly, closing her eyes and taking a deliberate, calming breath before stepping into the space. Once inside, the air is so thick with dust that she has to lift her hand to her mouth to prevent herself from coughing.

Moving forward, she squints her eyes to adapt to the darkness surrounding her.

The Holy Scribe withdraws.

Her heart quickens its pace, beating rapidly, and her fingertips hum with nervous energy. She had dreamed of this moment for so long that the reality of it felt surreal.

She calls out into the darkness, straining her eyes to catch any sign of movement.

"Acheron, my love?"

The Holy Scribe reaches beneath his black cloak and wraps his fingers around a cold, smooth object. As she continues to call out, he pulls out his hand and takes slow steps toward Odette. Suddenly, she comes to a halt. Rushing in, she feels her breath catch in the back of her throat, and she falls to her knees.

The remains of a large snake, with blue skin still clinging to sections of its bone, can be seen curled along the bottom of the wall. At first, her wailing is barely audible, almost too faint to hear, until she manages to catch her breath and let out another cry. In a poignant display of grief, she presses her hand against her chest in a comforting gesture, the other hand finding solace on the frigid stone floor of the prison where her beloved had been confined until his death. Her hand trembles as she reaches for him, determined to gather the courage to rise to her feet.

"My love—I blame myself for this. But you must believe me that I tried. Once I knew that you were here, I agreed to do the most horrible things to reach you. I traded my soul for the promise of your release. But it seems I was too late."

As the Holy Scribe shifts behind her, Odette quickly reacts by turning around and floating towards him. With her hand outstretched, she swiftly wraps it around his throat. With an intense burst of strength, she forcefully slams him against the wall, causing him to be lifted off his feet while he desperately tries to break free. In a powerful display of emotion, she leans closer to him, allowing all of her hatred and anger to surge forth, her eyes fixed on his as she carefully examines him.

"You did this!" she cries. "You killed him!"

He tries to shake his head, his voice barely audible as he speaks. "No—it seems he died of a broken heart—simply wasting away because you never came for him, Odette. You left your husband here to rot."

As Odette raises her free hand, her nails elongate into sharp points, a clear indication that she is getting ready to disembowel The Holy Scribe. However, just as she is about to swing her arm, the eerie sound of flesh being torn apart and bones shattering echoes throughout the room. The moments stretch out, almost as if time is playing a trick, as Odette's hand relaxes, and the man slips away from her wrath. Stumbling back, she gasps in pain and feels a large fang piercing her stomach, slicing through her diaphragm and emerging next to her bony spine.

She shakes her head in disbelief as The Holy Scribe massages his throat, trying to regain his voice.

"It is poetic that you would be ended this way, with the very thing that made Acheron so feared."

She attempts to move closer to him but loses her balance, collapsing onto her knees as the mortal wound drains her strength. Even after death, the venom in Acheron's fang remains deadly. Long ago, during the War of Brumah, her love, who possessed the power to transform into a serpent, had been taken captive. Since then, he was confined here, and fed countless women who were a threat.

"He never shifted back to his other form, and eventually he was unable to remember what he once was, only feeling his heartache for losing his true love. You, Odette Ender."

Pacing back and forth, the Holy Scribe's eyes never leave Odette, who desperately clings to the stone floor for balance. With each passing moment, the poison takes hold, slowly robbing her of her ability to move.

"I will kill you," she coughs, blood glistening on her lips.

"Shift for me and become a God," he whispers. "Do this and I will give you the antidote to his poison."

As she looks at him, a playful smile spreads across her face, and laughter bubbles up from deep within her.

"Never," she hisses.

"Then this will become your tomb." He shakes his head. "I offered you everything and in the end you deny yourself so much—now I must go. I have a king to bury and a war to win."

With a cautious step back, the Holy Scribe retreats and secures the door, making sure it is firmly locked. Meanwhile, Odette's eyes shift upwards, and a delighted grin illuminates her face. With a strained neck, she tightly grasps the end of Acheron's massive fang and lets out a low, painful moan as she pulls it out of her stomach. Covered in her blood, she lets go of it and watches as it falls onto the hard stone floor. As she glances over her shoulder, she sees the remains of Acheron. Her gaze shifts upwards, and she spots the small openings in the ceiling, a clear sign of what she must do for the last time.

"Before I depart from this realm to be with you," she swears, her voice filled with determination, "I will seek vengeance on your behalf, my love. But I fear I will find no peace, as my transgressions have doomed me, yet there may be solace in saving another's soul. I should have killed him and escaped with the girl. This I know."

She fights to stand, feeling the sting of pain as she places her trembling hand over the gaping wound. The metallic smell of blood fills the air as it seeps over her fingers, painting them a vivid shade of red. Closing her eyes, she summons her remaining strength, causing a black mist to materialize and swirl around her, carrying with it the scent of bone dust. As if by magick, her body transforms into a swirling flock of ravens. The spinning mass rises, creating a whirlwind of feathers and cawing as every raven escapes the room, following the slivers of light through a maze of tunnels until taking flight in the sky.

EVERLEIGH STANDS BEFORE CULLEN, feeling the weight of his presence on the throne. He has decided to don his ornately adorned gold neck armor, a present from his mother.

"You should leave this place."

Everleigh looks at him with such sorrow. "And where would I go?"

"Away from me."

"Do you not love me?" she asks.

The silence that greets her is so profound, it feels like it is peeling away layers of her being.

"It seems I was mistaken." She bitterly admits.

"As most are about me."

"How can you be so cruel?" Everleigh pleads.

"Cruel? Have you not understood what I am?" Like a powerful force, his voice reverberates through the hall, reaching every corner like a massive wave crashing against the shore. She can feel it move through her. Her thoughts drift to the gentle caress of his touch—the lingering sweetness of his kiss. The way his mouth moved against hers sent shivers down her spine. She knows he must feel something for her.

He has to love her.

"Why do you let me linger here like a ghost?" she asks.

"It seems I am no good at being alone."

"So, that's it? That's all I am to you?" she questions, her voice trembling with disappointment.

He releases an unneeded sigh.

"You are a bad habit I find difficult to let go. But I will, in time."

She wipes away a tear. "Your heart doesn't look like mine," she half-whispers, but the vampire, with his keen hearing, can understand her.

"I'm aware of what I am, Everleigh Aeress."

She takes a step closer.

"No—your heart doesn't look like mine because mine is broken."

With every word she utters, Cullen can feel her sadness seeping into his core, resonating within him. He longs to express the depth of his emotions. If what stood between them was a tangible thing, he would lay it to waste for her.

"Did you not hear me?" she asks.

He says nothing.

"I will not—"

In a matter of seconds, he is right in front of her, his face mere inches away, and she finds herself transfixed by his piercing crimson eyes. Cullen wishes to frighten her away, but she remains resolute. It stirs up conflicting emotions of frustration and fascination in him. Her courage is truly remarkable, deserving of his utmost admiration.

But he is sensing something and turns his gaze toward the window.

∿

As the ravens move westward, their wings beat in a frenzy, creating a symphony of fluttering and cawing. Some of them, worn out, drop to the ground and meet their end, until the sky turns gloomy, and raindrops lash against their weary wings. By the time they reach the Black Gates, the group has dwindled to just half of its original size. The unkindness of ravens swirl and churn like a bubbling cauldron, until they gradually converge into a swirling frenzy, leaving Odette standing there, her complexion paler than before and her eyes starting to glaze over. As she looks upward, her voice echoes through the air as she cries out one name.

"Cullen Moore!"

In a flash of movement imperceptible to mortal eyes, the vampire prince glides past Everleigh, leaving only a hint of cool air in his wake. The scent of him lingers, now guiding her. Everleigh sprints down one corridor after another, her determination grows with each moment, until she reaches the imposing castle steps.

Cullen's voice carries in a hushed whisper as he recites the ancient magickal words, and slowly, the gate begins to creak open. He steps through.

As Everleigh slips outside the gate, she comes to an abrupt stop, her eyes widening in surprise at the sight of the shifter, Odette Ender.

"You dare come here!?" His voice is deep and powerful, resonating like thunder rolling in the distance. Everleigh lifts her hand and places it to her chest, feeling the resonance of his words reverberating through her entire being once again.

Odette stumbles, her hand covered in blood, and begins to collapse, but Cullen is quick to catch her, aware that she is his only source of information on Talen's whereabouts. Looking down upon her, he can feel her heart beating slower and see the blood seeping from her abdomen. She is mortally wounded. Cullen must act swiftly to retrieve the information he desires since he cannot save her.

Rushing in, Everleigh falls to her knees. As she takes Odette's hand, the shifter holds on tightly and glances at her. As death beckons, she finds solace in not being alone. Gasping for air, the shifter is calmed by the Stone Maiden's emerald-green eyes and tender touch. Everleigh moves closer, her heart breaking at the sight of her suffering.

"Do something," she pleads, her eyes filled with desperation.

"I am unable," he admits.

The rain mingles with her tears, leaving her face and hair wet and glistening.

"But you helped me."

"That was before."

"Before what?" Everleigh asks.

"Before I became sick with the same disease that drove my father into The Sorrow and my mother to her deathbed," he says, his voice filled with contempt as he begrudgingly reveals his truth.

Everleigh's eyes widen.

He looks to Odette. "Where is she? Tell me so I may go to her."

With each passing moment, the shifter's heart grows weaker, its beats becoming fainter and more sluggish.

Odette inhales sharply, feeling the acrid air sear her lungs.

"I took the memory from her, leaving behind only a faint trace of her pain. Yet, despite everything, she pleaded for the memory of you to stay. She said you would come for her, and I am here to let you know that Talen Freeborn is in The Kingdom of Stone, but her life will soon end. The Holy Scribe will do this, but not before he hurts her further. He's done terrible things—unspeakable things to her already." Tears flow from Odette's eyes. "You must know that I did what I could, I even gave her something to escape this world if needed."

Cullen's body tenses up, his once bright crimson eyes now turning pitch black. As anger consumes him, his fangs extend, sharp and menacing, in his mouth.

"Please—save her and set me free," Odette begs.

In a single fluid movement, Cullen brings her near and, without hesitation, snaps her neck before gently placing her lifeless body onto the ground. Everleigh gasps for air, and at that moment, he gets up, towering over her. The shifter's hold on Everleigh weakens, and her pale hand slips away.

The young Witch's cries mingle with the booming thunder and crackling lightning that fill the sky. She wishes she had unlocked the secrets of immortality before the book was taken from her, as she now feels utterly powerless. As Everleigh looks at her hands, she notices tiny beams of light darting beneath her skin. Cullen clenches his fist and grits his teeth, emitting a fierce growl that causes birds to take flight and small creatures to seek refuge underground, fearing his wrath.

"If the end of my story is the beginning of hers, then so be it. I will not have lived in vain," he speaks determinedly, his voice filled with conviction.

Everleigh knows what she must do. She must release him.

"Save her," she begs.

Everleigh's hair is swept away from her face as Cullen races past, leaving an empty space where the rain is momentarily displaced by his speed.

The Heir of Shadow comes to a sudden stop. He now stands at the edge of the Forest of Blood Roses, the scent of iron mingling with the sweet fragrance of the budding flowers. With each step he takes, the storm grows fiercer, the sky filling with gathering black clouds and the wind whipping through the air with a menacing force. The lightning streaks across the sky, casting an eerie glow on his face, emphasizing his full lips and the unmistakable madness in his eyes. Blood oozes from the corner of his lips, slowly trickling down his chin and staining the ground below. Venom fills his mouth. Cullen is no longer burdened by worry. To guide his actions, he sets free the untamed creature that dwells inside, surrendering to its power. With each flash of lightning, his detached shadow stretches and expands, a visual manifestation of his growing hatred. Soon, their efforts will harmonize into a unified force.

A sense of determination fills his every step. He gradually increases his speed until he reaches the gates, where he launches himself over with a powerful jump, landing on the other side with a graceful thud. To his surprise, there is not a single soul present to receive him. All have gathered in the cathedral to pay their respects to their fallen king. With a flick of his wrist, Cullen's shadow begins to converge around his feet, adding an ominous touch to his presence.

With a rush of adrenaline, he bounds up the steps and forcefully pushes open the doors, causing them to swing wide and reveal two Stone Guardsmen standing frozen in their tracks. With a swift motion, they charge towards him, their blades raised high, and Cullen, fueled by his rage, willingly lets them impale him, savoring the surge of adrenaline. They stand in silence, their breaths heavy in the air, until Cullen's grin spreads across his face. Suddenly, his shadow elongates, contorting and entangling around the necks of the two men. In one swift motion, their heads are severed and flung in opposite directions. As their bodies convulse uncontrollably, they eventually collapse to the ground, causing a rush of blood that stains the pristine white stone beneath their feet.

Cullen's grin widens as he pulls the two blades out of his flesh, savoring the delightful sensation. The feeling of metal smoothly moving through his skin is exhilarating. The level of pain is truly exquisite. The only thing that could possibly compare to such an experience is the intense pleasure of reaching a climax while fully immersed in the desires of a passionate lover. Despite Everleigh crossing his mind, he forcefully shakes his head and emits a deep growl as a means to ward off such thoughts. His overwhelming love for her threatens to distract him from his crucial task, a risk he cannot afford at this moment. Especially not when Talen's life hangs in the balance.

As he lifts the blades, his eyes ignite with a fiery glow upon witnessing the presence of blood. With a swift motion, he extends his tongue and skillfully runs it along the edge of the razor-sharp blade, causing it to slice into the soft pink flesh and creating a noticeable split. With the grace of a serpent, the vampire prince flicks it before it effortlessly fuses back together. His gaze shifts downward as he witnesses the miraculous mending of the holes in his sides, as if invisible forces are at work. Rolling his shoulders, he tightens his grip on the blades and presses forward, venturing deeper into the royal house of stone.

Rounding a corner, he is met with another Stone Guardsman. With swift, precise strikes, he dispatches the enemy, driving each blade deep into his chest. He lifts him off the ground, his powerful arms outstretched, and with a single motion, rips the man's body apart, causing blood to spray like a gushing fountain. Cullen raises his chin, letting the blood splatter onto his face and into his open mouth. He extends his tongue and indulges in the delectable taste on his lips. As his shadow gracefully moves along the wall, it revels in the sheer brutality and finds pleasure in the spectacle.

As Cullen takes a step forward, he is suddenly brought to a halt by a familiar scent that he immediately recognizes. It is Talen Freeborn, the Witch he has come to rescue from this hellish prison. With his eyes fixed on the cathedral, he suddenly diverts his attention to a seemingly endless corridor that stretches out before him. Despite the fact that he could easily indulge in a feast fit for a king by attacking them at this very moment, he resists his primal instincts. Although he is not unwilling to consider doing so once she is safe, his main priority is to fulfill his promise and save her. Nonetheless, the vampire's ravenous hunger shows no signs of abating.

As Cullen approaches the large door, he can sense her presence on the other side, but he notices that something has changed. With a seemingly effortless touch, he firmly presses his hand against the unyielding hard wood, resulting in the door being forced off its hinges and lifted away.

Upon entering the room, his eyes narrow, and he carefully scans the area to distinguish the shape of her body leaning against the wall. The closer he gets to her, the more his teeth begin to grind against each other, his senses heightened by the overwhelming scent of blood that fills the air around them.

As she takes a step into the light, he is granted the opportunity to witness some of the profound damage that has been inflicted upon her. The change in his expression is noticeable as anger fades away and is replaced by sorrow, while his eyes scan her from head to toe, eventually focusing on the drying blood on her thighs and knees.

Cullen's voice trembles as he struggles to ask, "What have they done to you?"

With a sudden burst of energy, she lunges forward, her arms instantly encircling his neck.

Cullen gasps. Her desperate need for him now apparent.

Excited by the sight of him, she quickly fires off question after question.

"Is this a dream? Are you really here? Have you come for me, Cullen?"

Cullen's eyes widen, their crisp crimson hue reflecting his struggle to come to terms with her condition. Talen's innocence was cruelly taken from her. Her body bore the marks of their brutality, with blackened bruises serving as grim reminders of their evil deeds. With his eyes closed, he lets go of the blades, feeling the weight of them hit the floor, and embraces her tightly, savoring the feeling of her in his arms.

"I have failed you," he mutters.

With tears streaming down her face, she vigorously shakes her head in disbelief.

"No—you have saved me as you promised you would."

"But you are—" he pauses, remembering that Odette

said she took this horrible memory away from her so that she could heal.

"With you now and always," she whispers.

He gently moves her away, allowing his hands to glide to her wrists. He senses the metal and tries to take them off, causing her to wince.

"Only magick can remove them," Talen says. "They were placed on me with a powerful spell."

He effortlessly lifts her up with a gentle motion, her weight disappearing in his strong arms. Resting her head against his shoulder, she is comforted by his presence. With the intention of ensuring her safety and sparing his revenge for a different moment, he makes the decision to bring her as far away from this dreadful place as he can.

Exiting the room, he is able to catch a glimpse of her face due to the light streaming through the corridor. Filled with an intense rage, he trembles uncontrollably, fully aware that the harm inflicted upon her could not have been the work of a single man alone. She was taken against her will by those who would leave her with wounds that would never fully mend.

He glides through the corridor, his footsteps nonexistent, until he freezes in place, catching a whiff of the lingering scent of the men who violated her. His teeth grow longer and more pronounced in his mouth in a display of fury and disgust.

Stepping forward, he forcefully kicks in the doors to the cathedral, revealing the pews filled with worshippers. Positioned at the farthest end of the room, his eyes are drawn to a massive statue of their revered serpent God, while just below it lies a transparent glass coffin containing the deteriorating remains of none other than his brother, Cassius Brumah.

As the vampire gracefully walks down the aisle, carrying Talen in his strong embrace, all eyes are fixated on them. Upon seeing her, some individuals are taken aback and cannot help but gasp. She is wearing no shoes and no pants. Just a white dress that is tattered and torn. It clings to her bones like a shroud.

"I strongly advise you to leave this house of sin and depravity or face my wrath. I only seek the men who foolishly chose to lay hands upon her."

As he passes by, the royals quickly slip from the pews, their fear evident in their eyes and the way they tremble. They hastily flee the cathedral, their pounding footsteps fading into the distance, leaving behind only The Holy Scribe, dozens of Stone Guardsmen, Visha Aeress, and Arrowe Brumah.

"Who is this girl, Niam?" Arrowe demands.

The Holy Scribe lets out a tired sigh, his disapproval clear as he clicks his tongue, and taps his hands on the pulpit where he was reciting the prayer to honor their late king.

"She is no one, my Lord."

Taking a moment to ensure Talen's safety and comfort, Cullen gently sets her down on the plush cushions of the first pew. He kneels before her.

"She is no one!" Niam repeats, his laughter betraying his nerves.

"Cleary not, and she appears to be injured," Arrowe insists while noticing the bruises on her body and cuts to her lip.

Niam lifts his hand. "That is an abomination—a vampire from the north who has entered our kingdom not once but twice, and the girl is his whore—a WITCH, the same Witch who came within these walls and stole away with Everleigh Aeress and the magickal book! I was going to take you to her after the ceremony, to allow you to meet the evil that works against you."

As Cullen cups Talen's cheek, she can't help but keep her eyes locked with his, feeling a deep connection between them. She will forever be indebted to the vampire.

"I have to do something before we leave. Something I wish for you not to see. It will be most unpleasant. Can I?" Cullen effortlessly tears a strip of fabric from his sleeve. With a nod, she grants him permission to blindfold her. He delicately secures it behind her head.

"I won't be long," he whispers.

"What are you waiting for?! Attack him!" The Holy Scribe's voice echoes through the vast space, yet the Stone Guardsmen hesitate, seeking Arrowe's guidance.

Cullen stands up, looking down at Talen as she touches the lace covering her eyes. He crooks his neck, stretching his muscles before facing The Holy Scribe.

Arrowe steps forward. "I assure you. I don't know who she is or why she's here in such a state, vampire. I am the Heir of Stone and I give you permission to take her and go. Return to your lands before you declare war upon us."

As Cullen's spine straightens, an astonishing transformation takes place, causing him to grow at least a foot taller, with his bones effortlessly separating. His fingernails elongate into delicate, needle-like tips and his teeth become fully erect. His hands flex at his sides, ready for action. His eyes expand and darken like the depths of night, granting him the ability to perceive even the slightest movement in the room. Without looking, Cullen can detect every breath, every twitching muscle, and even the slightest drop of sweat. His senses are ignited, his mouth watering with venom.

Cullen narrows his eyes. "Like you, I, too, once lived within these walls, my mortal footsteps echoing alongside yours. And now, as I stand here, I know this was never my home, and it is not the company I would want to keep."

"Who are you?" Arrowe asks.

"I am retribution," Cullen growls.

"A name," Arrowe demands.

"I rode in on the thunder and the lightning, so you can call me *The Storm*."

Without warning, a Stone Guardsman silently sneaks up on Cullen from behind. In a split second, Cullen is in the man's face, his hand piercing through the Stone Guardsman's chest like a sharpened spear, as he grips the man's heart in his hand. He forcefully retracts his arm, causing the man's body to collapse onto the floor. He lifts his hand, revealing the pulsating heart to The Holy Scribe, and begins to devour it, chewing and swallowing the quivering organ. As he rolls what remains of the heart down the aisle, it makes a soft thumping sound before landing at The Holy Scribe's feet.

"Kill him!" The sound of Niam's scream fills the air as the Stone Guardsmen charge in, their footsteps pounding against the stone.

Grinning, Cullen quickly assesses the situation before smoothly slicing through one man's throat with a swift hand movement. He then drops to one knee and delivers a powerful punch, burying his fist between another man's legs. The moment he pulls his hand back, a searing sensation courses through the man's body, leaving him writhing in agony. Cullen's growl reverberates through the air as he tosses the limp flesh aside, a visceral reminder of the consequences for those who lay hands on Talen Freeborn or any woman against their will.

The Guardsman's agonizing screams fill the air as Cullen slowly rises above him, his eyes filled with rage. In one swift motion, he forcefully tears the man's tongue out and flings it aside. Then, without hesitation, he grabs the lower part of the man's jaw and violently rips it off. He uses the jawbone like a bone dagger, complete with teeth, to run it through the eye of another man before he can attack with his blade. Cullen then jumps into the air, his feet finding firm ground on another man's shoulders before he twists his head until bones snap and flesh tears. With a fluid motion, he pops his head right off and propels himself into the air, performing a graceful backflip. He lands on the stone floor, effortlessly balancing the head in one hand and the jawbone in the other. The prince of darkness callously throws them aside while his ominous shadow mercilessly cuts through the room, leaving a trail of destruction in its wake. With limbs soaring above his head, a twisted smile dances on his lips. His teeth now drenched in a macabre blend of blood and venom. With a firm grip, he intertwines his fingers and pushes his arms out, feeling the satisfying crack of his bones.

The Holy Scribe, with wide eyes filled with fear, finally reaches his breaking point and impulsively snatches up a discarded blade. With a tight grip, he lifts it, his knuckles turning white around the hilt. Cullen walks towards him, the sound of bones crunching as he breaks the back of one man, the screams of pain filling the air. He then proceeds to tear the arms off another and uses them to beat the third man to the ground, the sickening thuds echoing through the air as his body is flattened against the white stone. Finally, he casually tosses the severed arms aside, a chilling display of his strength and brutality. The remaining Stone Guardsmen are frozen in fear, their frantic footsteps echoing through the cathedral. But amidst the chaos, Cullen's keen senses detect the presence of another assailant among them. With lightning speed, he darts ahead and stands face-to-face with the man. As Cullen tilts his head, his complexion drains of color, leaving him paler than the moon, his eyes reflecting a darkness deeper than the night, and his teeth gleaming with an unnerving sharpness.

With a swift, powerful punch, he obliterates the man's face, resulting in a grotesque hole and a spray of blood. Unfazed by the violence, he begins to pull the lifeless corpse along behind him, leaving a disturbing trail of crimson in his wake. The twitching of the man's foot against the floor serves as a haunting testament to the merciless act. He effortlessly swings the body in front of him, forcefully tearing it in half and casually tossing the severed pieces in opposite directions.

Niam's hand trembles with nerves while Cullen's face lights up with a mischievous grin.

The vampire prince lifts his index finger.

"Only one left."

The Holy Scribe's eyes dart between his daughter and Cullen, uncertainty etched on his face. The women who live within these walls have suffered greatly from his actions, and it appears that his reign of terror may finally reach its end.

Visha understands this, but she is unwilling to help her

father. Remembering how often Niam had placed his hands on her and left similar bruises.

The vampire prince points at The Holy Scribe.

"You are undeserving of life."

Cullen's gaze shifts towards Talen, who remains seated and unmoving, her eyes shielded by the blindfold. Her chest rises and falls in a steady rhythm, the only audible sound in the room as she waits for him to return to her.

"I'm almost done," he says as she offers a small nod.

"Your existence is a sickness that cannot be cured, a disease that spreads without end." Niam screams, his voice cracking with fear and hatred.

"Perhaps, but not as terrible as yours."

Displaying his dark nature, the Heir of Shadow wipes his bottom lip with his thumb, then licks off the blood, reveling in his own wickedness.

With a burst of energy, Niam rushes toward him, his heart pounding in his chest. With a graceful pivot on his heel, Cullen disarms the man, effortlessly taking the blade from his grasp. With impressive skill, the vampire manages to position himself stealthily behind The Holy Scribe, encircling his chest with a firm arm and pressing the sharp blade against his vulnerable throat. A small trickle of blood forms, causing The Holy Scribe to break into a sinister grin.

Knowing he must be able to bribe the vampire with something, Niam asks, his mind racing for a solution. "What do you want? I know that every man has his price."

The Heir of Shadow leans into his ear.

"For you to bleed until we're even."

The blade begins to move across The Holy Scribe's throat in a sawing motion, causing blood to spurt out and fill his mouth. The vampire takes his time so that the man can feel every single slice. Cullen sets him free. Niam stumbles forward, his vision blurring as he hears his own heartbeat pounding in his ears. He stares in horror at Talen, still sitting on the pew, her blindfold tightly secured.

"Yes," Cullen hisses, his voice dripping with venom, "look at the last woman you will ever torment you filth."

Desperately, he clutches his throat, trying to stop the flow of blood, but it seeps through his fingers and stains the floor. Despite his efforts to suppress his thirst, Cullen's resolve crumbles as he lunges at the man, sinking his fangs into his neck with a savage force that pierces through muscle, penetrating all the way to the bone. With a forceful grip, he mercilessly crushes his spine, causing excruciating pain and leaving behind a gruesome scene of torn flesh and shattered vertebrae.

Niam twists around, feeling the intensity in his daughter's eyes, before collapsing onto the floor. His hand trembles against the rough surface of the stone as his lips part, but no sound escapes. His mouth fills with blood, which spills over and collects into an ominous puddle on the floor.

Cullen places his hand on his armor, feeling the cold metal against his skin, protecting his vulnerable throat, only to realize that his hands are now drenched in blood. Taking in the aftermath of his destructive path, his gaze eventually finds Talen. Stepping towards her, he's abruptly interrupted by a slight stinging sensation on his side. As he turns, he catches sight of Visha wielding a small blade, an insignificant weapon for his kind. But then, he notices the blood dripping from her hand, staining the blade with her own essence. She has poisoned it.

A strange sensation begins to surge through him. He blinks a few times, trying to make sense of it all. Without hesitation, he effortlessly lifts Talen and dashes out of the cathedral, propelling them through the open field and into the haunting depths of the Forest of Blood Roses. Finally, he reaches the Black Gates, their imposing presence looming before him. His shadow is quick to catch up, lingering only a few steps behind.

His steps gradually become more labored until he eventually halts, giving Talen the chance to stand independently. She removes the blindfold, and her eyes widen at the sight of his face, smeared with the blood of their enemies. Tenderly, she cups his face in her hands. Her eyes show unmistakable gratitude as she looks into his, acknowledging what he has done.

As the pain in his side continues to grow, he turns away, grimacing. Her heart pounding, she runs after him, desperate to catch up before he reaches the bridge overlooking The Sorrow. He is desperate to reach Everleigh. The relentless storm continues to rage, and the forceful wind nearly knocks Talen over as she reaches the open doorway.

Everleigh bursts out of his room and eagerly rushes to meet him. She must travel halfway across the bridge without falling. Seeing him sway on his feet, she instinctively moves closer to provide support. He is holding his side, wincing in pain. Everleigh's eyes dart from Talen to Cullen, a creeping sense of unease settling in.

As he removes his hand, she recoils at the sight of it covered in his blood.

"You're hurt!" she exclaims.

His intense gaze lingers on her as if mapping out every delicate contour of her features, her essence fueling his desire. Cullen wants to capture every detail, every moment

—the way her eyes sparkle with adoration when she gazes at him as if he's the sole focus of her world.

He reaches out, gently clasping her hand, and brings it to rest against his chest. Lowering his chin, Cullen holds it there, his grip firm.

She moves closer.

Cullen grins as his vision becomes hazy.

"She will need you as you will need her. War is coming. You must prepare yourselves, but Koa will be loyal to you. He will not fail me. Trust in him. Travel south—you will find allies there. You cannot linger in this place. It will become your tomb," he warns.

Everleigh shakes her head, unable to process the moment.

"Cullen—please, please stay with me. I need you."

Glancing over, she catches Talen's intense gaze fixed on them from the doorway. Witnessing their love, Talen's eyes grow dull with sadness. She yearns for a love that she could call her own, a life she wishes to live with the vampire prince.

"I fear that I am no longer a master of death."

"Cullen—no. Come with me. I can help you. I know I can. I—I know I can do this. I can—I can do this," she chokes out the words, desperate to convince him.

The weight of the moment settles on Cullen's shoulders as he lets out a resigned sigh, acknowledging that death has finally arrived. He rotates them to give her a view of The Sorrow's turbulent expanse. Leaning close to her, he uses his remaining strength to speak his truth, revealing himself to her for the first time.

"I will love you until forever falls apart, and The Sorrow runs dry."

As he stumbles backward, his desperate shadow clings to his body. Wrapping around him like a burial shroud. Time seems to stretch, allowing Cullen to savor one last glimpse of Everleigh's radiant beauty before he descends into the unknown. His eyes flutter closed, consumed by the deafening roar of the churning abyss below.

NOTE FROM THE AUTHOR

I appreciate you joining me on this journey! We have reached the end of ACT I in The Isles of Ellian. It's all good, no need to worry! We are not done yet. ACT II will be a two-part duology, marking the end of the series. The plan is to launch both books together in early 2025.

It would mean a lot to me if you could review this book on Amazon, Goodreads, Bookbub, or any other social media site you're active on.

Don't forget to tag me! I go by Rue Volley on all of those sites. Add me as a friend, as well! There's nothing I enjoy more than engaging with my readers.

Finally, my love for you is endless. I'm grateful for your continuous support of my art throughout the years. You've made it possible for me to share my stories with the world.

See you on the other side of the page,

Rue

OTHER BOOKS BY RUE

The Isles of Ellian

The Heir of Shadow and Stone (The Isles of Ellian, Book #1)

The King of Blood and Bone (The Isles of Ellian, Book #2)

The Midnight Saga

13 Ways to Midnight (Books 1-5)

The Devil's Gate Trilogy

The End of August

Parts 1-3

All The Ways You Never Loved Me

Hemlock

The Dead Boy's Club

ABOUT THE AUTHOR

USAT Bestselling author and award-winning screenwriter, wife, pug mom, and chocolate lover. Author of romance in multiple genres, Rue Volley combines her unique sense of humor, intriguing plots and multi-layered characters into every story.

PRONUNCIATIONS:

The War of **BRUMAH** (BREW-MA)
RAIDEN Moore (RAY-DIN)
NAYA Freeborn (NIE-YA)
CASSIUS Brumah (CASS-E-US)
SANJA AERESS (SAWN-JAH AIR-S)
VISHA AERESS (VEE-SHA AIR-S)
EVERLEIGH AERESS (EVER-LEE AIR-S)
IZEL AERESS (E-ZELL AIR-S)
CORDELIA AERESS (CORE-DEAL-EAH AIR-S)
EMBERLY AERESS (M-BURR-LEE AIR-S)
ROWE EFHREN (ROW F-REN)
CULLEN Moore (CALL-IN)
EZLEN Moore (EZZ-LIN)
MARA (MAR-RAH)
ARCADIA MIAKODA (R-K-DEE-A ME-A-CO-DAH)
ARREN VERRICK (AIR-IN VHERE-RICK)
NYX Miakoda (NICKS)
ALTHEA Miakoda (AL-THEE-AH)
NEEMA Freeborn (KNEE-MAH)
ARROWE Brumah (AIR-ROW)
ODETTE Ender (OH-DEBT)
TALEN Freeborn (TELL-LYNN)
NIAM JAZINE (KNEE-UM JAZZ-EEN)
Grim DASHIELL (DASH-EEL)
PAXTON (PACK-SUN)
FAERYN ZABINA (FAY-REN ZAM-BEE-NAH)
ZIMORA (ZAH-MORE-AH)
HIRO (HERO)

Terminology:

KEEPER OF WORDS – Someone who can read and write.

STONE MAIDEN – Girls born on a blood moon and groomed to birth an heir.

ASCENTION – A holy ceremony to choose which Stone Maidens will birth an heir.

FATES – A race of FAE and ELVEN.

ACHERON – Serpent God of the mortals.

ELIXERS OR TONICS – Different tea blends to control the mood.

VISIONS – Dreams.

FINGER CLAWS – Sharpened metal jewelry.

MOTHER WARD – Surrogate mother in The Kingdom of Stone.

BLOOD ROSES – Roses that are brewed by vampires.

STONE GUARDSMAN – Protectors of the King and Queen of Stone.

DRAGON'S KEEP – The island of dragons.

THE LIBRARY OF ACHERON -The library in The Kingdom of Stone.

THE WAR OF BRUMAH – The thousand-year war.

THE RIVER WILDE – The only fresh water that runs through Ellian.

THE SORROW – The sea

ECLIPSING THE SUN– A FATES coming-of-age ceremony.

MOONRISE and STARFALL – The two magickal books.

THE BOOK OF ALL KNOWING – Holy book in The Kingdom of Stone.

THE HOLY SCRIBE – The priest who receives the holy word from Acheron.

ACOLYTE – A boy who serves The Holy Scribe.

THE VOID - Beyond the edge of the world.

WILDLINGS - Those who refused to live in The Kingdom of Silver Flame. More Fae and Elven.

Made in the USA
Columbia, SC
11 April 2024

dbcd96cb-86a0-42db-99d4-73bb7a37dfa1R02